Is she being disloyal to her friend?
Or simply following her heart . . . ?

"You just seem like someone who doesn't do stuff just
'cause everyone else is doing it," he said. "You're different
than that."

I didn't say anything, and then neither did he. We just
looked at each other. Neither one of us squirmed or said
something stupid or teasing or anything. We just really held
each other's gazes for longer than I've ever stared at another
person.

"I think about you a lot, Lima," he said. "A lot."

"Have you thought about doing, about having it with me?"
I asked.

He rolled onto his back so he wasn't facing me and took a
deep breath in and out.

"Yeah," he said.

He had thought about it. His imagination would be so
much more vivid than mine, because he had actually done
it before. The thought made me scared and excited at the
same time.

"I think about you, too," I said.

Other Books You May Enjoy

first

there was

forever

first

there was

forever

A NOVEL

juliana

romano

∞

speak

SPEAK
An imprint of Penguin Random House LLC
375 Hudson Street
New York, New York 10014

First published in the United States of America by Dial Books,
an imprint of Penguin Group (USA) LLC, 2015
Published by Speak, an imprint of Penguin Random House LLC, 2016

THE LIBRARY OF CONGRESS HAS CATALOGED THE DIAL BOOKS EDITION AS FOLLOWS:
Romano, Juliana.
First there was forever / by Juliana Romano. pages cm
Summary: Los Angeles, California, tenth-graders Lima and Hailey have
always been best friends, but now Hailey is chasing after a more popular crowd,
and Lima connects not only with a different popular group, she also begins
getting close to Hailey's long-term crush, Nate.
ISBN 978-0-8037-4168-3 (hardcover)
[1. Best friends—Fiction. 2. Friendship—Fiction. 3. Conduct of life—Fiction.
4. Popularity—Fiction. 5. High schools—Fiction. 6. Schools—Fiction.
7. Family life—California—Fiction. 8. Malibu (Calif.)—Fiction.] I. Title.
PZ7.R6603635Fir 2015 [Fic]—dc23 2014012983

Speak ISBN 978-0-14-751391-5

Printed in the United States of America

1 3 5 7 9 10 8 6 4 2

Designed by Mina Chung

for my family

first

there was

forever

chapter

one

ailey and I were sitting on the beach behind my house in Malibu, on the smooth, damp sand by the edge of the water. The Pacific Ocean stretched out before us. Tiny, razor-sharp shards of light sparkled across its surface like glitter. A wave nipped at our bare feet and Hailey squealed.

"Tell me everything," I said.

"I told you already," she replied, squinting out toward the horizon. A gauzy sheet of clouds hung across the sky, diffusing the late summer sun. "He was really cute and it was fine. It was whatever. I'm just glad it's over with."

Hailey, my best friend in the world, had lost her virginity the day before to a guy she met at a barbecue while she was visiting her dad in San Diego. She called from the bathroom immediately after it happened to tell me. But now her story was strangely empty, colorless. Usually, Hailey was an amazing storyteller.

"So, you're not going to see him again, like, ever?" I pressed. "San Diego isn't that far from LA. You guys could meet up."

"It wasn't like that," she said. "And besides, I only want Nate. I don't care about anyone else."

Hailey had been in love with Nate Reed since the fifth grade. She wasn't discouraged by the fact that he had never liked her back.

"Don't look so serious." Hailey laughed and flicked a loose chunk of sand in my direction. "Anyway, do you think I look different? Will Nate be able to tell?"

"Yes?" I said it like a question, just in case it wasn't the right answer. I was accustomed to knowing exactly what Hailey was thinking, but there was something slippery and hard to read about her right then.

"Skyler says guys like it when you've had sex," she said, digging her toes into the sand. "So maybe it'll help."

"You told Skyler already? When?" I asked.

"I saw her this morning," Hailey said. "We got manicures." Then, she lay back in the sand and closed her eyes.

I stared out at the ocean and tried to imagine that I could actually see the curve of the earth a thousand miles away.

In a few days, tenth grade would start and summer would be officially over. It had been perfect. Peaceful, long, and lazy. All I did was hang out with Hailey, work on my garden, listen to music, and cook elaborate meals for me and Mom and Dad. The three of us ate on the back deck with the waxy beach air wrapping itself around us like blankets almost every single night. Once school started, everything would change. I wouldn't have time to go to the farmers' market and pick out strange fruits to turn into pie fillings or jams. I wouldn't be able to lie in bed with Hailey all day, having old movie marathons and eating candy.

I turned to Hailey. In the sunless, natural light, I could see every detail of her skin—even the grayish layer of concealer she had smeared under her hazel eyes and the goose bumps that rose up on her thighs like Braille. I couldn't believe she wasn't a virgin anymore. Even if she didn't think it was a big deal, I did.

Hailey's eyes snapped open as if she could sense me staring at her.

"What are you thinking?" she asked.

"I just . . ." I began. "I just still can't believe you had sex."

Hailey looked away before she spoke. "I'm telling you. It's not what you think."

I waited for her to continue, but instead she sat up and brushed the sand off her forearms.

A slightly denser cloud moved in front of the sun, and the world seemed to grow a shade darker. The tail end of another icy wave sliced at our feet and we both flinched.

"It's freezing out here," Hailey said. "I'm so over the beach. Can we go inside and pick at your mom's weird health food?"

Inside, Mom made us almond milk smoothies, and we curled up on the big white couch to drink them. The first floor of our house was one open sprawling space with the kitchen, the living area, and the dining area all flowing together. The back wall was made entirely of sliding glass doors that opened onto the beach, so salty air was always blowing in. Even our closets smelled like the ocean. Our furniture was mostly white and minimal, but Mom scattered Mexican blankets and painted pots from Africa around the room for color. Mom and Dad used to travel a lot and collect things before I was born. That's actually how I got my name: Lima. Lima is the city in Peru where my dad proposed.

"'*Trust your instincts this week, Cancer,*'" Hailey read aloud from the *LA Times* horoscope section. "'*When it comes to a big decision, your intuition will guide you. Be willing to take a financial risk, but discuss your options first with a trusted few.*'" Hailey rolled her eyes. "This is so not helpful."

Mom perched on the arm of the couch. With her long blond hair swept into a ponytail, and wearing jeans and a

T-shirt, she almost looked like a high school student.

"How's your mom, Hail?" she asked.

"Crazy," Hailey deadpanned. "Her new thing is she smokes in the bathroom and then lights all this incense to cover it up. I'm, like, 'Mom, all the Nag Champa in the world isn't going to disguise the smell of cigarettes in a room with no windows.'"

Mom frowned. She was always protective of Hailey. When we were in fourth grade and Hailey's parents were getting divorced, she actually lived with us for three weeks. One night, she and Mom slept together in the guest room because Hailey's nightmares had gotten so bad. I confessed to Mom later that I had been jealous, but she explained to me that sometimes when you have a lot of something, like love, you have to share.

"Anyway, these horoscopes are bullshit," Hailey continued. "Sorry for cursing, Laura. I'll put a penny in the swear-word jar."

Mom laughed. We didn't actually have a swear-word jar but somehow Hailey always knew what to say to lighten the mood.

Hailey sunk deeper into the couch and flipped to a new page of the newspaper.

It bothered me that she was acting like having sex was no big deal. I had barely ever made out with someone, so it's not like I could relate to her experience, but I still wanted to know what it had been like. I wanted her to share more, to include me in everything she was feeling. Instead, it was the opposite. All afternoon, she had seemed like she was only half there.

I gazed outside at the flat white sky. The afternoon tide was coming in. A big wave crashed on the beach, and the foam gnashed at the sand like teeth.

chapter

two

On the first day of school, I went straight to the vending machine after second period to meet Hailey at our spot. She wasn't there, so I leaned against the cool plastic shell of the machine and waited.

"Excuse us," a ninth-grade girl said. She and her friend both had crisp back-to-school haircuts and fresh tans. They talked quickly while they shoved quarters down the throat of the machine. After they got their Diet Cokes, they left behind the smell of sunscreen and flowery shampoo.

Emily Friedlander spotted me from across the patio and waved. I waved back. Emily lived down the beach from me in Malibu, and we'd known each other forever without ever really being friends. All Emily cared about was surfing.

"What do you have next?" Emily asked after we'd

exchanged an awkward hug. Her blond hair glowed like a fluorescent light. It looked almost white next to her ruddy, sun-stained skin.

"Honors Chemistry," I said. "With Patty."

"Really? Me too!" Emily said. "I'm freaking out. It's going to be so hard. I'm so glad I know someone in the class. Maybe we can even study together."

"Yeah," I agreed absently.

The crowded patio had begun to thin out as people made their way to class.

"Should we go?" Emily asked. "I'm not even sure where the classroom is."

I checked my phone to see if Hailey had texted, but my screen was blank.

"Yeah," I said. "Let's go."

Honors Chemistry was in a big, bright room on the top floor of the science building. It must have been the highest point on campus because the view out the enormous glass windows was amazing. Sitting at a desk in the front row, I could see all the way past the ramshackle industrial buildings outside to the San Fernando Mountain range that divided the city from the valley. The ridge of the mountains cut a jagged line along the horizon, and the sky above them was a vivid, glossy blue.

"What is the second kind of scientific experiment?" Patty asked.

A senior in the front row raised his hand.

"Yuri?" Patty said.

Patty had memorized all of our names during roll. She was one of those teachers who you could tell was a good teacher right away because she had an even, patient way of talking.

"Exploratory," Yuri said.

"Right. So, the candle wax lab tomorrow, will that be testing a specific hypothesis, or an exploratory investigation?"

I knew the answer but I didn't raise my hand.

"Lima?" Patty asked, as if she had heard my thoughts.

"Testing a hypothesis," I said.

"Which will be?" she continued.

"That the wick, not the wax, is the primary fuel for a burning candle," I answered. Even though I knew the answer was right, I felt my face get hot.

Science had always been my favorite subject. I liked how everything promised to make sense. There were rules. In labs, I marveled at the way a written formula could match the reality of an experiment so neatly. Not very different from baking something from a recipe.

Patty turned her back to us and started writing on the

board. She had white hair, cut within an inch of her skull. It wasn't styled like a pixie cut, or some fashion statement. It was just plain, short hair, like a little boy would have. Everything about Patty was practical and comfortable. She wore a fleece jacket, khaki shorts, and hiking sneakers.

Most of the teachers at our school, Rustic Canyon Day, dressed like Patty: outdoorsy and casual. Rustic was founded in the seventies by a bunch of hippies in the Santa Monica Canyon. The elementary and middle schools were still run out of the original location, but the high school moved to a set of converted factories in West LA when I was a kid.

Patty ran over by ten minutes, cutting into lunch. When we got out, I texted Hailey and she wrote back that she'd left campus. She said she'd be at the smoking tree after school.

By the time I arrived at the tree, Hailey and Skyler were already sharing a giant drink from the gas station across the street. They had been becoming friends ever since they had easy-math together the year before, but Skyler and I had zero in common. Now they were wearing identical heart-shaped sunglasses. Their faces were pointed in my direction and, because I couldn't see their eyes behind their lenses, they possessed a blind, animal-like quality, like deer.

"Hey, Li," Hailey said.

"Cute shoes," said Skyler. I looked down at my dirty red Converse and wondered if she was being serious or not. She and Hailey were both wearing wedge sandals and short, colorful dresses, while I was in beat-up jeans and a gray T-shirt. I nervously touched my hair, checking to see if the knot-bun I'd tied it in that morning was still in place.

"I haven't seen you all day," I said. "How were your classes?"

Skyler yanked the drink out of Hailey's hand.

"Classes were whatever," Hailey said. "But guess what? We went out to lunch with Ryan and Nate today. It was awesome. I think Nate got literally hotter over the summer."

Skyler wrinkled her nose and inspected the waxy straw of their drink. "Hailey, you're so nasty, you chewed up the tip. That's so gross. I don't want to put this in my mouth."

"You've put plenty of dirtier shit in your mouth, Sky," Hailey replied.

Skyler cackled.

"Anyway," I said awkwardly. "My classes were whatever, too. Chemistry is gonna be so hard."

Hailey nodded.

"Do you want to come over later?" I continued. "My mom and I got these zucchini flowers at the farmers' market yesterday. We're gonna stuff them with cheese and fry them for dinner. They're gonna be amazing."

"I don't know," she said vaguely. "Maybe."

She glanced at Skyler, who had taken the lid off of the soda and was drinking straight from the cup.

"I'll call you, okay?" Hailey said to me.

Mom, Dad, and I ate on the back porch that night and afterward I went up to my room to do homework. It was seven o'clock and Hailey still hadn't called. I stared out my bedroom window. The setting sun hovered over the ocean, a melting crimson bulb.

My computer beeped. It was a chat request from Emily, seeing if I had done the chemistry reading yet. I wrote back and told her I was about to start. I checked my phone one last time to make sure I hadn't missed any texts from Hailey, and then I plopped on my bed and opened the textbook to page 35. I ran my hands firmly down the center to flatten the pages, pressing hard until I heard the soft crack of its cardboard spine.

chapter

three

"Lima, oh my God, I miss you," Hailey said, throwing her arms around me. We were halfway through the second week of school and this was the first day Hailey had showed up at our meeting spot.

"I've been here at break every day," I said. "Where have you been?"

The year was off to a bad start. Hailey was impossible to pin down at school, and my time at home was being devoured by hours of nightly homework. I'd been so busy I had neglected to take care of my garden, and last night I discovered that my strawberry plants had wilted and died. I'd tended to those plants all summer, watering them and pruning them and watching them transform from a packet of seeds to perfect living organisms. There is an indescribable joy that comes from seeing a plant you have grown yourself produce actual edible fruit. Each strawberry, even if it was small and lopsided and soft, had felt like a miracle.

"I know it's totally my fault that we haven't seen each other lately," Hailey confessed. "It's just that now that we have off-campus privileges, I leave at, like, every single break."

"Just 'cause we're allowed to go off campus doesn't mean you have to go," I said softly. As the words came out, I could hear how lame I sounded.

"You're right. I'll probably get sick of it soon. But it just feels exciting. And Nate is usually there. And you know me: when it comes to Nate, I have no self-control. Actually, when it comes to anything, I have no self-control."

We both laughed, and I felt comforted by Hailey's honesty. She wasn't avoiding me. She was just chasing something else.

"Come out to lunch with me and Skyler today," she said. "You might like her more than you think."

It turned out "going out to lunch" with Skyler and Hailey meant getting iced coffees and driving in circles around the neighborhood. I was starving. I couldn't believe we weren't actually going to get food.

"Slow down," Hailey yelled as Skyler swung a sharp turn and the car fishtailed. "I'm gonna mess up my makeup!"

Hailey was sitting shotgun and using the flip-down mirror to smudge cover-up onto the circles under her eyes.

"Don't put so much on. It looks fake," Skyler ordered.

"Yeah, but I look worse without it," Hailey replied. "And Nate is in my fifth period."

"Nate's not that cool," Skyler said. "Don't be so into him. He thinks he's the shit."

"There's more to him than you think."

Skyler moaned. "There is so not more to him than I think." Hailey laughed.

"Whatever, I'm sure if you actually hooked up with him, you'd stop liking him," Skyler continued. "That's how I am. I just like guys until I get them. What do you think about Hailey and Nate, Lima?"

"I don't know," I said lamely. "I don't really know Nate. But she likes him." I wished I hadn't agreed to come. I was so hungry I could hardly think.

Skyler laughed. Her nails were painted a midnight blue. "So," she said, glancing over her shoulder at me, "who do you like?"

"I don't like anyone," I said.

"You must like someone," she tried. I couldn't read her expression behind the hard black shells of her sunglasses. "Not even Ryan? He's so cute. I mean, I could never be attracted to him because we're basically like brother and sister. But he's definitely, like, boy-band cute."

Ryan Masterson had always been the best-looking guy

in our grade, with movie-star dimples and silvery eyes that reflected light like mirrors. I'd gone to school with him since pre-K and he'd always been nice, but I'd never had anything even close to a crush on him. I tried to imagine being alone with Ryan, maybe even kissing him, but those thoughts didn't make me feel anything. It was like pinching myself somewhere that had been numbed.

When I realized Skyler was waiting for me to respond, I said, "Oh, no, I seriously don't like anyone."

"Really?" Skyler asked, glancing at Hailey for confirmation.

"No, she genuinely doesn't," Hailey said, patting lip gloss onto her lower lip. "Lima never likes anyone."

"Lemme use that when you're done," Skyler commanded Hailey. "Want some, Lima?"

I shook my head no.

"Lima doesn't need to wear any makeup," Hailey said. "It's insane. She just looks like that all the time. It's weird. If we were living in medieval times, like pre-makeup and blow-dryers, Lima would be, like, the only person who would still be pretty. She's the only person who would look the same!"

"Thanks a lot, biatch!" Skyler snapped. "Are you calling me ugly?"

"Don't pretend you don't know how hot you are," Hailey retorted drily.

Hailey always had a way of giving me compliments that made me feel small and almost ashamed. I had looked exactly the same since I was five years old. My hair had turned gradually from platinum to a darker blond, the color of sand or dust. I had blue eyes and skin that freckled or burned but never tanned. For the last few years, I had been waiting for my soft features to give way to harder, more grown-up ones, but they never had. Even my smile hadn't changed because Mom didn't let the orthodontist give me braces. She said my slightly crooked teeth gave me character.

"Well, whatever," Skyler said. "I don't wear makeup 'cause I have to. It's just fun." She twisted the volume knob on her stereo so the music thumped violently through the car.

When we were in elementary school, Hailey invented the every-other rule. Every other day is good. Every other birthday is perfect. Every other test is easy. Even though we stopped talking about it in middle school, and even though I knew it was just a silly superstition, part of me still believed in it. Eighth grade had been miserable, but ninth grade had been okay, which meant that, according to the every-other rule, tenth was destined to be terrible.

chapter

four

Going to Hailey's apartment on Fridays was one of our rituals. But this week Skyler, Ryan, and Nate came, too. Skyler had made the arrangements a few days earlier, and since then Hailey had been talking about it nonstop. She went on and on about what she would wear, what kind of drinks she should have, and whether or not Nate would think her room was cool.

Yellow afternoon light cut sideways across us where we stood on her balcony. "Dare me to walk on the railing," Hailey said, taking a big gulp of her vodka and soda.

"I dare you, Hailey," Skyler said, sounding bored. She was leaning her whole body into Ryan's side, his tan, smooth arm slung around her shoulders. My mind flashed on my conversation with Skyler earlier in the week. She was right: Ryan was good-looking.

"Nate, do you dare me?" Hailey asked.

Nate was standing a little separate from the rest of us, leaning against the wall with a beer in his hand.

"Hailey, please don't," I said. I was the only one not drinking, so maybe I was the only one who realized what a stupid idea walking on the railing was. "You're being insane."

Hailey lived on the sixth floor of an apartment building a few blocks east of the 405 freeway. The sprawl of West LA stretched out beneath us: rooftops, backyards, artificially blue pools, the intricate crisscross of sagging telephone wires, and somewhere, lurking behind the city, the blurry smudge of the ocean.

"Don't worry, Li. I got this," Hailey said, hoisting herself onto the railing. It was no wider than a gymnast's balance beam, and she crouched on it for a second before unfurling into a standing position. She stood toe-to-heel, her arms extended like a tightrope walker's.

I squeezed my eyes shut, afraid to watch, and when I opened them, Nate was looking at me. He wasn't smiling, but his expression wasn't unfriendly. It was like he was just contemplating me or something. I glanced quickly at my shoes, and then looked up at him again. I expected him to turn away, but instead he held my gaze steadily, the way you might hold a glass brimming with water that you didn't want to spill.

Maybe it was because of the color of his T-shirt, or maybe

it was the way the afternoon light was hitting him, but I had never realized until then that Nate's eyes were so blue. Our gazes hooked together and everything around me seemed to grow quiet.

"Oh my God, Hailey, I can see everything from where I am." Skyler laughed, shielding her eyes with her hand. "Get down."

Everyone's attention snapped up to Hailey. A gust of wind had made Hailey's skirt float up above her waist, suspended in midair like a hot-air balloon.

When the sun slid down behind the wall of the ocean, we went inside. Hailey turned on her stereo and blasted a synthetic pop song. The apartment was dark and Hailey was too drunk to switch on the overhead lights.

"Come here, Li. Dance with us!" Hailey called out to me. She and Skyler danced with their arms wrapped around each other's necks.

"In a minute," I said. I slipped into the kitchen. Doing dishes was the perfect excuse to be alone.

I was washing out a glass when Nate came in.

He passed behind me, where I stood at the sink. He didn't say anything or offer to help. I didn't turn around, but I felt his eyes on my back, felt him moving across the room to the trash can and crossing back to the door. Right before he left,

I turned and looked at him and our eyes met. For the second time that day, something passed between us.

And then he sort of winced, and said, "What?"

"Nothing," I stammered, suddenly embarrassed.

He stared at me for another second like I was crazy, rolled his eyes, and left the kitchen.

chapter

five

Hailey and Skyler passed out in a sticky drunken sleep as soon as the boys left, but I wasn't tired. The alcohol emanating from their bodies gave the room an antiseptic scent, like hand sanitizer, or the way it smelled right after the janitor had passed through the hallways of school with his industrial cleaning supplies.

I had only been drunk once. Last fall, Hailey and I broke into Dad's fancy liquor one morning when he and Mom were out at brunch. Before then, I had taken sips of alcohol at parties, and sometimes Mom shared her glass of Chardonnay with me at dinner, but I never drank enough to feel anything. So when Hailey and I started swigging from Dad's whiskey, we got drunk fast.

Dad kept his whiskey in the room he called his office, which was really just his private hangout room. He had a record player, a vintage typewriter, and a framed Bob Dylan poster on the wall. There was also this really pretty black-and-white picture of Mom on his desk. In the picture, the wind was whipping her blond hair across her face, but you could still see her freckles and her strong eyebrows and the shape of her straight nose. She's smiling in it, but there's sadness to her expression, too. Something about that photo always looked like love to me. Like that's what being in love would look like, if it could look like something.

Being drunk made Dad's office look different. The walls warped. The room swarmed around me, and everything grew rubbery and funny. We played Dad's records and danced sloppily, falling onto the floor and knocking into the bookshelves.

I remember Hailey was laughing so hard at my drunken rendition of "Livin' on a Prayer" that she actually peed in her pants. She stood there with her legs crossed, her face beet red, as she laughed and cried at the same time, and the dark liquid spread across her pajamas. I convinced her she needed a bath; she convinced me I needed one too, and the next thing I knew we were taking off our clothes and stepping into a bubble bath in our bras and undies.

By the time Mom and Dad came home at two p.m., we were already napping on my bed.

When I woke up, my bedroom was full of this dusty end-of-the-day light. My mouth was dry and I felt stiff and unsettled. We all ate dinner on the back porch that night, which was usually my favorite thing, but that night, I couldn't shake my irritability. Nothing that had seemed funny that morning seemed funny anymore. Even the memory of Hailey peeing in her pants, which had made me laugh so much, just seemed depressing.

That same year, Hailey had smoked pot a bunch of times, and I finally decided to do it with her.

"Listen," she told me as she pulled a pair of black jeans off her floor and inspected them for stains, "we'll smoke this joint and then we'll call a taxi and go to Skyler's party. You'll love being high, it's amazing."

"What's it like?" I rolled the joint around in my palm. I knew a lot of people who smoked pot. Even grown-ups. My aunt Caroline had a medical marijuana prescription because she had breast cancer when we were in elementary school. Her cancer was in remission now, but she still kept her prescription, and I suspected that even Dad got stoned with her occasionally.

"Ugh, my favorite jeans are dirty," Hailey said, tossing the jeans back onto the floor. Then she looked at me. "I can't explain it. It makes stuff funny. Just try it. It's even less of a big deal than getting drunk."

We smoked the joint on the balcony, and Hailey made me hold my breath for three full seconds to be sure I inhaled.

"Are you high?" Hailey asked me after a few minutes. Behind her, the red polka dots of brake lights on the 405 freeway flickered on and off.

"I don't think so," I said. But my voice sounded far away, and I had a sudden craving for something sweet.

"Are you ready to go?" Hailey asked. Her eyes looked like they were dipped in honey.

"I can't go to a party," I giggled. "I think I might be stoned. Let's just go to the kitchen and make root beer floats."

And then I started laughing uncontrollably, because it dawned on me that even the kitchen seemed far away at that instant. "The kitchen is literally—and I mean literally—as far as I can go."

Hailey laughed a little. Sweets must have sounded good to her, too.

We didn't have the right stuff for root beer floats, but we made all kinds of other creations. We put chocolate ice cream in the microwave and drank it out of straws. I made a cookie sandwich out of graham crackers, peanut butter, and Froot Loops. Then we watched an old *Saturday Night Live* on Hailey's laptop and passed out on her bed.

The next morning, Hailey's mom knocked on her door.

"Can I talk to you out here, Hailey?" she asked.

Brenda's dyed blond hair was pulled into a ponytail, and I could see a full inch of her dark roots. She was wrapped in a fluffy pink terrycloth robe. Every time I saw Brenda she looked a little older.

Hailey stepped into the hallway with her mom, and I could hear them arguing, but I couldn't make out the words.

"We have to clean the kitchen," Hailey said when she came back in, and her eyes slid all over the room without meeting mine.

The kitchen looked terrible, but I was a good cleaner, so it went fast. Hailey was super quiet while we did dishes.

"Look at this fork!" I said, laughing. "There's a Froot Loop stuck in it!"

Hailey didn't crack a smile. "I feel so fat," was all she said.

I sucked my lips between my teeth. I hated when Hailey was in a bad mood, and I felt guilty that it was partly my fault.

"Your mom won't stay mad, Hailey," I offered quietly.

"I don't care about that," she said. "I got, like, a million texts from Skyler asking me where I was. She's pissed at me for not going to her party."

"She'll get over it," I said.

"Maybe," said Hailey.

I hadn't smoked pot or been drunk since then. It wasn't that I didn't like how it had felt, but both times it left me feeling emptier than before. Like it dug something out of my insides and left a hollow, quarter-sized vortex behind.

chapter

six

∞

The following Friday, Mom and I spent the afternoon making peach cobbler from scratch. Mom showed me how if you drop peaches in boiling water for thirty seconds and then take them out, their skin comes right off in your hands. Easy as taking off a piece of clothing.

After we cleaned the kitchen, I went upstairs to pack. We were leaving the next day to go to Santa Barbara for my grandmother's birthday. We'd pick Hailey up early on Saturday morning and head out before traffic. That's how we always did it when we went to Nana's.

Outside my window the sky was a pale blue, but the moon had already appeared. It looked yellow and disproportionately big, like it had been painted onto the artificial backdrop of the sky.

My phone lit up with a text message from Hailey.

Can't go to Santa Barbara. Sad face.

I perched on the edge of my bed and called her.

"What's up?" I asked.

"I'm so sorry, Li. I just really can't go away this weekend," she said.

"Oh," I said. "Okay. Why?"

Hailey sighed. "I have so much homework. I have three quizzes on Monday, and I'm already behind in everything. It's just, like, I have to stay."

"You can do homework at Nana's," I said. "I'm gonna bring mine."

Hailey paused. "Well, there's also, like, this party at Skyler's friend's house from outside of school on Saturday."

My heart sank. That's what this was about?

After we got off the phone, the silence in my room felt loud. I gazed out the window at the fake-looking sky, trying to ignore the disappointment that spread through my chest like sand.

chapter

seven

Nana lived with Dad's sister, Caroline, in a huge, mustard-colored Spanish-style house overlooking the ocean in the prettiest part of Santa Barbara.

"Come in, ladies," Caroline greeted us. "And gentleman."

Caroline's shoulder-length hair was white as powdered sugar. Light seemed to shoot through it, giving the impression that she was always standing in front of a lamp. My cousins were away at college, so I was the only kid around. I actually didn't mind being alone with grown-ups. Sometimes I even preferred it to being with people my own age.

Nana was sitting under an umbrella on a white canvas recliner by the pool when we came in. Every time we visited, Nana looked smaller. I must have been growing up at exactly the same rate that she was growing old, like we were sitting on opposite sides of a seesaw.

"How are you, Nana?" I asked.

Nana wrapped her fingers around mine and they clung tight, like claws.

"I can't complain," she said. Even though Nana was old, she still always wore red lipstick and blue eye shadow. "How are you? Tell me about school."

Everyone always said I looked like Nana when she was young, but that was hard for me to imagine. The only thing that I could tell for sure was that Nana, Dad, and I all had the exact same eyes. They were clear, even pools of blue.

"School's hard," I said. "Harder than last year."

"You're a smart girl," she said. "You'll do fine."

Mom and Dad made lunch while I swam in the pool. The water was warm and velvety. I did flips, handstands, and somersaults until my fingertips turned into raisins. And then I climbed out of the water and ate under the sun. The taste of chlorine mingled with the salty food. The sun grew lazy and tired and sunk lower in the sky. The light changed to that mild orangey afternoon color and soon we all went inside.

During the car ride home on Sunday, Mom, Dad, and I listened to the Rolling Stones. My favorite Rolling Stones song had always been "Wild Horses," and it was easy to sing along to. We took the Pacific Coast Highway all the way back to LA.

When we were about twenty minutes from home, I got a text message from Hailey: Nate and I kissed last night. My life has finally begun.

chapter

eight

∞

Hailey texted me during lunch on Monday to come find her in the bathroom in the science building. She was sitting on the floor of the handicap stall, her face in her hands. She looked up at me, revealing puffy red eyes. The way she had tucked her knees up to her chest, I could see her underwear. Even though Skyler was acting like Hailey's new best friend, I was clearly still the one Hailey wanted to cry to.

"I thought I looked so pretty today," she stammered between sobs.

"You do!" I said, crouching down and putting my hands on her knees.

Her bottom lip quivered as more tears came. She flicked them away with the tips of her fingers. She always cried like that—wiping away tears before they could run down her face and ruin her makeup. I leaned in and gave her a hug. My cheek touched her forehead, and her skin felt oily and hot.

"He doesn't like me, Lima," Hailey said, her voice cracking. "He told Ryan, who told Sara, who told Skyler that he only kissed me 'cause he was really drunk. He said it was a mistake."

"Nate? What a moron," I said, rolling my eyes. "You can do better."

She looked at me with empty eyes. "I can't," she said softly. "I can't do better than him."

"He's a spoiled, rude, too skinny, cocky, stupid sixteen-year-old," I said, trying to come up with accurate insults. "He thinks he's so cool and edgy, but he's just the same as everyone else."

She half smiled, and then her eyes went blank with pain again. "Lima, he was such a good kisser."

I hated that detail, but I tried to keep my tone light.

"Just forget about it. Think about that hot guy you hooked up with in San Diego."

"Everyone hooks up with random guys from out of town. Out-of-town guys don't count."

I laughed; I couldn't help it. And then Hailey started laughing. After a few minutes I think she actually seemed a little less sad.

chapter

nine

Saturday morning I woke up early enough to watch Dad surf behind our house. He usually went in around six or seven, not like the hard-core surfers who went in at five, or even four in the morning. Sometimes I'd see those surfers piling into their cars on the Pacific Coast Highway, sunburned and raw, already having been in the ocean for several hours by the time I was leaving for school.

Now I sat beneath a damp gray sky, watching Dad ride the choppy waves. I wore a fleece jacket over my sweatshirt but I was still cold. I wondered how Dad could stand to be in the icy water.

I know it's weird, because I grew up practically on the beach, but for the longest time, I was afraid to go in the ocean. I liked swimming in pools, where the water was predictable and calm. But the ocean was ragged and wild, always threatening to pull you in and never let you go.

I finally went in when I was twelve. It was perfect beach weather that day, hot and sunny, with only a few dense clouds in the sky, like scoops of vanilla ice cream. Hailey and Dad were wave-diving, and I was lying on the sand reading and eating chips. Every now and then I'd look up and see their heads, bobbing just beyond where the waves were breaking.

"There's no time like the present, Lima," Dad announced when they came out to shore. They were both all wet, an even layer of sand stuck to their calves and feet, like a rough second skin.

"C'mon, Li," Hailey said. "The ocean isn't scary. You're being totally psycho."

I looked from Hailey to Dad and back to Hailey, and I knew I wasn't getting out of it.

We walked toward the ocean. The sand felt slimy under my feet, and the water felt sharp and cold, like a million needles on my thighs. I froze. I looked at Hailey, but she didn't look scared or cold at all. She looked back at me, rolled her eyes, and grabbed my hand, pulling me in farther. Just when my feet started to lose contact with the floor, Dad yelled: "Dive!"

I held my nose with my right hand and lurched forward through the tense surface of the water. I felt the wave crash overhead, but it didn't hurt. Being under the wave felt like being inside of a pulse, or a big heartbeat.

I popped up out of the water and Hailey was screaming and cheering. I was treading water and gasping for breath, but I was laughing, too.

"You did it, Li." Dad beamed.

The water felt thick and muscular, not like the limp water of a swimming pool. It was actually easy to swim out here. I remember thinking, This is it? This is what I've been so afraid of? I'm just *here* now. Only a hundred feet away from where I've always been. I'm still me. I'm just in the ocean.

chapter

ten

"It's back on with Nate," Hailey announced. It was a cool fall day, and we were walking toward the car-pool line where Mom would pick us up.

"Really?" I asked. This was the first time she had mentioned Nate in the two weeks since her meltdown in the bathroom.

"Yeah. We hung out at Max's house last night, and he seemed really into me."

"You went to Max's house? On a school night?" I asked, feeling vaguely left out.

"Yeah, I've had, like, zero homework all week," she said. "It's been amazing. Anyway, Nate sat next to me on the couch while we watched a movie, and I could just, like, tell he wanted to be near me. Our shoulders were touching, like, the whole time. I can't wait to see him tomorrow night, now that we have some momentum."

"What's tomorrow night?" I asked. "The dance?" Hailey and I hadn't gone to a school dance since sixth grade, and I was shocked she wanted to start going again now.

"Are you joking? The dance?" She laughed. "I feel awkward just thinking about all those streamers hanging from the ceiling in the gym."

I laughed, too. "It's not that bad."

"Well, you should go," Hailey said. "Say hi to the fruit punch for me if you do."

"So if you're not going, where are you planning on seeing Nate?" I asked.

"Max's. He's having people over. His house is so fun when his parents are out of town."

"Have you gone there a lot?" I asked.

"Not like, a-lot a-lot, but a few times," she said. She pulled her cell phone out of her pocket and started typing.

"Why don't you ever bring me, too?"

"I just didn't think it was your kind of thing," she said.

"What do you mean?" I was starting to feel unsteady.

"You know," she sighed. "It's just, like, smoking cigarettes and weed and watching dumb TV."

"I like that sometimes," I said shakily.

Hailey rolled her eyes. "Don't get all bent out of shape, Li. Just come tomorrow night if you're curious."

"Do you want me to come?" I asked.

"Yeah. Totally," she said, but her tone was opaque. And then, after a pause, she added, in a softer voice, "Of course I want you come."

She pulled me into a tight hug. She smelled like cigarettes and a perfume I didn't recognize.

chapter

eleven

ailey got a ride to Max's with some of Skyler's friends, so Mom drove me. We listened to Simon and Garfunkel in the car and sang along to "April Come She Will." Mom and I both preferred Simon and Garfunkel to The Beatles, a fact that drove Dad crazy.

Max lived in a mansion on a broad street in Beverly Hills. The house looked like a dollhouse. It was light blue with white-shuttered windows and a neat, triangular roof.

The front door was open, and I followed the sound of music up a set of stairs to Max's room. There were maybe ten or fifteen people from school in there, a few sitting on his massive bed and a few on the floor.

"Lima!" Hailey said happily when she saw me. "You made it! Come here, baby!"

Hailey handed me a pipe and, without thinking about what I was doing, I took a long inhale. It burned. I started to cough. And cough. And cough. I felt like my body was splitting down the middle.

"Oh wow," I said finally, over the music and the laughter. "I need water. Will you come find some with me?"

Hailey didn't look at me, and I had the distinct feeling that she was pretending she couldn't hear.

"Hailey!" I practically shouted. "I need water!"

She looked at me then with wide eyes. "Calm down. Just go to the kitchen if you need water."

I left the room and voices chased me down the stairs. Max's house felt like a maze and I paused, worried I'd never find my way to the kitchen or find my way back to his room.

"Lima."

I looked up and Nate was standing a step below me. The stair compensated for our height difference so we were face-to-face.

"Wow. Your eyes are red. You're pretty faded, huh?" He suppressed a laugh.

I nodded, realizing that I was. I tried to speak, but I didn't know what to say.

"Let's go outside for a second," he said. "I think you should get some air."

Air sounded good. I followed Nate.

Outside, the night was still. I longed for a beachy wind. The houses on this street looked too big and were set too far back from the wide road. I missed my own house. The feeling came on so quickly and so strongly that it felt like a punch.

"You okay?" Nate asked, as if he could read my mind.

"I don't know. I can't stop thinking."

"Do you get high often?" he asked me, a crooked smile spreading across his lips.

I bit my lip. "Are you teasing me?"

He looked surprised. "No, not at all."

Looking into Nate's eyes actually made me feel a little better. He looked sober, mellow. I could kind of rest my thoughts when I was looking at him.

"I smoked pot once before with Hailey," I said unsteadily. "But it was different. Right now I feel really weird."

"It'll be over before you know it," he said, and he sat down next to me on the steps. "And I can sit here with you for a minute."

Everything about this night was wrong. I knew I had only been at Max's for a little while, but it felt like a lifetime ago that Mom had dropped me off. Getting high seemed to have severed me from the person I had been on the way over.

"Don't you want to go inside and say hi?" I asked.

"I'm sure they're fine inside without me," Nate replied.

Nate pulled a cough drop out of his pocket and unwrapped it. I studied him unselfconsciously for a moment as he slipped it into his mouth. He had a slightly crooked nose and traces of lavender circles under his eyes, but his mouth was surprisingly nice. His lips were red and full and perfectly shaped, even though his bottom lip was a little chapped. He wasn't as conventionally good-looking as someone like Ryan, but it occurred to me now that that made him even cuter. Maybe that was why he got so many girls and also part of why Hailey had always liked him so much.

I turned my attention out to the street and let my mind unwind. Being stoned made me focus on small, strange things, like the faint buzz of electricity that I could practically hear coming out of the houses. The fog created strange orange halos around each streetlight, and the perfectly trimmed plants that lined Max's driveway were so neat they looked fake. Max's house looked like a stage set, bright and hollow.

"So," Nate said. "How do you feel now?"

I had almost forgotten he was there. Suddenly I felt terribly guilty that he was out here with me instead of with Hailey.

"I should go home," I said.

He nodded. "Give me your phone."

"Who are you calling?" I asked.

"A taxi."

I watched and listened as he ordered the taxi, grateful that Nate was there, and that he was taking care of things.

"Thank you," I said softly.

"It's nothing," he said. And then his voice had a mean, condescending tone in it. "Are you gonna say good-bye to your friend or just ditch her here?"

It was weird the way he called Hailey "my friend." Like he didn't know her, too. Like he hadn't kissed her just a few weeks ago.

I texted Hailey. When she came outside, Nate and I were still sitting side by side on the steps.

"Hey, stranger," she said to Nate in a weird, overly flirty voice. I felt embarrassed for her.

Nate looked at her for a moment before answering. Then he said coolly, "Hi."

The three of us waited on the curb for my taxi to come without talking. Nate was so weird, the way he could be helpful and nice one minute and withdrawn and impatient the next.

"I love you, Li. Feel better," Hailey said to me as I climbed into the taxi, but her words contorted in my mind and all I heard was: "I told you so."

I had completely failed at proving that I could keep up with her. I looked out the rear window as the car drove away, watching her and Nate talk on the sidewalk. As they disappeared from view, I wondered what would happen between them now that I was gone.

chapter

twelve

"**D**o you think I should wear Caroline's prom dress again this year?" I asked, draping the pink 1980s dress across my desk. Mom and Dad's twentieth-anniversary party was starting soon. The caterers and band and bartenders were already set up downstairs. I laid the dress down carefully and ran my hands over the silk.

"I don't know." Hailey was lying on my bed with her laptop on her stomach. She had been glued to the computer all afternoon. "Skyler just chatted me and said people might be going to the pier."

I deliberately didn't respond. Instead, I held up a long, patterned dress with an empire waist. "Or maybe I should wear this hippie dress," I said, "and you can wear Caroline's dress."

Hailey and I always had fun at Mom and Dad's anniversary parties. Last year, Hailey snuck enough champagne to get drunk and then made out with one of the hired bartenders on the beach. He was at least twenty-one.

"Oh my God, and she just sent me pictures from Max's party last weekend. The one where Nate had to babysit you. Wow, I look so wasted," Hailey said. "Come see."

Thinking about that night at Max's house filled me with embarrassment, but I went to the bed and peered over at the picture on her screen anyway. Her face was flushed and sort of wet looking, her lips open.

"Do I look good here?" she asked. Before I could even answer, Hailey's cell phone lit up with a new message.

I walked back to my closet and started hunting for shoes. I could hear Hailey tapping hard on her phone, texting.

"Skyler says Nate is definitely going to be there tonight," Hailey said. "I have to go. You understand, right?"

I turned and looked at Hailey. I mean really looked at her. She hadn't taken her eyes off the computer or her cell phone all afternoon. Even now, she avoided my gaze.

"Really?" I asked. "You can't *not* have a crush on Nate for one night? You promised me you'd stay."

Hailey looked up at me and her eyes were closed doors. "You don't understand because you've never had a crush," she said plainly.

I turned back to my reflection in the mirror, suddenly ashamed to be getting all dressed up with nowhere to go. I felt inexperienced and immature. Here I was all giddy to be hanging out with my parents, when Hailey had a real life and new friends.

Skyler picked Hailey up at my house before the guests had even started to arrive. In my room, I put the dresses away. I decided to stay in the jeans and shirt I'd worn to school. If I was going to be the girl with no life, who stayed home on a Friday night, at least I could be comfortable.

I took a fish taco off of one of the caterer's trays and ate it while I walked around the party. Mom and Dad's friends were a mix of neighbors and people that Dad worked with. I had known most of them my whole life.

"Lima?"

I turned and was momentarily stunned. Meredith Hayes was standing in my living room. And next to her was her twin brother, Walker.

I knew who Meredith and Walker were because everyone did. They were the most aloof, most gossiped-about, most mysterious seniors at our school. But it surprised me that Meredith knew my name. *I* was a nobody. *She* was Meredith Hayes.

The twins dressed like celebrities. Meredith wore high-waisted bell-bottom jeans and lots of bulky, exotic jewelry. Walker had a beard and long hair and always wore perfectly beat-up corduroys or vintage suits. You never saw one twin without the other. All kinds of rumors circulated about them. The weirdest one I ever heard was that they liked to have sex with the same people. I wasn't even sure how that would work, but I didn't want to sound naive so I never asked.

"Hey, hi," I stammered. "I live here."

"I know," Meredith said, beaming. I'd never been up close to her before, and she was startlingly pretty and exotic looking, with a wide face, large, almond-shaped brown eyes, and dimples. Her elbow-length brown hair was pin straight and parted in the middle.

"Your house is amazing," she said.

I marveled at her sweet, benevolent manner. She wasn't at all scary like I'd imagined.

"Our dad is a client of your dad's. He's out of town but he forwarded us the invitation," she continued. "And we decided to come in his place."

"A Peruvian-themed party in Malibu sounded weird and awesome," Walker added.

I almost laughed. I couldn't imagine my parents' anniversary party sounding weird and awesome, but I liked that they saw it that way.

"Give us the tour," Meredith said.

"This is pretty much it," I said. "The whole first floor is just this one room."

"There must be a secret room somewhere," she said slyly. "All houses have secrets."

They were being so nice to me and I didn't want to say anything that might burst the bubble, so I said, "Follow me," and led them upstairs.

Meredith looked around Dad's office in the dim lamplight. "This is totally the magic room."

"Good music," Walker said, scanning Dad's record collection. "Lots of hippie stuff."

I laughed. "My parents love that kind of music. So do I."

"You do?" Meredith cocked her head. "Like who?"

"My favorite singer is Joni Mitchell," I said, feeling my face flush. Talking about music felt like sharing something private. "My parents saw her in concert when my mom was pregnant with me. They say that's why I love her so much."

Meredith wrinkled her nose. "That's sweet."

"Joni's cool," Walker said. "That stuff is actually really musically complicated. Hard to play."

"Have you heard *Court and Spark*?" Meredith asked.

"I love *Court and Spark*!" I said, getting excited. "That's my favorite Joni album."

And then, without any prompting, Meredith starting singing the words to one of my favorite songs. She sang as naturally as if she were speaking. Her voice fluctuated between being raspy and clear in the most mesmerizing way, like a violin.

Walker picked up Dad's whiskey bottle and examined it.

"That's my dad's," I said quickly. "He'd notice if we drank it."

Meredith laughed. "He's not gonna take it, don't worry."

Walker opened the lapel of his jacket and a metal flask caught the light. "See, Court and Spark? Relax. I brought my own."

"Let's go drink that by the water," Meredith said.

Sounds of the party drifted out to the beach. As we sat outside, the sky changed from a pastel dusk to a black night. After the twins finished their flask, they sent me back in to get something else. I brought them back a bottle of red wine that I snuck off the caterer's bar.

The twins passed it back and forth, taking long sips that dripped down their chins. They talked aimlessly. They weren't like other people. They didn't talk about school or gossip or their parents.

"What would you rather: no music for the rest of your life, or no stories?" Meredith asked at one point.

"No stories," Walker said, taking the bottle from his sister.

"Me too," Meredith said. "Lima?"

"No stories," I agreed.

"What would you rather," she started again, "Africa or India?"

"India," Walker said.

"Me too!" Meredith said, sounding surprised. She gave her brother a high five. "Lima?"

"It's impossible to choose," I said. "I want to go to both."

"You are so right," Meredith said sincerely.

Walker nodded slowly and handed the wine to me.

They watched as I took my first sip of the night. It tasted like warmth. I lay back and listened to the loud crashing of the waves. I took a deep breath and felt the cold night air crawl all over my body. Tonight had turned out to be amazing. Hailey was really missing out.

"Lima!" Meredith called. She was standing now, and had to shout to be heard over the ocean.

I propped myself up on my elbows. "Yeah?"

"We like you a lot!" Meredith shouted into the night air. She was barefoot, and stumbling, the bottle of wine swinging from her hand, catching and refracting little bits of moonlight.

"You do?" I asked.

"We do!" she shouted, dropping the bottle in the sand. "And we're going swimming and we want you to come!"

Walker stood up and started pulling off his clothing.

"No!" I screamed, laughing. "It's too cold! You'll die."

Walker started singing a song I didn't recognize at the top of his lungs, his voice cracking and disappearing beneath the sounds of the waves. Meredith stripped down to her bra and underwear. She was more fragile and skinny than I had imagined, her wrists and calves as thin as forks and knives.

She darted toward the ocean. Walker, pulling his pants off, ran in behind her in his boxers. They disappeared out of my view into the blackness until I couldn't see or hear them at all. I walked down closer to the shore, to the place where the sand feels cold and wet from the lapping water.

Ten long seconds later I saw them splashing and running toward me, and I heard their shrieks.

"Fuck!" Walker screamed.

Meredith ran to me, shivering, and put her hand on my cheek. It was like ice. Her skin was goose bumped and pale, almost blue. "Can you feel that?" she asked, through chattering teeth.

Later, I walked them to their car. They smoked a joint as we wove through the line of parked cars on the Pacific Coast Highway. "Want some?" Meredith asked. Her hair was a wet coil, twisting over her shoulder.

I shook my head no.

"Tonight ruled," Walker said when we got to their car.

"I know," Meredith agreed. "It was magic." She was looking right at me, but somehow I felt as if she was seeing someone else. Someone cooler, wilder. Someone unforgettable.

chapter

thirteen

"My parents' party ended up being really amazing," I told Hailey at break on Monday. I knew it wasn't nice of me, but I wanted her to feel a little left out.

"Sure," she said absently, bored already. "My night sucked. Nate never even showed up."

I ignored her. "Meredith and Walker Hayes came. I guess their dad knows my dad."

Hailey grabbed my forearm, her jaw hanging open. "WHAT?! The Hayeses came to your party? Did they steal anything?"

"No, stop it!" I scoffed. "They were—"

"Honestly, Lima," she said, "you should check your cabinets. I heard they've stolen a ton of stuff, like clothes and jewelry from the end-of-the-year party at Hannah Kelley's house."

"You're wrong," I said. "They were cool."

Hailey rolled her eyes, "I give that friendship five minutes."

Hailey was making it really difficult for me to explain how exciting Friday night was. Feeling flustered, I stormed off to get a Coke from the vending machine.

I pounded quarters into the machine, our conversation echoing in my head. Hailey didn't know anything, I decided. The twins were fun and too cool for her anyway. She probably just felt threatened.

My Coke banged its way out of the machine. I bent down to grab it, and when I stood up Nate was standing next to me.

I froze. I wanted to just say hi, or walk away, but I felt somehow caught.

"Coke, not Pepsi?" he asked.

I smiled, relieved by his lightness. "Always," I said. I looked down at my Coke and popped the tab. It fizzed up.

"Can I . . .?" He gestured to the vending machine, and I realized I was still standing right in front of it. I scooted out of the way. Why did I always act like such an idiot around him?

I hurried away from the vending machine and, after about a minute, I glanced quickly back over my shoulder. He was gone.

chapter

fourteen

𝕴 wasn't sure if the Hayes twins would ever talk to me again, but Meredith surprised me by offering to give me a ride home from school the next day. She was wearing a Fair Isle sweater, high-waisted skinny black jeans, and her hair was pulled back into a neat ponytail. She looked ordinary and glamorous at once.

"This place is amazing in the daylight," she cooed when we got to my house. She crossed the living room, walked up to the back doors, and pressed her palms against the glass. "Can we go down to the ocean?"

The late-afternoon sky was getting white, but the sun setting on the water turned the clouds an electric pink. It was a postcard-perfect California sunset.

Meredith and I rolled up our jeans and walked barefoot in the cold, damp sand.

After a moment she said, "I hope Walker and I weren't too weird the other night."

"You weren't weird," I lied.

"Well," she said. "We were very wasted."

"You were fun," I said.

Meredith laughed. "Yeah, people are fun to be around when they're high on something."

"I'm not," I said. "I'm really awkward."

"You?" she asked.

"I've tried smoking pot a couple of times," I said. "But I don't think I really like it. The last time I did it was at this guy's house with some people from school, and I had to go home. I felt like I couldn't be around anyone."

"I get that. I used to hate getting high when I had to do it in big groups and be around people who I didn't even like," she said. "But once you get older, it's different. Walker and I just smoke on our terms now, like at home or on a hike, or with really good people. Drugs can be really magical. You just have to be with people you love and trust."

I thought about this for a second. Meredith had described the other night as magical, too.

"Magical? Do you believe in magic?" I asked.

"Don't you?" she asked cryptically.

"I don't think so," I said.

Meredith laughed. I liked her laugh. It was very knowing.

She put her hands on my shoulders and pointed me toward the ocean and the brilliant setting sun. "What would you call that?"

The sky was neon pink and lavender, and I breathed in a deep ocean-y breath. Maybe Meredith and I weren't so different after all.

I was doing homework in my room later that evening when Hailey called.

"Lima. What are you doing for community service this year?"

Rustic required fifty hours of community service a year. Last year, I worked at a soup kitchen in Santa Monica. I actually sort of liked it. This year, Mom had done some research and found out that we could help plant gardens in public schools in downtown LA. Mom said she would do it with me, and I was really looking forward to it. I rarely got to venture to the east side of LA, and I loved gardening, so the whole thing seemed cool.

"I'm gonna work at a garden," I said. "Why?"

"Have you signed up yet?" she asked.

"No. Why?"

"Fantastic! Because we are doing Clean the Bay! Together! And so is Nate!" she said excitedly. "It starts tomorrow."

I groaned. "I don't think so, Hailey. I love you, but I really don't want to do Clean the Bay."

Clean the Bay was the worst community service. It was community service for slackers. You just rode the school bus down to the beach and spent a few hours picking up trash.

"Please, Lima," Hailey continued in a baby voice. "I really think if I can spend some quality time with Nate, doing something that doesn't involve booze or weed, we can get closer."

"But why do I have to be there?" I asked.

"If I sign up by myself, he might think it's because I like him 'cause I know he knows. But if you sign up with me, I can say I'm doing it because you're doing it!"

"What about Skyler?" For once I wanted Hailey to choose Skyler over me.

"Skyler's dad donated all this money to some foundation in the school's name, and it got her out of community service for, like, forever," she said. And then she added, "But that's a huge secret, so don't tell anyone."

I sighed.

"Come on, Li. I need you. You promised you'd help me get Nate."

"I did?" I said meekly. I could feel myself starting to give in.

"You promised by virtue of our friendship. It's implicit in the best-friend contract."

I really didn't want to do Clean the Bay. And I had a queasy feeling about spending all that time with Nate and Hailey, but I couldn't put my finger on why.

"Honestly," she said, her voice a little softer, "I just feel more comfortable when you're around."

Hailey obviously wanted this really badly. And I could put Hailey first this one time. If the tables were turned, I told myself, she'd do the same for me.

chapter

fifteen

∞

The bus to Clean the Bay was full of just the kinds of people I'd expect to sign up for it. Hailey insisted that we try and find a seat in the back of the bus, even though I would have much preferred to sit in the front row across from the supervisor, Leo.

Leo had a bushy beard and glasses. He wore khaki shorts and a hemp necklace and rode his bike to work every day. We had him for American History in ninth grade, and he was a really good teacher. Hailey made fun of him for being such an eco-nerd, but I thought he was interesting.

When Nate darted onto the bus at the last minute and sat in the second row, Hailey's eyes burned with disappointment.

"See," I said. "We should have sat in the front."

Hailey rolled her eyes at me and sulked the whole way there.

At the beach, Leo told us we could go as far north as the lifeguard stand and as far south as the Santa Monica Pier.

Beach cleanup wasn't as terrible as I'd thought it would be. The beach down here was different from the one near my house—it was bigger and louder and dirtier. There were tourists walking on the sand with cameras and knee-high socks, and police officers on bikes.

I liked the way being near the ocean made me feel a little dirty and earthy. The air coming off the water was thick with minerals, and the wind wrapped itself around me and climbed inside my clothes.

The class was spread out over the whole beach. I could make out Nate, about a hundred yards away, bending over and depositing little bits of trash into his plastic orange "Clean the Bay!" sack.

At one point Hailey ran up to talk to him, and I watched but couldn't hear them. The wind and waves swallowed their voices. She returned a few minutes later, walking toward me in the slow, painful way people do when they're walking in sand, like it hurts to move.

"He's in a terrible mood," she declared. "What an asshole."

I didn't ask.

. . .

"You're unusually quiet, Hailey," Mom said, glancing at her in the rearview mirror as she drove us home that afternoon. "Is there something on your mind?"

"I hate boys," Hailey grumbled.

"I doubt that," Mom teased.

"You're right. I don't hate boys; I love boys," Hailey said. And then she added, "Well, I actually love one boy."

"The same one you've told me about?" Mom asked. "Nick?"

I shifted around uncomfortably in my seat. It always annoyed me when Hailey talked to Mom about Nate.

"Nate," Hailey corrected. "I'm so confused. Like, he's nice to me one second and then he's all mean and weird the next. I can't tell what he wants."

"Maybe he doesn't know what he wants," Mom said. "Boys at your age are different from girls. And in your case, it's especially true. You're a romantic. I can pretty much guarantee you spend more time thinking about love than this boy does."

"Maybe," Hailey agreed. "I mean, I do think about him like twenty-four/seven. I just want him to like me as much as I like him. I like him so much it, like, physically hurts."

"I know, sweetie," Mom said. "And he probably does feel

the same way as you, whether or not he can show it. You're such a wonderful, fun, fantastic girl. If he can't see that, well, he might not be worth liking."

Hailey let out a long, whistle of breath. "I love you, Laura."

Mom beamed at Hailey in the rearview mirror and I tried not to roll my eyes. She looked like she was ready to pull over on the PCH just to give Hailey a hug. I looked out the window. The sun had started to go down, and reddish, late afternoon light splintered across the surface of the water.

Maybe Mom noticed my silence, because she glanced suspiciously at me. "Are you still with us, Li?"

"Yeah, totally," I said, and scanned my fingernails for a good one to bite.

chapter

sixteen

"We're five minutes away from your house and we're picking you up," Meredith said over the phone that Friday night. "We're going to get food."

I was home alone watching reruns of *House* and eating popcorn in the living room. I was wearing my favorite fluffy bunny slippers and boxer shorts. The idea of getting dressed and getting on the freeway sounded unbearable, but Meredith was hard to deny. "You're gonna drive me all the way back to Malibu afterward?"

"You can stay over at our house," Meredith said. "We have lots of extra beds."

I texted Mom to ask if I could go over to Meredith's, but she and Dad were at the movies and they still hadn't responded by the time the twins' car pulled up in our driveway. For a moment, I contemplated telling Meredith I couldn't go because I wasn't sure if I was allowed to, but that would sound ridiculous. They had come all this way just to see me; it would be insane to make them leave now.

The Hayeses drove a big, noisy 1955 Chevy. It was painted black and upholstered with bright red vinyl. The lining of all the seats was splitting in multiple places, and yellow spongy stuffing was bursting out.

Next to me in the backseat was a girl named Lily who I recognized from school. Lily was round and baby-faced, like a doll, and she dressed like a pinup girl from the fifties. She curled her dyed black bangs into a perfect coil, as hard and shiny as a pole, and she wore tights, high-heel pumps, and orangey red lipstick to school every single day.

Now that I was so close to her, I noticed other things about Lily. She had skin as smooth and white as porcelain. Her arms were pale and almost hairless looking, as if she was covered in flour. She had a small Celtic pattern tattooed onto the inside of her left wrist.

In the front seat, a boy I didn't recognize sat between Meredith and Walker. In old cars like the twins', the front seat is like a bench.

"The famous Lima," he said, craning his neck around to see me. "We've been hearing all about the wild party you had a few weeks ago. We heard y'all went skinny-dipping in the ocean."

"Well—" I began to clarify, but stopped myself. Why ruin

the glamorous image he had in his head by telling him it was my parents' party and I didn't even go in the ocean? Instead I said, "Who are you?"

Everybody laughed.

"I'm Henry," he said.

"He's my boyfriend," Lily said. She stretched out her arm so she could just skim Henry's cheek with her fingers. He turned to face her, made a kind of a barking sound, and then clamped down on her fingers with his teeth. She squealed with glee.

"So, Lima," Henry continued. He had honey-colored skin and high cheekbones, and his voice was slow and sultry. "You're named after the capital of Peru."

I nodded. "Most people don't know that. Where do you go to school?"

He smiled a little. "I'm not in school anymore."

"Oh. How old are you?"

Everyone laughed again.

"I'm eighteen," he said. "School just wasn't my thing. I dropped out last year and moved to LA."

"From where?" I asked.

He shook his head. "Lots of questions."

I laughed. "Sorry."

"From all over," he said. "Last place I went to school was Indiana."

"Wow." What he said—dropping out of high school, living in lots of places, ending up in LA—it just implied so much more than I could imagine. I had a million questions, but didn't even know where to start.

"We went down to the beach for a little fresh air," Meredith said, twisting back to look at me. She must not have been wearing a seat belt because she curled around the back of Henry's body to face me. She rested her bejeweled fingers on his shoulder and let her long hair tumble down into his face. He didn't flinch. "And now we're all starving. We're going get some food on the way home."

I'd never been to Canter's Deli before. I had seen the big 1950s neon sign and wondered about it, but it wasn't the kind of place Mom and Dad would ever go, with its retro, seedy-looking storefront. Inside, it was livelier and more crowded than its exterior promised. I scanned the enormous room, registering right away that we were the youngest people there.

The five of us squeezed into a big, red vinyl booth and Walker ordered a round of milk shakes while we perused enormous sticky menus. At the table next to us, a man with long hair and weathered, sunken cheeks was eating breakfast: eggs, bacon, even coffee.

"We're going to the Rose Bowl Flea Market tomorrow, Lima," Meredith said. "You have to come. It's so fantastic."

"I'm obsessed with flea markets," said Lily. "They're lame if you don't know what you're doing, but I go all the time so I know all the good vendors."

"My buddy has a booth there. Old records and shit," Henry added. His arm was draped around Lily's shoulders, and his fingers hovered near her breast. He leaned in and bit her earlobe.

These people have touched each other everywhere, I thought. Contact wasn't even a big deal to them anymore. Their hands and eyes had slipped all over one another's bodies. It seemed impossible that I would ever, in a million years, feel that comfortable with another person's body. For some reason, my mind flashed to Hailey and Nate.

"Remember that eight-track player we found last summer?" Lily asked Henry, ignoring his nibbling.

"What's an A track?" I asked.

They all laughed.

"I get it," Henry said to Meredith. "This girl is sweet."

The Hayeses lived in Laurel Canyon, the hills above West Hollywood. The road wound up and up for what seemed like forever. The streets got narrower and steeper as we drove. Hidden houses lined one side and mountains the other.

"Does anyone else from school live around here?" I asked.

"Someone just moved in to a house at the bottom of our

street," Meredith said vaguely. "Brian? Or Ryan? He's in your grade."

"Ryan," Walker corrected.

"Ryan Masterson?" I asked.

"Maybe," Meredith replied. And then, after a minute, she pressed her forefinger to the window as if it were a screen. "There. His dad just bought that house. You can't really see it."

Finally we arrived at the twins' house. It was enormous and modern, with walls of glass and strange concrete additions. It appeared to have innumerable stories and wings and balconies.

The furniture inside was dark and sleek except for one glittering white grand piano. The ceilings were high, which made the rooms feel cavernous, glamorous. Everything was immaculate. The whole place was a surprise. I guess I'd pictured the Hayeses living in a shack with tiki torches everywhere and Christmas lights hanging from the roof. I hadn't realized they were so insanely rich.

"Where's your dad?" I asked, trying to sound casual.

"Saint Barts," Walker said.

Meredith told me I'd be sleeping in her bed with her, and for a second I was nervous. I'd only ever shared a bed with Hailey. But once I saw Meredith's decadent, king-size canopy bed, I relaxed. We would both have plenty of space. Even Meredith's bathroom was bigger than my bedroom at home.

Meredith had a TV mounted on the wall across from her bed. We climbed under her satin sheets, watched *Seinfeld*, and played with her cat, Leonard Cohen. Meredith was surprisingly easy to be around. Sometimes she seemed all complex and mysterious, but she was really disarmingly normal.

I reached for a framed photograph that was resting on her bedside table. "Can I look at this?"

Her eyes drifted over to my hands, and she nodded slowly, pensively.

It was a photograph of a woman with the wind in her hair, standing on a big wooden deck. At first I thought it was a picture of Meredith—it looked just like her, with the long dark hair and heart-shaped face—but then I saw that there were two tiny children standing at her feet. *Meredith and Walker.*

"That's my mother," she said. "Anne."

"She looks exactly like you."

Meredith smiled vaguely. "She was pretty. She was a model."

I grew quiet. It worried me to hear her referred to in the past tense.

Meredith laughed. "Oh, no, don't worry. She's alive. She just lives in Paris. We almost never see her."

"Why?" I asked.

Meredith shrugged, *"C'est la vie."*

It was just the kind of cryptic answer I was starting to

expect from her. She seemed so at peace with everything. Not angsty. Not confused.

She stared off into a space for a moment, and then she said, in response to nothing in particular, "Paris."

But this time she pronounced Paris like "puh-ree," like a real French person would. After she said it, there was a strange pause. And then she giggled.

chapter

seventeen

The next morning we headed to the Rose Bowl Flea Market, which turned out to be loud and exhausting. The others seemed fascinated by everything they saw. They handled pots and old picture frames and dusty records. And the amazing thing was, it seemed like they were actually able to assess the quality of this stuff.

Meredith thumbed through a bin full of jewelry and produced a glittering necklace.

"That's pretty!" I said, admiring the way it reflected daylight.

She looked at it thoughtfully. "No. Not special."

And then she moved on. To me, it was all the same. Special because it was old and weird, but also just stuff that you wouldn't actually wear.

I was getting pretty bored and cranky. It was hot in Pasadena, and the flea market was crowded and dirty. I wanted to go home and talk to Mom. I was feigning interest in some vintage posters when Meredith called my name.

"This. You." She was holding up a leather jacket.

It didn't look like much to me. It was smallish and black, with slightly beat-up leather that was starting to crack around the elbows and collar. It had two zipper breast pockets and another set of pockets lower down.

"Cute!" I lied. "But I'm too hot to try it on. And I have no money."

"Don't worry about that. Get over here," she said affectionately.

I begrudgingly dropped my purse and let her put my arms into the sleeves. I knew right away that it was a perfect fit. The leather felt cool and mild on my skin.

Meredith turned me toward a mirror that the vendor had leaned up against the side of his van, and I looked at my reflection. I was stunned. There was a hardness to the jacket, a dark history you could sense from looking at it. It was the jacket of someone who had done bad things, who had taken risks, lived a dangerous life. Wearing it, I seemed to assume some of those qualities. I was transformed. Even I could see the magic.

"This is so cool," I said, my eyes finding Meredith's in the mirror. "But, still. I literally only have seven dollars with me."

Meredith wrapped her arms around me from behind. I

liked seeing the two of us together in the reflection. Even though we didn't look alike, our faces seemed to match. Like people who belonged together.

"You have to have this jacket," she said matter-of-factly. "I'll get it for you."

I looked at the handwritten price tag hanging off the sleeve. It was over a hundred dollars. My heart sank.

"You can't do that," I said. "It's too much. I won't be able to pay you back."

Meredith slid out from behind me and cupped my face in her hands. Her eyes were smiling. "Shush. It's a present. I seriously don't care."

The sun sparkled through the big trees of Laurel Canyon while I waited on the steps of the twins' house for Mom and Dad to pick me up, and bits of yellow light swam around me like a million shimmering fish. It was so pretty here, and the last twenty-four hours had been an amazing adventure, but it felt incomplete without being able to share it with someone. I wished Hailey were here. We could analyze Henry and Lily and how foreign but cool Meredith's world felt.

I picked up my phone and called her. After a few rings, it went to voice mail and the sound of her voice on the recording stung. Missing her felt physical, like an icy wind blowing through my rib cage.

Hailey hated voice mails so I sent her a text instead.

Tried calling you. I miss you! Love you! Call
me! xoxox

What was Hailey doing right now? What had she done all weekend? I couldn't remember a time when a weekend had passed and I'd had no idea what she'd done. A high breeze moved through the trees and the rustling leaves made a sound like the ocean.

"Where'd that jacket come from?" Mom asked when they arrived. Mom was sitting in the passenger seat and Dad was behind the wheel.

"I got it at the Rose Bowl this morning. Meredith bought it for me," I said.

Instead of backing out of the driveway, Dad turned the engine off and turned to face me.

"Aren't we leaving?" I asked.

"What you did last night was not okay," Dad said.

"What did I do?" I asked, growing hot. Images of the night before flashed through my mind.

"You went out without asking if you could," Mom said. "And you got in the car with a driver who we don't know."

"I asked!" I protested. "And you know Meredith and Walker. They came to your anniversary party."

"Asking is not the same thing as getting permission," Dad said. "You should have waited. You can't just leave."

"And to be honest, Li, I probably would have said no," Mom added.

"Why? Why in the world would you say no?" I asked, even though I had a feeling I knew the answer. Meredith and Walker were just the kind of people parents were afraid of.

"Meredith seems very independent," Mom replied.

"You say that like it's a bad thing," I said. "Isn't it a good thing?"

"What Mommy means," Dad said, "is that they're fast."

"Fast?" I repeated. "Really?"

"Look," Dad said. "We're here. Why don't we go inside and talk to Howie Hayes. You know he's a client and I haven't seen him in a while. If you're planning on sleeping over here again, we'd just like to know that you'll be safe. That he's a responsible parent."

"You can't," I blurted, panicking. They would freak out if they knew there hadn't been any adults here the night before. I would never be allowed to come over again. "He went out to lunch. He's not here."

I didn't have a lot of practice lying to Mom and Dad, and I held my breath while I waited for them to see through me. Instead, Dad turned on the car and started down the driveway.

"Okay. But this conversation isn't over," he said. "You can't just go out without permission."

"I know," I said. "I promise I won't do that again. Ever."

Dad turned onto the twisty street that led back to Laurel Canyon Boulevard and I started to relax. There were colorful, stucco houses tucked into the hills and big, gnarled trees that canopied the road.

"We haven't seen Hailey lately," Mom added, after a moment. "Is she friendly with Meredith Hayes?"

"Not really," I said. I glanced at my phone and a hard pebble of sadness formed in my throat. She still hadn't texted me back.

chapter

eighteen

Q decided to meet Hailey outside of her second-period class Monday morning. The hollow feeling of missing her hadn't gone away, and even though she never got back to me, I was dying to give her a hug and smell that familiar Hailey smell. I was wearing my new leather jacket, and it made me feel brave and optimistic. Hailey and I had started tenth grade on the wrong foot, but I was ready to right things. I could forgive her for ditching me at my parents' anniversary party, and for not including me in her social life. We could get past that.

Hailey and Skyler stepped out of the classroom side by side, and I waved at them from across the hall. Even though I didn't really want to talk to Skyler, I was glad she was seeing me in my new jacket. She always had to have the coolest things, and I was sure she'd be super impressed.

Skyler looked me up and down and then ignored me. She

hooked her arm tight around Hailey's neck and said, "I have to get something from my locker. Come with me?"

"I called you yesterday, Hailey," I blurted out, a mix of hot emotions rising in my throat.

Hailey stopped. She was quiet for a second, and then she said simply, "My phone died."

I stood there awkwardly, not sure what to say next. My face burned with shame and hurt. There was no way I could tell her I missed her. Not with Skyler hanging on to her like that.

Hailey looked at me for a moment longer, and then a concerned expression slowly transformed her face. She opened her mouth to say something but Skyler cut her off.

"C'mon, Hailey," Skyler whined, toddler-like.

Hailey laughed and allowed Skyler to steer her down the hall away from me.

chapter

nineteen

The noise level in the library during lunch was the perfect amount of loud for studying. Too much quiet could be even more distracting to me than too much sound. Maybe it was because I had grown up listening to the constant thrumming of the waves on the beach and the grinding buzz of cars on the road, but true silence rang in my ears like an alarm.

I was working at my favorite library table when I got that heavy feeling you get when someone is standing behind you. I turned to check and there was Nate. Gray hoodie. Dirty jeans. Ballpoint pen clamped between his lips like a cigarette. He walked around the table and slid into the seat across from me.

"What Spanish class are you in?" he asked, nodding to my textbook.

"Spanish two. Sixth period," I said,

"I have that class fifth," he said. "Are you studying for the quiz?"

I looked up at him, and felt my cheeks grow immediately hot under his warm blue gaze. "Yeah."

He took the pen out of his mouth and placed in on the desk.

"Quiz me," he said, giving me this lopsided smile.

"*Me gustaría ir a España, pero no puedo*," I read cautiously.

"I would like to go to Spain, but I can't?" he translated.

"Right," I said. "Conditional of *hablar*?"

"*Hablaria, hablarias, hablaria, habliaramos, hablariais, hablarian*," Nate recited.

I was impressed. "Right."

"Give me something hard," he said.

I searched. "Second person conditional of *poner* versus *poder*. They're similar."

Nate closed his eyes for a minute and I watched him think.

Finally he said, "Shit, I don't know. Tell me."

We quizzed each other back and forth for the rest of lunch. When one o'clock arrived, Nate stood up.

"Are you going to Cole's Halloween party this weekend?" he asked. And then he teased. "I know how much you love to party."

"I didn't know about it," I confessed. "Are you going?" A strange bubble of nervousness formed in my throat when I said it.

He flicked his ballpoint pen on the desk so it spun around and around, like a top. When it had slowed to a stop, he shrugged and said, "Maybe."

"I heard Cole is having a Halloween party," I said to Hailey in the car-pool line later. "Maybe we should go and dress up as something together. Like, I know we've always said we'd do Thelma and Louise."

"I'm going with Skyler," she said casually, "and we're dressing as fucked-up fairies."

"Oh," I said, deflating a little. I hadn't been planning on dressing up this year until I'd heard about the party from Nate, but since then I'd started to get excited. I'd spent all sixth period brainstorming. I could wear overalls and be Shelley Duvall from *The Shining*. Or wear Dad's clothes and be Annie Hall. Or Hailey and I could do something together. In fifth grade we'd gone as conjoined twins, and even though it was basically impossible to walk in the three-legged jumpsuit Mom made us, it was the best Halloween ever.

"Cole's is going to be stupid anyway," Hailey said, checking her cell phone. She was barely paying attention to me.

"We might, like, not even go, 'cause we're going to Bridget's brother's friend's house first. And if that's fun, we might just stay there."

I felt myself being pulled under a wave of disappointment. Hailey must have sensed it because she put her phone away and focused on me.

"I'm sorry, Li. Are you mad?" she asked in the baby voice that she reserved for times when she was trying to get something from me. "I didn't think you would want to go."

"I'm not mad," I said quickly. "It's not a big deal."

The autumn Los Angeles sun was sitting low, shedding a pallid light over the cars and washing out the concrete walls of our building.

Hailey's mom's car pulled up in front of us. Hailey had been resting her backpack on her feet and now she scooped it up and climbed into the car.

I waved to Brenda and she waved back, her face hidden behind a plaster mask of make-up.

Hailey stared straight ahead as they drove away, and I watched them go, wondering what they would talk about in the car, or if they would talk at all.

chapter

twenty

om and Dad and I were watching *Chinatown* and eating Chinese food that Saturday night when the landline rang.

"It's Meredith Hayes," Mom said. "For you, honey."

"Walker and I are going to this Halloween party at someone named Cole's house, and we want you to come," Meredith told me over the phone. "It's an old-fashioned all-school rager. Not really our thing, but Walker is convinced it'll be good for us to participate in some mainstream social activities."

I laughed. "I don't have a costume. I'm just watching a movie with my parents."

Suddenly it was Walker on the other end of the line.

"We're coming for you in an hour," he said.

"Oh—hi, Walker," I replied.

"Be ready." The line went dead.

Mom was really supportive of me going to the party.

Maybe she was feeling bad for me because I was hanging out with her and Dad and clearly had nothing better to do. We stopped the movie, and Mom and I went upstairs to scrape together a costume. We rummaged through the old costume chest, discarding some ratty angel wings and a tutu, and finally decided I should be something really easy and classic, like a black cat.

Mom painted whiskers on my cheeks with black eyeliner and put my hair in pigtails. I wore a long-sleeve black leotard and black skinny jeans. Over it I wore the black leather jacket, and the costume was complete.

Studying my reflection in Mom's full-length mirror, I found myself wondering who would be there. I looked like the kind of girl who things happened to. The kind of girl who had exciting nights.

Billie Holiday blared from the scratchy stereo as we zoomed along the Pacific Coast Highway. Walker and Meredith passed a cigarette back and forth, and the salty air slammed into the car and washed the smell of smoke away as quickly as it was being produced.

I texted Hailey on our way to the party to see if she was there. I knew it was petty and stupid, but I wanted her to see me show up with the Hayeses. I hoped she'd be jealous. Even though she thought they were scary, they were still undeniably ultracool.

Meredith and Walker hadn't even made an attempt at wearing costumes, not that they needed to. Dressed in their regular clothing they looked like rock stars.

"Where are Lily and Henry?" I asked.

"Being lame," Meredith said simply. "Having 'couple time.'"

"Probably braiding each other's hair," Walker added.

That made Meredith laugh and laugh.

When we pulled up to the party, Hailey was waiting for us outside, shivering in her costume. She was covered in glitter, and her white tights were ripped with big holes showing her skin. Her little white dress was a few sizes too small.

Her jaw dropped when I got out of the car. My costume was so simple and so cute, and I could feel her envy.

"Let's go in. I'm freezing out here," was all she said.

"I like your costume," I said. I knew I was fishing for a compliment.

"Thanks. I made it in, like, twenty minutes," she said, and as soon as we walked through the door, she turned to me. "I gotta find Sky, she has my cigarettes. You're okay, right?"

I nodded, stunned, and immediately was alone. Cole's steamy, windowless living room was packed with people in makeshift costumes that were already falling apart. The floor was sticky from spilled beer and smashed fun-size candy bars.

"Hey!" Emily shouted, weaving across the room toward me and wearing a wet suit and Aqua Socks. "Your costume rules!" She smiled as she arrived beside me. Her eyes were full of genuine awe. "That jacket is so cool," she said, touching the leather with her fingertips. "Wow. It's, like, a real biker jacket."

"I got it at the Rose Bowl Flea Market," I said.

"You shop at flea markets?" Emily asked. "If you ever want to go again, I'll go with you. We can carpool from Malibu."

I nodded and then moved on my way, scanning the room for Hailey or Meredith or Walker. Not seeing anyone, I followed two confident-looking older girls up the stairs. They stepped into a room at the end of the hall, and I could smell the smoke and hear the music leaking out.

I knocked.

A boy with a paper bag over his head and two tiny eyeholes cut out opened the door. He was tall and slim and I wondered if it was Nate.

"Yo, Hailey, your friend's here," said the voice from the bag. Not Nate.

Hailey was sitting on the floor between the two older girls, her back propped up against the wall, sipping a 40.

"Come here, Lima—have a malt beverage," she said. "Make room for Lima! Scoot down!"

Her sudden warmth surprised me, and in a weird way, it

bothered me more than when she had ditched me earlier. Or maybe it wasn't her warmth that bothered me but the way that she managed to turn it on and off like a faucet.

"Nate isn't coming," Hailey whispered. Her breath was warm and smelled like sugar. She rested her head on my shoulder.

"How do you know?"

"I texted him to see if he was coming, and he said no," she sighed. "And I look so hot! Don't I look hot?"

"You look amazing," I said.

"Fuck it," she said, abruptly popping up. "Let's dance."

She jumped up, cranked the volume on the stereo, and started dancing. The rest of the room joined in and I stood awkwardly in the corner for a few minutes, pretending to enjoy myself.

Finally I inserted myself in the dance party just long enough to grab Hailey and shout over the music, "Hailey! Come downstairs with me. I want to see people's costumes."

She shook her head. "I can't hear you!"

She waved at me, and I stumbled out of the dance party and down the stairs. After circulating through the first floor, I found Meredith and Walker lounging on a couch. They agreed that the party sucked, but Meredith said Walker was waiting for some guy to show up, so they couldn't leave. I called Mom to come get me. I felt like such an overdressed loser going home at 9:30 p.m., but I had no desire to stay out. Halloween was a big, stupid disappointment.

Sitting on the steps outside Cole's house waiting for Mom, I found myself thinking about Nate. I wondered what had he done instead tonight. Did he stay home and watch movies with his parents, like I usually did? Had he gone out and hooked up with a girl from outside of school?

A pair of girls in identical jailbird jumpsuits walked past me into the party. Their arms were linked, and they were laughing so hard they could barely walk. They left an extra-sharp silence in the space behind them.

chapter

twenty-one

I brought my books into the library on Monday at lunch and dropped them on the desk. I cracked open my history reading and stared at the page. I heard footsteps behind me and snapped my head around to see who it was. A boy in Coke-bottle glasses padded past my desk.

Emily and I walked to fifth period together through the old gym, the one that smelled like sweat and chlorine. A pack of boys walked toward us from the opposite entrance. They were shouting, but the claustrophobic acoustics in the hallway kind of made their voices disappear—like the opposite of an echo. As they came closer, I could see that Nate was among them. He dragged a little behind the others, kicking a basketball gently between his feet, coaxing it with him.

Hunter was at the front of the group. He was tall and gangly and goofy. We had carpooled together in elementary school, but I hardly ever spoke to him anymore.

"Hey," Hunter said. "Lima. Like the city in Peru."

I kind of smiled. I could feel that my face was starting to burn from his attention. How is it possible, I wondered, that some girls my age could already be having sex and I was still blushing when I talked to boys?

"Maybe that's why you're so much better than me at Spanish. Although, pretty much everyone is better than me at Spanish," he joked.

I could feel Nate looking at me, and I tried to hold Hunter's gaze firmly. Nate scooped up the basketball and held it with one arm, pressing it casually to his side.

"I'm not that good at Spanish," I lied.

Hunter spun around and slammed hard on the basketball, snapping it forward out of Nate's grip, and it bounced toward me. It came at me fast. I tried to catch it, but it hit my shins and trickled back toward Hunter. I felt clumsy and ashamed.

The cluster of boys began to move away, but Nate seemed to hesitate. I let my eyes slide over in his direction, and our gazes met. I think I expected him to smile or say hi, or to offer up some reason why he hadn't gone to Cole's party. Instead, he just looked at me, unflinching.

"Nathan, come on," Hunter called.

Nate turned and followed his friends into the locker room.

I stared at the door through which they had disappeared.

"That was so awkward," I said.

"What was?" Emily asked.

Right, I thought. It was nothing. It was a twenty-second interaction. Snap out of it, Lima.

chapter
twenty-two

The following Monday, Mom had an appointment and couldn't pick me up until four thirty. Staying late at school had always been one of my least-favorite things. Campus was eerie after school. Without people, familiar places seemed distorted, the way they would in an anxious dream.

I decided to do homework on the patio behind the administration building, which was my favorite spot on campus because of the two huge jacaranda trees that bloomed there in the fall and spring.

I unlatched the gate and walked in. Purple flowers, as bright as a highlighter, canopied the whole patio like a net of stars. I took another step and froze. Nate was sitting at the picnic table, wearing a long-sleeve, light blue button-down shirt, and I hadn't even noticed him. He looked dressed up. I wondered if I should try and leave without him seeing me, but it was too late.

"Hey," he said.

I swallowed. "Hi."

He looked at me for a long moment before he spoke again. "Whatsup?" he finally said.

"I was going to do some homework back here. I'm not getting picked up for a while."

He nodded. "I was just leaving."

I felt a strange knot in my stomach, and I wasn't sure if it was relief or disappointment.

Nate stood up and walked toward the gate, stopping just before he passed me.

"I'm going to the gas station across the street," he said. "You want to come?"

I hesitated, and then I said, "Okay."

We walked across the empty campus and out the back gate, not speaking. I wondered what Hailey would think if she saw us walking together.

"Do you always stay late after school?" I asked as I filled a big cup with an electric-blue slushie.

Nate was standing next to me, already digging into a big bag of Doritos. "Well," he said, "I was on academic probation, so I still have these monthly meetings with Leslie and Rick."

I stuck a big straw in my slushie and looked up at him. "Really?"

He popped three Doritos in his mouth at once and nodded. We made our way to the cash register. "It's not like school is hard for me. I just fucked up a lot last year 'cause I stopped caring."

"Oh," I said. "So do you care now?"

He laughed. "Good question."

Nate reached into the pocket of his pants and pulled out his wallet. I watched his hands as he opened it up and found a five-dollar bill. His hands were so nice. Strong and defined, with these clean, hard bones pressing out from under the skin.

He glanced down at me—maybe he could sense me staring—and I flushed.

"I'll get her slushie, too," he said to the man behind the counter.

"You don't have to," I said.

He ignored me.

Outside, the hot afternoon sun glowed yellow.

"Do you mind if we just chill here?" he asked, gesturing to a dirty bench. "I can't go back to school right now."

"Okay," I said.

We sat down on the bench, the sunlight burning down on us. But I didn't mind.

"Anyway, the dean says I have to start doing better in school," he said. "Put in a little more effort." He made air quotes around the word "effort."

"I never considered not caring about school," I said. "I think I just follow rules. I'm a rule follower."

He laughed. "I like that."

I looked at him. And when our gazes touched, I felt my insides heat up.

"This shirt is so stuffy," he said abruptly, jerking around like he was uncomfortable in his own skin, adjusting his tie, shirt, and pants. "My mom makes me dress nice on days when I meet with Rick."

I giggled.

"I guess she wants me to look more like a rule follower," he said.

I tried not to laugh anymore. I was almost embarrassed by how much fun I was having, just sitting here next to Nate. I sucked hard on my slushie straw.

"You really like that drink, huh?" he said.

"It's so good," I said. "It's the best flavor I've ever had."

He looked at me, and his eyes moved over my face slowly. "Your lips are blue," he said.

I sucked my lips between my teeth.

A car pulled up at one of the pumps, and we both watched as a short man in a Hawaiian shirt got out and filled up his tank. I don't know what Nate was thinking about, and I didn't really know what I was thinking about either, but somehow the silence felt velvety and warm.

"Do you drive?" I asked.

Nate nodded. "Yeah. I'm old for the grade. I turned sixteen last summer. My stepdad borrowed my car today though, 'cause his is in the shop. Do you drive?"

"No," I said. "I'm still fifteen. I haven't even started driver's ed."

He nodded. And then he sunk down onto the bench and let his head knock back, as if he was soaking up the sun. I stared at him, just taking it all in—the bony bump on his nose, the color in his cheeks, the faint freckles, the perfect symmetry of his mouth, the way his skin got just a tiny bit rough as it got closer to his neck. The top button of his shirt was unbuttoned, and his collarbone protruded a little. I felt an urge to see his whole shirt unbuttoned, to know the shapes of all of the parts of his body. The thought made me feel ashamed, and not just because of what a terrible friend I was being to Hailey for thinking those things.

When I finished my drink, I tossed it in the trash and we walked back to campus. The late-afternoon light cut sideways across us, casting long shadows on the asphalt. Nate told me he was going to take the bus home, but then instead of leaving, he just walked back to the picnic bench behind the administration building and sat down.

I'm not really sure if he was following me or if I was following him, but it felt natural. We sat across the picnic table from each other. I leaned forward, propped my elbows on the table, and rested my chin in my hands. A bright purple petal fell off the tree over our heads and the sunlight hit it so directly, it looked like it was on fire.

"I have a sugar high," I said.

He smiled. "Are you sure you're almost sixteen? You seem like you're about twelve right now."

He looked right at me and my stomach dropped. His eyes seemed to swallow me up. Suddenly, my mind flashed on Hailey, and I instinctively withdrew to my side of the table.

"Do you feel older than you did a year ago?" he continued, like he didn't even notice my movement.

"I don't know," I said. "Do you?"

"Sometimes," he said. "Sometimes I feel ancient."

"Like when?" I asked.

He frowned and looked off far into space. "I don't know. Sometimes, I have to stand up for my sister 'cause my stepdad is kind of a dick. And that always makes me feel old, even though I'm younger than her. I don't know if that makes sense."

"I think so," I said. And then I added, "Why is your stepdad a dick? Or not why, but, like, how?"

Nate ran his hand over his face and forehead.

"You know what?" he said. "He's not a dick. He's just kind of a control freak."

"What does that mean?" I asked.

"You ask a lot of questions," Nate said.

"Sorry," I said, dropping my gaze.

"No, it's good," he said. "It makes me think about what I'm saying."

I blushed.

"He's a control freak 'cause he's just, like, closed-minded. Like he thinks things should always be only one way. And happen at a certain time in a certain way," he said.

"Maybe this sounds dumb or obvious," I said, "but listening to you talk about your family is making me think about how hard it is to know what it would feel like to be in someone else's family. Or even just to, like, have someone else's life for a day."

"That's not dumb at all," Nate said.

I felt good knowing that he understood.

"You think a lot," he continued.

"I think too much," I replied quickly.

"I do, too," he said. "I try not to. When I'm thinking too much, I try and do something that will just get me out of my head. Just, like . . . whatever."

"Like what?" I asked.

"Like, I don't know. Whatever. Ride my bike. Listen to loud music. I just hate getting stuck in my head."

"Me too," I said.

Nate ran his finger through one of the grooves in the picnic table. The wood was old and waxy. My eyes followed his hand as it moved slowly across the table toward me. When he stopped, my eyes flicked up from his hand and we looked at each other.

chapter

twenty-three

"Are you going to invite Hailey over for Thanksgiving?" Mom asked on the way to school a few days later.

Hearing Mom mention Hailey's name punctured my sense of calm.

"She's seeing her dad," I lied. I stared out the window at a thin, sharp streak of white cloud. It looked like a crack in the smooth, glossy blue sky.

The truth was that I had no idea what Hailey was doing for Thanksgiving because we had barely spoken since Halloween. The past two Saturday nights I'd gone to Meredith's house and hadn't even checked in with Hailey.

I liked Meredith. She always invited me over with a plan. "Teach me to bake a pie this weekend," she said one Friday. And the following week, she said she wanted me to help her write lyrics to a song. But Meredith was easily distracted, and both times we just ended up listening to music and playing with her cat. Still, it was more fun than trying to tag along with Hailey and Skyler.

"Really?" Mom exclaimed. "That's good to hear. I feel bad for her that they don't have much of a relationship. I know what it's like to not have a dad around when you're young."

Mom's dad died when she was ten. I never knew what to say when she brought it up.

"Does Hailey talk about her dad a lot?" she asked.

"Not really," I said.

Someone in the car behind us honked. I bit my nails.

"Stop that," Mom said, reaching across the center console and lightly pushing my hand back into my lap.

That afternoon was Clean the Bay. I sat in the second row of the bus and pretended to study my chem notes.

"Hey," Hailey said. "Can I sit here?"

I looked up at her. It was weird that she even had to ask. Our whole lives she had never once asked if she could sit next to me. It was like we were becoming half strangers, half friends. It's one thing, I thought, to get to know someone. It's another to get to un-know them.

"Of course," I said.

As soon as she sat down, she rested her head on my shoulder.

I stiffened.

"You're the best," she said, out of nowhere.

I stalled, trying to figure out what to say, how to angle myself in response to Hailey's sudden affection. I felt stingy for not wanting to reciprocate.

Hailey's hand shot up to her face, and I heard her snivel as she wiped her nose with the palm of her hand. It was a really disgusting habit that she'd had since she was a kid.

"Are you crying?" I asked, pulling away from her so I could see her face.

She opened her eyes really wide, looking not at me but past the window, and two fresh tears pooled in her eyes.

"What's wrong?"

"Nothing," she said, wiping her face. She let her eyes meet mine. "I'm just getting my period. I'm bloated. And stupid."

I rolled my eyes. "No, you're not."

"I'm gonna grow up and be fat and single, just like my mean, single, evil mom," she said. "You're so lucky that your mom is so cool."

"She's still a mom," I said, not sure what to say. "She still, like, nags me about cleaning my room."

Her eyes suddenly focused on me. "How are you? I haven't seen you in forever, and I seriously miss you."

I wanted to say that she hadn't seen me because she had

been avoiding me, but all that came out was, "I'm okay." I had the sensation that everything that had been on my mind for the last few weeks about the problems with our friendship was being erased by Hailey right that second.

"What are you doing for Thanksgiving?" she asked. "I love Thanksgiving with your family, and my mom doesn't want to do a whole thing this year. Can I tag along with you?"

I hesitated, looking at the people still filing on to the bus.

"It's okay," Hailey said. "I don't know why I'm inviting myself; that's rude."

"No," I said quickly, "of course you can come. We're having it at our house. My mom already asked me if you were coming."

Nate appeared on the bus behind a girl with a yellow backpack.

"I love your mom," Hailey said, not smiling. "Let's make something really awesome and fattening like pumpkin pie. I'm fucking tired of yogurt."

The flow of traffic down the aisle of the bus had come to a halt with Nate standing right next to the seat that Hailey and I were in. He stared straight ahead, either not seeing us or pretending not to. His hand rested on the cracking leather of the seat in front of Hailey's face. I stared at his hands. His fingertips were chapped.

Hailey followed my gaze and realized that Nate was standing right next to her. She brightened immediately and flicked his thigh.

He looked at her, not smiling.

"Nate Reed. In the flesh," she said drily.

He took a deep breath.

"You never talk to me anymore, Nate," she said, beaming up at him. "Do you even know my name?"

"Hailey," he replied, and then put his hand on the shoulder of the yellow backpack girl. "Go."

"I love it when he says my name!" Hailey whispered to me, smiling from ear to ear. "How is he so hot?!"

I frowned.

"Do you think he could tell I was crying, like, two minutes ago?" she asked.

I certainly couldn't.

"It's okay if he can," she said. "Maybe it's even good. I mean, maybe it'll make him wonder about me."

I craned my neck up and backward over the sea of heads. Nate was still standing, waiting to sit in the back of the bus, his backpack draped languidly over his right shoulder. Somehow I just didn't really think he was wondering anything whatsoever about Hailey.

chapter

twenty-four

"Why aren't you guys doing Thanksgiving in Santa Barbara this year?" Hailey asked, dipping a piece of turkey in her cranberry sauce and taking a bite.

"I'm in the middle of a big case," Dad said, and he and Mom exchanged a look.

"I told him to let himself off the hook and stay here and rest," Mom said, beaming at Dad.

"Nana's gonna miss you, Jim!" Hailey said, wagging her fork at Dad in mock disapproval.

Dad chuckled a little.

"Are you not eating your marshmallows?" Hailey asked, glancing at my plate.

I had eaten the sweet potato bottom out of my casserole, leaving a glistening pile of burned white marshmallow on my plate. "It's too sweet for me."

"I hate you," Hailey said affectionately, reaching over and scooping up the marshmallows with her fork.

Mom and Dad laughed.

"I guess that's what friends are for," Mom said, a teasing gleam in her eye. "To hate each other."

Dad laughed.

I could tell they were happy to see Hailey back in my life.

After dinner, Hailey and I watched an eighties movie on my laptop, lying side by side on my bed. It felt like old times, the way our bodies just intertwined with each other, as if the other person was neutral space, or an extension of ourselves.

"I'm not tired," Hailey said in that strange, hollow quiet that comes right after you turn off the TV or end a movie.

"Me neither," I said.

We put on fleece jackets and sweatpants, grabbed the extra blanket that I kept stuffed in the back of my closet, and padded silently out through the house to the beach.

The wind was howling, raking across the darkness with ragged edges. The ocean looked like a black desert. Hailey and I lay on the blanket and looked up at the sky. The stars were bright. The waves were loud. I felt a million feelings storm through me and then a sharp emptiness. That's how the stars always made me feel.

"What are you thinking about?" Hailey asked.

"Nothing," I said. "Just the stars. They're so crazy. They're so far away. We're so tiny."

I kind of expected Hailey to laugh at me or tease me for trying to be deep, but instead she reached for my hand in the dark and wove her fingers into mine.

"I know," she said. "It's almost scary."

We lay listening to the waves for what seemed like forever.

"I feel bad that my mom is alone tonight," Hailey said after a while.

I didn't speak. When Hailey really opened up about stuff, I got kind of frozen, like I didn't want to scare her and make her be all sarcastic again.

"I know I make fun of her a lot," she continued, "but the truth is I just feel bad for her. And I'm mad at her, too, I think. I'm mad at her for being so locked up."

"Locked up?" I said.

"Not locked up," Hailey corrected. "Buried."

"What do you mean?" I asked.

"Like, I don't know. I just feel like she's buried beneath all this stuff. Like even literally. She's literally buried in hair dye and makeup."

"That's really intense," I said.

"I know." Hailey's voice was calm. "And she's totally obsessed with online dating. She just sits there eating hummus and drinking Diet Coke and sending e-mails to gross old guys. And I just wonder—is this what it means to grow up? Is that what adulthood is? Online dating has got to be the most unromantic thing in the world. I wish I could have known her when she was happy. I feel like the person I know now isn't even her."

"I remember her being different," I said, "when we were younger."

"You do?" Hailey asked, and turned her head to face me, her eyes wide with surprise. Then she turned back up to the sky and said, "I don't. I don't remember her being any other way."

"I remember this one time, I think it was after the Halloween parade in third grade, she picked us up and took us to get frozen yogurt on the way home. And she was wearing this hot pink sweater with rhinestones. And I thought it was the coolest, fanciest-looking thing I had ever seen."

Hailey laughed. "I remember that sweater. It was pretty cool. It made her boobs look huge."

"They are huge." I giggled.

Hailey laughed a little. "Yeah, why didn't I get those?"

"But she wasn't unhappy back then," I said. "You made her laugh all the time. Like you make everybody laugh."

We grew quiet again, the sound of the ocean sucking up our conversation.

"Do you ever wish your parents were different? Honestly?"

I frowned. Did I? I guess I wished Mom and I shared more than just practical stuff.

Before I could answer, Hailey continued. "What I mean is, your parents are basically perfect. Does that ever get annoying? Like, how can you ever fuck up when your parents are, like, so well adjusted?"

I'd never thought about it like that.

"I don't know," I said. "I know this is lame, but I haven't ever really wanted to fuck up."

Hailey sighed. "You are so lucky."

I glanced at Hailey. Being near her felt lucky, I wanted to say it. I could feel the words forming on my lips, the heat rising to my face. It was so true it almost felt embarrassing.

"I'm hungry," she said, interrupting my thoughts. "Want to pick at some leftovers?"

As we brushed sand off each other's bodies, I resolved never to think any more bad, ungrateful thoughts about Hailey ever again. She was the best friend in the world. The deepest, kindest, most interesting person I knew. It had been a rough couple of months for us, but I needed her in my life. My mind suddenly flashed on Nate, and I felt a knot of guilt in my stomach for talking to him for so long last week. I vowed I would never, ever do that again.

chapter

twenty-five

"**H**ey."

I looked up from my laptop and Nate was standing in front of me. It was the first day back from break, and the library was uncomfortably quiet. Nate was wearing his backpack and a gray wool sweater that looked itchy. He didn't wait for me to say anything; he just sat down across the table from me.

"You work too hard," he said. His cheeks were glowing next to his pale sweater. I could see the top of a button-down shirt peering out from under his sweater, and I had the impulse to reach across the table and touch it.

"I don't think so," I said softly, looking back at my computer screen. "I have lots of homework all of a sudden. I'm trying not to fall behind."

He kind of half nodded. "Rule follower, right?" He joked.

I wanted to laugh with him, but I couldn't. There was

something dangerous about our friendship. We couldn't keep getting closer. Thanksgiving had reset my priorities. Nate belonged to Hailey, and Hailey was my best friend. Nate was nobody.

I fixed my gaze on my notebook, willing myself not to get pulled in to another conversation, but I could still feel his eyes on me. Finally, I looked up at him. It made my stomach flip.

"How was your break?" he asked.

Nate's expression, that mix of playfulness and intensity, stirred something inside me, but the feeling was coupled with guilt. *This can't happen*, I wanted to tell him. *Leave me alone. Stop doing whatever it is that you're doing to me. Do this to Hailey. She is in love with you.*

"What about Hailey?" I whispered. As soon as I said it, I regretted it.

Nate looked surprised, and then he slumped back in his seat for a second before he placed his hands on the table and stood up to go.

"Wait," I said, feeling suddenly desperate. I reached across the table and put my hand on top of his. The action happened so fast, I didn't even know where it came from. It was like instinct, or reflex. We both stared in surprise at our hands and the moment seemed to expand and stretch out. Nate's hand felt soft and cool beneath mine. And then Nate pulled his hand away and straightened up.

I was too embarrassed to look at him at first, but when I finally did, he had an apologetic, almost sad expression on his face.

"I get it," he said softly. "It's cool."

As he walked away, I wanted so badly to undo everything that had just happened. I hated to see him leave.

chapter

twenty-six

Meredith always had stories about her clothing and jewelry. Nothing she owned seemed to be bought at a mall.

"This one," she said, fingering a smooth, brown stone encased in a gold band, "is petrified wood from the Atlantic Ocean. It represents transformation. Touch it. It's so smooth."

I reached up and fingered the stone. It was almost cold to the touch and smooth as glass. We were sitting cross-legged under a tree by lower campus.

"I like it," I cooed.

Just then I caught Hailey walking by, headphones shoved into her ears. She was wearing her heart-shaped sunglasses.

"Hailey!" I said.

She didn't hear.

"Hailey!" I called again.

This time she heard, and she stopped walking.

I beckoned her over, and she came, not bothering to take off her sunglasses.

"I texted you last night—where were you?" I asked.

"Nowhere," she said, her voice cold and tired. "I can't go to community service today. I have too much homework."

Meredith stretched one of her long delicate arms up toward Hailey. "I am just wild about your sunglasses!"

I sighed. "I wish you'd told me. I don't want to go if you're not going, and my mom isn't coming for me until five."

"Sorry," Hailey said irritably. "But you're a big girl. Figure it out. You'll be fine."

And then she just started walking away, not even acknowledging Meredith. I jumped up after her and touched her shoulder. She turned to face me. I felt suddenly enraged. What happened to all that closeness we had felt the other night?

"Are you okay?" I asked. My heart was pounding.

"I'm fine," she said. "I'm sorry if I'm being weird. I'm just beyond tired. I'm on, like, another planet of exhaustion."

I tried to look in her eyes but all I could see was my own insect-like reflection in her big black glasses.

I wanted to say something, to tell her it wasn't fair that she kept turning our friendship on and off like a light switch. But I couldn't find the words.

"Lima," Meredith called from behind me. "Are you going to finish this?"

I turned to Meredith, who was holding up my half-eaten apple.

"No, you can have it," I said. I looked back at Hailey, who was looking at her phone. I felt the moment dissolve away.

Clean the Bay was different without Hailey. For one thing, I got to sit in the front and talk to Leo on the way there. He told me what it was like to get around in LA on buses and bikes. It sounded like a ton of work to me, but I was impressed. I thought about how much Dad would like Leo. Dad secretly wished he was the kind of guy who rode bikes and boycotted cars instead of a lawyer who watched football and drove a Lexus.

It was cold on the beach that day. And there wasn't very much trash. Maybe another group had come before us. I found myself sort of meandering, waiting for the hour to pass. I wove in and around the pillars under the pier. Years of ocean water splashing against them had transformed the wood into a black, sooty material. I wondered how long the pier had been there. It had probably been a real pier for fishermen before it got turned into an amusement park for tourists. I was so busy imagining this history that as I rounded the final pillar, I practically walked right into Nate.

"Whoops, sorry," I said quickly.

"It's okay," he said. "Have you found any trash?"

"Not really."

He stood there for a second looking like there was something he wanted to say.

"I'm sorry about the other day," I said before he got the chance.

He didn't look surprised. "It's fine."

"It is?" I asked.

"Yeah," he said.

Nate started walking toward the water, and I followed.

"Why'd you sign up for Clean the Bay?" I asked after a while.

"Lizzie did it," he replied simply.

I thought it was cute that he called his older sister Lizzie. I had only ever known her as Liz.

"Do you miss her now that she's at college?" I felt a little shy asking him more questions, but I was gripped with curiosity. I wanted to know everything about him.

He snorted. "No. She's fucking nuts."

And then he broke into a run and dove into the sand and grabbed the only piece of trash either of us had seen all day. It was a tiny silvery gum wrapper, and he waved it over his head, victorious. "Finally! Trash!"

We both laughed.

Even though he had said he didn't miss his sister, something about the way he said no made it clear he was lying. I knew he missed her a lot. It was like I was starting to figure him out. He was made up of a million noes that were actually yeses.

On the bus ride back to school there was traffic, so I read from *Great Expectations*, and Nate sat next to me with his headphones on. The air between us was soft.

Back at school, Mom was waiting for me. I descended the bus and headed in her direction, not saying good-bye to Nate. But before I had walked away, he reached out and flicked my shoulder. I turned and looked at him, and his eyes were full of a message I couldn't quite decipher. Something mischievous.

In the car, Mom said, "Who was that boy?"

I groaned. "What boy?"

"That boy who just said good-bye to you?"

"Oh, that's just Nate," I said nonchalantly.

"Nate," Mom repeated slowly, pulling out into traffic. "The one that Hailey is dating?"

"They're not dating," I said. "But yeah, that's him. So what's for dinner?"

"Lima, listen," Mom said, ignoring my question. "If you have a crush on the boy . . ."

"Stop," I said, covering my face with my hands. "Mommy, please."

"It's a really bad idea to get involved with someone your friend likes," she continued. "It can cause a lot of pain for everyone. Even for you."

"Oh my God, Mom," I said. "This is insane. I told you, he's just a friend. He's, like, less than a friend. There's nothing going on."

When we came to a red light, Mom turned her head and looked at me. When I allowed myself to meet her gaze, her eyes were as still and impossible to read as rocks.

"What?" I asked defensively. "What are you thinking?"

Mom blinked and then looked back at the road and sighed. "Nothing."

chapter

twenty-seven

The next day, I spotted Hailey and Skyler sitting on the concrete slab outside the history building. I tried to walk past them unnoticed, but Hailey waved at me to come over.

"I'm sorry I was weird yesterday," she said. She looked refreshed.

"Yeah, you seemed like you were in a really bad mood," I said cautiously.

Hailey rolled her eyes. "Yes and no. But it was mainly just that Meredith gives me the heebie-jeebies."

"Meredith and Walker Hayes are the creepiest ever," Skyler added.

"You should give them a chance," I said lamely. I sounded like Mom.

"I should probably give a lot of people chances who I don't," Skyler said flatly.

Hailey snorted. "So, how was Clean the Bay alone with Nate?" she asked.

My mouth went dry. "I didn't really see him."

"So he didn't, like, ask where I was?" she asked.

I shook my head no.

"I thought maybe if I didn't come, he would wonder where I was," Hailey continued. "I just feel like he knows I like him. I want to play hard to get."

"You're such a moron," Skyler said, looking right at Hailey. "Remember what Sara told us yesterday?"

"What did Sara tell you guys?" I asked.

"Sara said Nate's been hooking up with that senior, Sophie, for, like, months," Hailey said.

"The one who dresses like a dude," Skyler added. "It's so weird. Guys, like, love her, and I swear, I've only ever seen her wear enormous sweatshirts and baggy jeans."

"Nate has a girlfriend?" I asked meekly.

Skyler scoffed. "Nate definitely does not have a girlfriend. That guy will probably never have a girlfriend."

"Sara said it's super-casual," Hailey said. "Sophie is still in love with her ex-boyfriend, but she just, like, hooks up with tons of guys. She's not into any of them, though."

"Oh," I said.

"Anyway, Sophie's nothing," Hailey said. "I am totally as hot as her."

Skyler scanned the tip of her ponytail for split ends. "I'm so over hearing about Nate. He's a douche bag."

Hailey ignored her. Her hazel eyes were fixed on me, suddenly focused, intense.

"What are you thinking, Li?" she asked.

"Nothing," I said, throwing on a quick smile. "Just, yeah, I agree with both of you. You are totally as hot as Sophie. But, also, Nate's probably, like, a douche bag. Like Skyler said."

Hailey laughed. "I can't believe you just said douche bag. That sounds so wrong coming out of you, Li."

I giggled. "Yeah, I know. It felt wrong."

Hailey stood up and linked her arm through mine.

"C'mon. I'll walk you to class," she said, and then quickly turned to Skyler. "See you at the smoking tree at three?"

"Same as always," Skyler said.

chapter

twenty-eight

"That quiz today killed me," Emily said as we waited for our parents in the car-pool line under a milky December sky.

"I know, me too," I said. "What did you get for the second question? Alkaline?"

It seemed like chemistry had gone from hard to impossible overnight. The first part of the year had been fine. I could look at the problems on the board and visualize how they would balance themselves out, like pieces fitting into a puzzle. But once we started reaction stoichiometry, solving the chemical equations felt like trying to reassemble a sheet of paper that had been shredded. Every piece of information was impossibly detailed and delicate and nuanced. If I forgot one teeny tiny characteristic or rule, an almost perfect answer would be wrong.

"I put alkaline and then I changed it at the last minute,"

Emily said, biting her lip. "Shoot. Maybe that was a mistake."

"Well, I don't know if I was right," I said, and then, spotting Mom's car, I added, "We'll find out tomorrow. I gotta go; that's my mom."

I bounded toward the car, but I stopped in my tracks before I got in. Dad was sitting in the passenger seat. In my whole life, Dad had never come with Mom to pick me up. He should be at work right now. Dread rose up inside me, thick and dark as molasses.

"What's going on?" I asked carefully when I got in.

"Nana's sick," Mom said.

My heart raced. "Like, how sick?"

Mom let out a ragged breath. "She's not going to get better. She's in the hospital."

Dad turned his head around to me and made this pained face, like a cross between sort of smile and a frown and a grimace. I hadn't buckled my seat belt yet, and I climbed forward and wrapped my arms around his neck. It was an awkward position to hug him in, but he hugged me back tight.

The next day, the three of us drove up to Santa Barbara together. We were quiet in the car.

Nana looked really different in the hospital bed. It was the first time I had seen her without her makeup on and she looked so much frailer because of it. But when she held my hand, she still had that clawlike firm grip.

We shifted around the hospital all day, alternating from the waiting area to Nana's bedside to the dreary café. Nana mostly slept. The drugs she was on made her tired. There was a window made of thick, tinted glass in Nana's room that looked out to a flat, concrete parking lot and a separate adjacent bleached-out medical building. Looking out the window was almost sadder than sitting there looking at Nana.

Mom and I drove back that night, but Dad stayed over at Caroline's. For long stretches between Santa Barbara and Los Angeles there's just farmland and mountains. At night, you can't see anything but darkness.

chapter

twenty - nine

When I told Hailey about Nana the next day at break, she stared at me blankly for a long moment, and then said, "Are you sad?"

"I'm really sad," I said. "And I'm especially sad for my dad and Caroline."

Skyler, who had been sitting silently next to Hailey and playing on her phone the whole time, finally spoke. "Grandparents die," she said. "That's what they do."

I looked at Skyler, with her gooey lips and glossy snake of a ponytail.

Hailey laughed a little. "It's true, Li. That is what they do."

I couldn't laugh about it. I just stared at the ground.

"Well, Skyler's holiday party is next weekend," Hailey said. "At least you can look forward to that."

I had forgotten about Skyler's party. It was the last thing on my mind.

"I've been planning it forever," Skyler said. "I invited, literally, the whole grade."

"I don't know if I'm going to feel like going to a party," I said, feeling suddenly really, really tired. "With all of this sad stuff happening."

Skyler gave Hailey a quick, loaded look. I recognized that look. It was the kind of look you gave people who know you really well, the people who can read your mind. That's the way Hailey and I used to be: telepathic.

Hailey squinted up at me. "Well, you have a whole week to decide. But, seriously, it would be stupid not to come just 'cause your grandmother's sick."

chapter

thirty

∞

The last day of school before Christmas vacation was one of those awkward filler days that come before a break. We had a holiday party in math, watched *The Motorcycle Diaries* with subtitles in Spanish, and played Literary Charades in English. Everything was supposed to be fun, but all I wanted to do was go home, climb into bed, and start making up for the sleep I'd lost since Nana had been in the hospital.

"Can we get ice cream on the way home?" I asked Mom when she picked me up after school. Finally, the day was over and the two weeks of vacation stretched out ahead of me like a perfect, unbroken ribbon.

"Of course," Mom said. "And you should do something fun tonight."

"I'm going to catch up on sleep," I said. "That is my idea of fun."

"Why don't you invite Hailey over?" Mom asked.

"Hailey's going to some party," I grumbled, kicking my feet up onto the dashboard.

"You're not going?" Mom asked. "Were you invited?"

"Sure, I was invited," I shrugged. "Everyone is invited. But, it's at this girl's house who isn't really my friend. It's gonna be more Hailey's friends. I don't really like those people."

Mom paused.

"Maybe you'll like them more if you get to know them better," she said carefully.

We didn't speak again for the rest of the ride, but her words rolled around in my head like gravel.

When we pulled into the parking lot at the Cold Stone on the PCH, Mom unsnapped her seat belt and turned to face me.

"I really think you should go to the party tonight, Lima," she declared.

"Mom, you're being so weird about this. It's not like I'm antisocial. I'm just tired," I said.

"I know you aren't antisocial," Mom said gently. She reached out and smoothed my hair back with her hand. "It's been a hard couple of weeks with Nana being sick and everything. I just want to see you have fun."

"I know," I whispered. I wished I could explain to Mom why Skyler's party wouldn't be fun for me, but I didn't know how to put it into words.

"Worst case scenario, you don't have a good time. And then you can come home and say 'I told you so,'" she said.

I laughed a little. "I can't believe I'm so pathetic that my mom has to convince me to go to a party."

"Don't call my favorite person pathetic," Mom said. And then she leaned across the center console and kissed my cheek.

Mom dropped me at Skyler's on the way to meet one of her friends for dinner. Dad was still with Nana. We called him from the car but he didn't answer, so we left him a silly, sing-songy voice mail. I hoped it would cheer him up.

I agreed to let Mom put makeup on me for the party. She powdered my nose and forehead, and when I flipped down the passenger side mirror and inspected her work, I thought it made me look strange and pastry-like.

Skyler lived in her own private, two-story guesthouse, totally separate from the enormous main house that her parents lived in. When I got there, I knocked on the front door and Hailey opened it. She was barefoot and wearing nothing except a towel, like she lived there.

"Am I super early?" I asked.

Hailey shrugged. "We told everyone seven, and it's like six forty-five . . . so . . . I don't know. People probably won't show up until eight or nine."

"This is the most beautiful house I've ever seen," I gushed nervously. "I can't believe Skyler has it all to herself."

"I know, right? She can do whatever. She's so lucky. She's upstairs getting dressed."

"Oh," I said. An awkward pause settled on us, and I looked around for something to talk about.

"Want a Coke?" Hailey asked, swinging open the door to a mini-fridge. It was crazy how comfortable she seemed here.

"I'm okay," I said.

Hailey looked at me strangely for a second and then shrugged. "Okay. I'm gonna go get dressed."

After trying on five outfits, Hailey had landed on a short black dress and one of those bright red Santa Claus hats with fake-fur trim. Her wet hair dried into perfectly tangled, messy locks so she looked wild and fresh all at once. She and Skyler blasted pop music and drank wine coolers while they set up, dimming the lights and filling glass pitchers with spiked punch.

It seemed like the whole school arrived at once, and everything grew dense and thick like the sky darkening before an unexpected storm. People shifted around in packs like rain clouds.

I watched Hailey from across the room. She was sharing a beer with a girl I didn't know, and she must have been saying something funny because the girl laughed. Then Hailey started laughing, dropping her head forward so that her long hair tumbled over her bare shoulders. She glowed. I suddenly felt like I looked all wrong with my neat, combed hair and painted face.

An older boy shoved past me in a rush to get to the kitchen and accidentally stepped on my foot. Instead of apologizing, he and his friend erupted into laughter and then blended into the crowd. I felt a terrible, sinking longing for my own room.

I glanced back up to where Hailey had been a moment ago, deciding I would go join her, but she was gone. I scanned the room but didn't see her anywhere. Why was she always disappearing? And why didn't she ever hang out with me at parties? Why was it always up to her when I was her best friend and when I was just a stranger?

I pushed through the crowded room and out the doors into Skyler's yard. I walked through the damp grass, trying to escape the sounds of the party. When I reached the far wall, I turned and looked back at Skyler's house. It pulsed with energy and light, like a heart in the night. Jealous, hot emotions pumped in my blood. Why couldn't I have fun like everyone else? Why couldn't I be like Hailey? Why was I so awkward, so sure that no one wanted to talk to me and that these parties were stupid? Maybe being social was good and healthy and I was just no fun. Maybe the problem wasn't Hailey—maybe the problem was me. I was so used to how I saw things, it felt uncomfortable to think there might be another way to see them.

A pack of people whose faces I couldn't make out were moving toward me. They were laughing and smoking, their beer bottles refracting little pieces of moonlight.

"Hey."

I recognized Nate's voice before I saw him.

"Hi," I said. I began to make out everyone's faces in the group: Ryan and a few girls I didn't recognize. They must have been from another school.

"Lima," Nate said, as if that was a complete sentence. He took a sip of beer that was tucked into a paper bag.

I stalled, unsure what to do or say.

"Talk to me. How are you?" Nate said.

I looked up at him, and he swayed. He was visibly drunk. But somehow drunkenness didn't seem sloppy and unflattering on him like it did on most people. On Nate, being drunk just seemed to magnify him.

"I'm having, like, the worst week ever," I said. "My grandmother is dying."

"Shit," he said. "I'm so sorry to hear that."

"Yeah, I feel really bad for my dad," I said. "'Cause it's,

like, his mom, you know? I'm sorry to be talking about this at a party. I'm such a downer."

"Nate—you want?" a girl with dyed black hair held a joint out to Nate. A series of small silver hoops ran up the side of her ear, like a metal spring.

"I'm good for now—thanks," Nate said, waving his hand away. "No, seriously, you were saying. It's hard. When my dad died, it really sucked."

"Your dad . . ." My voice trailed off. "I had no idea. I'm so sorry."

"Yeah, it's okay," he said, wincing. "It's okay now. Well, it's not okay, but it's okay. It was a really long time ago."

Nate's phone started buzzing, and he pulled it out of his pocket.

"It's Sophie," Nate said, holding the phone out to Ryan. "She probably wants directions. Talk to her."

Sophie. The girl that Hailey and Skyler had said he'd been hooking up with. I felt an inexplicable weight drop in my stomach.

"So, is Sophie, like, your girlfriend?" I asked, trying to sound nonchalant.

Nate looked genuinely surprised. "What? No. Where'd you get that?"

"Hailey said it, or something like it," I stammered.

He paused. "Truth?"

I nodded.

"We hooked up a couple times when she and her boyfriend broke up. But they're back together."

"Are you upset about it?" I asked.

He smiled, as if what I'd said amused him. He flicked my arm with his thumb and forefinger. "Nah. I'm okay."

"Catch," Ryan said, hurling the phone back at Nate. It slipped past him and fell into the dark grass.

"Fuck you, man," Nate laughed. He crouched down in the grass and started looking for his phone. I stood there awkwardly, suddenly wondering if I belonged out here with these people at all.

"I'm going back inside," I said.

Nate popped up with his phone, stumbled, and then steadied himself. He hovered over me. He was less than a foot away. Bending down to look for his phone had made all the blood rush to his face and his cheeks were pink, a lock of hair hanging down and covering one eye.

"I wasn't upset about Sophie because I like someone else," he said.

An unexpected wave of heat moved through me.

"You do?" I whispered. His words quickened my heartbeat, made me feel almost unsteady.

"Nate, give me your phone," the girl with the black hair said. "I want to show Ryan something."

"Jesus, what's wrong with you guys, you just had my phone," Nate said. "Just keep it."

"C'mon, Nate, don't be mad. You know you're gonna miss the shit out of me when you're in Hawaii next week," Ryan said. "You know you love me."

Everyone was drunk, murky, slippery.

"You love me more, man," Nate said, and jumped onto Ryan's back, tackling him to the ground.

I was stunned. What had just happened? Who did Nate like? This stranger with the black hair and the earrings? Why did I have the feeling that when Nate said he liked someone, he had meant me?

Nate and Ryan rolled around on the ground, laughing and kicking. The girl with the black hair and the earrings cackled, an audience of one.

"Lima, is that you?" Hailey's voice called. I turned and saw her approaching in the dark.

"Yeah," I said, hating her a little bit for showing up right at that moment.

Hailey stood next to me and linked her arm through mine. Now that I was standing near Nate, I was her best friend again.

"Hey, Nate," Hailey said, when the boys had stopped play fighting.

"Hey," Nate said.

I watched him as he stood up, brushing grass off his jeans, and his eyes slid up to meet Hailey's. The scooped neckline of her dress revealed just the tiniest bit of her lace bra, and her skin glowed in the moonlight. Her eyes were two enormous pools of black. She looked beautiful. I felt a pit of jealousy widening inside me, just seeing the two of them look at each other, and I knew I had to get away.

I pretended I had to pee, ran back to the house and into Skyler's upstairs bathroom. I closed the door and stared at my own reflection. After seeing Hailey, my hair looked limp and straight, and my whole body looked wan and small, like a dusty twig. I wondered what Nate saw when he looked at me.

chapter

thirty-one

The day after Skyler's party, Hailey left for San Diego to visit her dad. Hailey always had a way of falling off the grid a little when she went to San Diego, so I wasn't surprised not to hear from her until she got back to LA a week later.

"How was your Christmas?" I asked her over the phone. Outside my window, a thick, drizzling fog wrapped itself around our house. The sky was a dirty sponge resting on top of the gray carpet of ocean.

Hailey was shuffling something around on the other end of the line. "Wait, what did you say? Sorry, Li, I couldn't hear you 'cause my mom was talking to me."

"Did you have a good time in San Diego?" I tried again.

"It was fine," she said. Her words were clipped.

Then I asked her the question I had really been wanting to ask for the past week. "How was the rest of Skyler's party?"

"Fun," she replied absently.

"Did anything happen with you and Nate?" I asked. I had never in our whole friendship initiated a conversation with Hailey about Nate. But all week I kept thinking about him and her, wondering what had happened after I had left.

She paused. "Not really. Why?"

I tried to giggle. "I'm just being a good friend."

"You're a dork," Hailey said. And then she added, "I mean, Nate stayed really late and I slept over. But there were lots of people around the whole time. We were never alone together so nothing could happen."

I thought about how I always felt alone with Nate. Like whenever we spoke, it seemed as if we were separate from everything else, even if we were surrounded by people.

"Did you hear something about Nate?" she asked tentatively.

"Me?" I scoffed. "Like gossip? That'll be the day."

Hailey breathed a sigh of relief. "That's why I love you, Li. You're so above all this stuff."

Hailey's words didn't help untie the knot in my chest.

"So, what are you going to do for New Year's?" I asked, changing the topic.

"Sky and I are gonna go over to Bridget Howard's house and pregame. Then we're going to some party that Bridget heard of in the valley."

I didn't say anything. I waited for her to invite me along, or at least ask what I was planning on doing. When she didn't, I said, "I don't think I'm gonna do anything."

Hailey paused. "Do you want me to ask Bridget if you can come with us?"

I hated Bridget Howard. I had been to her house once before, and it was one of the worst nights of my life. But Meredith was in Italy, Mom and Dad were at the hospital with Nana, and I didn't want to stay home alone.

"Yeah," I said. "Would you?"

While I made dinner that night, I kept thinking about scary Bridget Howard. Bridget had always been popular and perky. She had blond hair that was thick and shiny and seemed to move in one solid sheet of yellow when she walked. She played soccer and wore trendy clothes and lip gloss to school for as long as I could remember.

One day, near the end of sixth grade, she came up to me in the car-pool line just after Hailey had been picked up by her mom. "Why do you hang out with her?" she asked me.

"Hailey's my best friend," I said defensively.

"She smells weird," Bridget said. "Why are you so anti-popularity?"

"What do you mean?" I asked.

"You know," she said, "you guys are always like, 'Whatever, I don't care about being popular, I just want to wear hippie skirts and listen to folk music and not do anything.'"

I was surprised to hear myself described like that.

"I mean you're, like, really pretty," Bridget said. "You could be, like, really popular."

I paused. I could?

"Come over on Saturday night," she told me. "It's my birthday. A bunch of girls are gonna sleep over, and we're gonna stay up all night watching movies."

For the first time in the conversation, she smiled. Even with her retainer in, her teeth were perfect and white. Her smile was shockingly sweet.

"Okay," I said.

I never should have gone. First of all, I had to explain to Hailey why she wasn't invited without telling her what Bridget had said about her, which was really hard to do.

Hailey started crying on the phone. "I don't understand," she said. "Why are you going without me?"

I felt guilty. But what if Bridget and I were meant to be friends? I had to find out.

At Bridget's Bel-Air house, everything—even the carpets and the doors and the telephones—looked polished. The wood floors were shiny. The picture frames glistened. There were crystal chandeliers in every room.

Despite how fancy their house was, Bridget and her

friends had already trashed the living room. There were candy wrappers and clothing and soda bottles strewn across every surface. Everyone was shrieking and dancing.

"I have such a sugar high!" I remember Bridget scream-ing as she jumped from one couch to another. The soles of her feet were dark gray with dirt, and she left stains on the couch's cream-colored leather.

I didn't know any of the girls very well. Skyler was there. She and Bridget used to be as inseparable as Hailey and me. All the girls were skinny and had long, stringy hair, and they were all wearing tiny cutoff jeans shorts, tank tops, and lots of bracelets.

After we ate pizza and birthday cake and Bridget's dad and stepmom had gone to sleep, the trouble began.

"Truth or dare!" Bridget shrieked. Bridget was always yelling. It was exhausting.

Skyler went first, and Bridget dared her to get naked and run around the pool.

She did it. We all laughed.

"Your turn," Bridget said, pointing at me. "Lima: truth or dare?"

"Truth."

Bridget started thinking, and then she went over to Skyler and whispered something in her ear. Eleven-year-old Skyler was just this tiny little insect of a person with enormous black eyes and long eyelashes. Skyler nodded and laughed approvingly.

"Okay," Bridget said. "But you have to answer honestly. That's the rule."

I sat up straight.

"Rank all of us from ugliest to prettiest, including yourself," she declared.

Skyler snorted.

"What?" I made a face. "No. Everybody's pretty."

"Oh, grow up," she said. "Not everyone is created equal. Just do it."

I looked around the room. Bridget, Skyler, Sara, Jen, Lauren—they all looked sort of the same. Well okay, Jen's eyes were beady and really close together, and Sara had almost no neck and skin that was blotchy and pale. I hated myself for noticing these things.

"You have ten seconds," she said.

"I really don't want to," I said.

"Don't be such a goody-goody," she countered. "It's my birthday party."

"Okay," I said. "I'm the least pretty—"

"Okay, stop," Bridget said. "You're lying already."

All eyes were on me. They were all waiting.

"I don't think anybody is ugly," I said.

"Ugh, this is boring," Bridget whined. "How about I make

it easier for you?" She stood up and pointed a finger at Jen. "Jen is the least pretty."

Jen's eyes welled up with tears.

"Don't freak out," she said to Jen. "You're still cute. You're not, like, ugly. You're just not as pretty as, like, Skyler."

Jen looked scared.

"Okay, so Jen, Sara, and Lauren are the bottom three," she said. "Sorry, guys."

Jen pushed herself to her feet and ran into the guest bathroom. Sara and Lauren followed, and they slammed the door behind them.

"Now you finish," Bridget said to me. Her green eyes were full of something awful. "Do me. Do Skyler. Do you."

"You're the prettiest, then Skyler, then me," I said. It seemed like the right answer. I looked at Skyler to see if she was annoyed, but she seemed fine with being second.

"Nice try," Bridget said. "But you're still lying."

"I am?" I asked.

"You're the prettiest," she said. "Just admit it."

"I don't think so," I stammered.

Bridget scoffed. "Just say it. Just say you're the prettiest, and then me and then Sky."

Skyler laughed. "Hey! I want to be number two!"

Bridget ignored her. "Come on, Lima. Stop being so perfect and sweet. Just say it. You're the prettiest person here."

"I'm the prettiest person here," I said. My voice was tiny.

And then Bridget just burst out laughing and screaming. "Lima said she's the prettiest person here! I knew it all along! Lima thinks she's prettier than everyone!"

"You made me," I said, my throat closing.

"It's a free country," she snapped. "Nobody can make you do anything. You said it because you think it's true."

chapter

thirty-two

Hailey put on makeup while I sat on the edge of her bathtub and watched.

"Aren't you gonna at least put on some mascara?" she asked me.

"Nope," I said.

"Tonight will be more fun if you at least try to get excited," she said. "It's New Year's. You're supposed to go all out."

"What does that have to do with mascara?" I asked.

"You just don't get it," she groaned, and started carefully applying fake eyelashes. "Of course, I don't even know why I'm getting all decked out. Nate is out of town."

"Yeah, I know," I said.

She snapped a look at me. "How do you know he's out of town?"

"I heard something about it at Skyler's party," I tried to sound casual.

All day, I had been rehearsing things I might say to ease into telling Hailey what was happening between me and Nate. I imagined saying, nonchalantly: "Nate and I have been talking a lot and we kind of have stuff in common." Or, "Nate and I have studied together in the library a few times. He's nice." Right now was the perfect opportunity but the words stuck in my throat.

"Lima?" Hailey said, interrupting my thoughts.

"Yeah?" I asked.

"Swear to me you'll never, ever, hook up with Nate," she said.

My heart sank. I felt like I wanted to throw up.

And then she turned her whole body to face me. "I know it's weird, but I just love him. I have always loved him. Please."

"Don't be silly. You know me; I never hook up with anyone. I'm the biggest prude ever," I finally said. Hailey let her eyes linger on me for a second, searching my face for something, but I couldn't tell what.

"Okay," she said, and turned back to the mirror.

"Well, do you like anybody else? Like for while Nate is out of town?" I wanted desperately to change the subject.

"Max is okay," she said, dabbing lip gloss onto her lower lip.

• • •

"Hey, girls," Bridget said when we arrived at her house. After my conversation with Hailey in the bathroom, I felt distracted and distant. Before, I had managed to seem at least sort of glad to have New Year's plans, but now I couldn't even fake a smile.

"Oh my God, you look uh-mazing." Hailey drooled. Bridget had shellacked her hair into a tight ponytail. It looked like it was carved out of wood and varnished. "I love your glitter eye shadow, Bridget."

"See, Sky!" Bridget screamed over her shoulder. "Hailey likes it!"

"Sky's already here?" Hailey asked.

"She's in my room getting ready. C'mon." Bridget grabbed Hailey's hand and yanked her up the stairs.

I stayed downstairs and wandered around the glossy foyer of Bridget's house. There were professional black-and-white photographs of Bridget and her sisters hanging in shiny silver frames on the pink wallpapered walls. I checked my phone nervously, not sure what I was expecting to find. I had no messages or missed calls.

After a few minutes, I went upstairs to join Hailey. There were giggles coming from behind one of the closed rooms. I tried the knob, but the door was locked. That's weird, I thought. I knocked and the giggles ceased.

"Who is it?" Skyler asked through the door. Laughter erupted.

"It's me," I said, confused.

"Hailey's not in here," Bridget said. More hysterical laughing and squealing.

My hands felt thick and heavy; I started to back away, unsure what was happening.

The door swung open and Hailey appeared. She was holding a bottle of whiskey in one hand and an unlit cigarette in the other.

"Want some?" Hailey asked, as if nothing weird had happened. Her face was sweaty and red, she already looked drunk.

I stepped tentatively in the room and shook my head no.

Skyler was splayed across Bridget's bed. "Gimme that," she whined, and pointed to the bottle.

"I'm already wasted!" Hailey laughed as she stumbled toward the bed and handed the bottle off.

Bridget was trying on a pair of high heels in front of her full-length mirror.

"Why do I have nothing to wear?" she moaned. She kicked off the shoes so they landed in the growing pile of discarded clothing on her floor.

"Just wear the white ones," Skyler commanded. "You're gonna make us late."

"I think the first pair you tried on was the best," Hailey added.

"What do I do?" Bridget cried exasperatedly. "I hate everything I own."

Skyler peeled herself off the bed, and wobbled on her stiletto heels over to the closet. She picked up one of the white patent leather sandals by the strap and swung the shoe in front of Bridget's face. "Just put these on. And then we're leaving."

Hailey cackled.

I stood stiff as a board, not laughing, not talking, not smiling. Why had I come here? Why had I thought this would be fun? This was horrible.

"I always wear those, but fine, whatever." Bridget sighed, sliding the shoes onto her feet. "Let's just go."

I followed them into the hallway, lagging a few feet behind.

Skyler and Bridget stumbled down the stairs, giggling and squealing.

"Hailey?" I said. "Can I talk to you for a second?"

Hailey turned to face me in the hall.

"Why did you guys pretend you weren't in the room before when I knocked?" I asked.

Hailey groaned and rolled her eyes. "What? That? I don't know. We were just being dumb."

"I feel strange," I stuttered, "like you don't want me here or something."

"Well, you're just lurking around being all quiet and weird. What am I supposed to do?" she snapped.

"I am not being quiet and weird," I said, stung.

"Yeah you are," she said. "You always are when we're around Skyler. You expect me to invite you to everything and then when I do, you just follow me around and cling to me and ignore everybody else."

"That's not true," I objected. My voice sounded tiny. I was thrown by the turn this conversation had taken. Wasn't Hailey supposed to be apologizing to me for making me feel unwelcome?

"Do you know what people say about you behind your back?" Hailey continued. Something hot flared behind her eyes. "They say you have no personality."

"What?" I breathed, shocked.

Hailey straightened up, gaining momentum. "And I'm sick of defending you. Just ten minutes ago Bridget was saying she feels like you think people should want you around just 'cause you're pretty. But the truth is, nobody cares how pretty you are if you're boring."

My chest contracted, like I'd been hit. Acid tears burned my eyes.

Hailey didn't say anything for a moment, and I struggled to catch my breath. When I finally managed to speak, all I could say was, "Why are you being like this?" I asked.

"I'm not being like anything," Hailey said. "This is who I am. And these girls are my friends."

"You're not like them," I said. "You're different."

"No, I'm not," she said. "I'm sick of trying to be the person you want me to be. I feel like myself with Skyler. And even with Bridget. I'm more myself with them than I am with you anymore."

Hurt welled up inside of me like a dark swamp. "I feel like you're, like, breaking up with me or something."

"Get down here, skanks!" Bridget shrieked from the bottom of the stairs. "The taxi is here!"

"Come on," Hailey said. "Let's go to the party. Just try and have a good time. It's New Year's."

I wiped tears out of my eyes.

"I want to go home," I whispered.

"Of course you do," Hailey seethed. "Just run home to hang out with Mommy like always."

I was too stunned to respond. I stared at Hailey. Her face was beaded with sweat and flecked with glittery makeup. Lipstick gathered in the cracked corners of her mouth, and the edge of one of her fake eyelashes had lifted away from her lid.

"I'm going," she said. She swayed and steadied herself on the banister. "Come if you want. Or don't."

I stood there, frozen in the hallway until I heard the front door slam and the taxi pull out of Bridget's driveway. When the house was silent and I was sure I was alone, I crumpled to the floor and sobbed. I wanted to tell Hailey she was wrong about me. I didn't have *no* personality, I just didn't have a loud, screeching personality like Bridget or Skyler. I wanted to tell Hailey that those girls were horrible, and they weren't really her friends at all. Someday they'd stab her in the back just like she was stabbing me in the back now. Suddenly, I wanted to hurt her. To tell Hailey no matter how popular she tried to be, she'd never be anything but the loser she feared she was.

chapter

thirty-three

nana died on January fifth. Dad was with her. He called us in the late afternoon to give us the news. It was a perfect blue-sky day. The worst kind.

Dad and Mom were all business right away, not talking about Nana or death or anything like that. They immediately started making phone calls, coordinating logistical things with Aunt Caroline, and planning the service.

"Ask Hailey if she's coming to the funeral," Mom said to me.

Hailey and I hadn't talked since New Year's. Hearing her name gave me a jolt, and I hoped Mom didn't see it. With each passing day that Hailey didn't call to apologize, my hurt and anger turned more into bitterness.

"Lima?" Hailey sounded surprised when I called her that afternoon.

"Hi," I said flatly. "Nana died."

She sighed. "Oh no. I'm so sorry. Is your dad okay?"

"I don't know," I said.

Hailey took a deep breath. "Lima, I am so sorry about New Year's! I'm such a terrible person!"

She didn't sound sorry at all. She said it in the same tone of voice she would have used if she'd forgotten to return my math book or something. Like, "Whoops! Silly Hailey!"

It wasn't what I'd expected, and it wasn't satisfying. She had been mean. She had been cruel.

"I was an asshole. I totally get it if you're mad," she continued cavalierly. "Just remember I was wasted. It was New Year's Eve. I mean, everything was crazy. Let's not fight."

My whole body suddenly burned with anger. I felt like screaming at her. Instead, I said icily, "You said some seriously hurtful things."

"I know. It was just a stressful, sloppy night," she said quickly. "I was probably being insane. I was trashed."

"And you left me at Bridget's house. By myself," I said, shaking.

"I thought you didn't want to come with us to the party," she said. "You told me you wanted to go home."

"Because I was so upset," I replied. "I mean, I didn't want to go to the party because we were fighting but . . ."

"Yeah, it was really complicated. It was such a messy

night," she said. "But whatever. I'm so sorry. So so sorry. I told you that already."

With every fake sorry, my level of anger seemed to rise. I was speechless.

"Lima? I'm sorry," now she sounded annoyed. "How many times do you want me to say it?"

"This actually isn't why I called," I said curtly, ignoring her question. "My mom wanted to know if you wanted to come to Nana's funeral. You knew her, too."

There was some rustling on the other end of the line, "Shit, Lima, can I call you back? My food is burning. I have to put the phone down."

"Okay," I said.

She never called me back. She didn't need to. I assumed she wouldn't go to the funeral, I just didn't want to be the bad friend who didn't invite her. I'd rather she be the bad friend who didn't come.

chapter
thirty-four

The morning of Nana's funeral, I got dressed in my room with the windows wide open so I could listen to the waves crashing on the beach. How strange, I thought, to be picking out an outfit for a funeral. Clothing just seemed so insignificant.

I fingered a wrinkled black dress that Mom had bought me in seventh grade for a classmate's bar mitzvah. It was tucked into the back of my closet. I pulled it off its hanger and shimmied into it. It was fading and flecked with dust, but it still fit. It had a high neck and cap sleeves. I put on black tights and a black cardigan, and braided my hair.

The cemetery was overcast and breezy, and the sound of the priest's voice got lost under the sound of the wind. My dress was itchy. I was cold, and my sweater didn't keep me warm. I had worn the wrong thing.

All afternoon, I waited for the fact that Nana was gone

to hit me. I waited for a big wave of sadness to crash over me. But instead, I felt self-involved and petty. I couldn't wrap my mind around Nana being dead, and every time I tried to understand it, my mind rebounded to something really stupid, like whether or not the food at the reception would be more like snacks or a sit-down meal. I even found myself getting impatient with Mom and Dad, who seemed distracted and barely looked at me when I tried to talk to them all day.

Dad stayed in Santa Barbara and Mom and I drove back to Malibu in the evening. We didn't talk or listen to the radio in the car. We hit traffic on the 405, so all of a sudden we were just inching along through the polluted, depressing outskirts of LA. Outlet malls, bland housing developments, and neglected diners punctuated the barren landscape. It was twilight, and the sky looked a grimy orange.

Mom was distant and, even though she wasn't complaining, I could tell she was sad.

"What are you thinking about, Mom?" I asked.

She sighed and shook her head slowly. "You know? Nana dying—it makes me feel so old."

Mom turned and looked at me then, and in that awful light I saw shadows underneath her eyes that I had never noticed before. Maybe it was because she'd been crying at the funeral, or maybe it was simply because she'd said it, but it was true—Mom looked old.

"Stop it, Mom," I scoffed, trying to be comforting. "You're forty-four. You're, like, the youngest mom ever."

She tried to smile. "Want to get dinner on the way home? I'm too tired to cook."

"Yes. I'm starving," I said. "Where?"

She shrugged. "McDonald's?"

My jaw dropped. In my whole entire life, Mom had never taken me to McDonald's. Not once. When I was little, Dad and I snuck there together a few times, but it was our secret. I couldn't believe what I was hearing. I know this is probably weird to say, but it made me sad to think about Mom eating McDonald's. It made me think she was more tired and sad than I could possibly imagine.

I nodded. "Okay."

We sat in a hard plastic booth and ate combo meals— burgers and French fries and milk shakes.

I was taking some of her leftover French fries, squishing them in my fingers, dipping them in a pile of salt, and eating them when I looked up and saw her looking at me with wet eyes. She was smiling.

"I love you so much," she said. She blinked and the tears spilled down her face.

I know it's not possible for your heart to actually break,

but I felt like mine was shattering into a million little pieces. Seeing Mom cry just made it hurt so much.

Back in my room that night, I put on *Blue* by Joni Mitchell and sat on the edge of my bed. The whole day had left me feeling out of sorts. Mom was sad. Dad was sad. Nana was dead. Our house felt so empty, as if all the people and all the music in the world couldn't fill it up again.

I could hear the sounds of Mom putting things away downstairs, the gentle patter of her footsteps. I knew I couldn't make her feel better. I knew she was sad for Dad and for Nana, and now I had this new knowledge that I didn't even really want. That Mom knew she was getting old.

Outside my window, the night sky was polluted and starless. A plane flickered slowly, moving in a straight line over the ocean. I couldn't believe how much everything was shifting around me, like the ground giving way underneath my feet. Life was feeling like nothing more than a disorganized, directionless series of events.

I picked up my cell phone, wanting to call someone, to be cheered up, to talk about something petty. I missed Hailey. Not the Hailey who had been around recently, but the old Hailey. I missed having a best friend. It was confusing to miss someone who wasn't actually gone. She was alive, but she was so different. It occurred to me for the first time that maybe Hailey wasn't going through some awful phase. Maybe she really had changed. Maybe sometimes people transform slowly into someone unrecognizable.

The person I really wanted to talk to and see was Nate. I wanted to feel his attention on me. I felt that telling him about Nana would actually make me feel better. I wanted him to tell me what he went through when his dad had died. That kind of loss was unimaginable to me. I wanted him to feel safe and cry, and I would understand and make it better. I wanted to hold him close to me and feel his heart pounding, and the pressure of his body against mine, and I wanted to smell his hair and his skin. I could almost imagine him here on the edge of the bed with me, the way his hot and cold blue eyes would look right now. How his hands would feel on my face.

chapter

thirty – five

The rest of January remained cold and overcast. The sun came out every afternoon, but it was weak and pale and it always went away quickly, receding into a veil of clouds. I caught a cold the morning after Nana's funeral and it lingered, coming and going for weeks.

As I walked to the car-pool lane one Wednesday at the beginning of February, people were already filing onto the big yellow bus that would take them to Clean the Bay. The week before, I hadn't done Clean the Bay because I was sick and today I had lied and told Mom it was canceled so I wouldn't have to go. I couldn't handle being around Hailey. And seeing Hailey and Nate at the same time would be even worse.

I barely saw Nate at school, but I didn't stop wondering about him. In spite of all the bad things that had happened over winter break, I still got this rush every time I thought about him. It had been almost two months since Skyler's holiday party, but still I replayed the moment we shared that night over and over in my mind, scanning the memory for clues.

Something had shifted in me that night and now I wanted to see him with an intensity that felt new. Every time I walked past the patio behind the administration building, I checked to see if he was there. Was this what a crush felt like? Was this how Hailey had been feeling about Nate forever? For the first time, I understood why she constantly talked about Nate, weaving him into every conversation we had.

I started to wonder how many girls Nate had been with and how far they had gone. I knew he had kissed Hailey, but how far had he gone with Sophie? And who else had there been? I had only kissed two guys in my life. The first was a guy from outside of school during spin the bottle at this girl's birthday party in seventh grade, and the second was a guy name Alec Foster who I kissed last year. He had been a senior when I was a freshman, which made it a really big deal when he asked me out.

Alec was really good-looking and easygoing. He had an angular, chiseled face and a lean, athletic body. He was super-nice and smart and well rounded. He had one girlfriend forever named Katie, who was equally perfect. A few weeks after they broke up, Alec came up to me out of the blue at lunch and invited me out. Hailey practically fainted.

That weekend, Alec picked me up and we went to some stupid movie. It didn't matter what movie we saw, though, because I couldn't focus on it at all. I was totally preoccupied with how I was supposed to behave and what was going to happen after the movie was over.

Hailey had dressed me that night, putting me in a baby blue cardigan that she said matched my eyes.

"Listen," she said, when I told her I wasn't sure if I wanted to kiss him. "It'll be easy. He'll know what to do. He's hooked up with tons of girls, I'm sure. Just try not to overthink it."

She was right. Alec knew just what to do, leaning across the center console of his car and cupping my face in his hand. It was just like it looked on TV. His mouth tasted like gum and something unfamiliar, but it wasn't horrible. While it was happening, all I was thinking about was making sure I paid attention to all the details so I could give Hailey the full scoop afterward.

When Alec asked me out again, I lied and said I wasn't feeling well. I don't know why I didn't go. I could have. It wasn't bad going out with Alec; it just wasn't anything.

I was lost in thought about Alec Foster when the front entrance to the school swung open and Nate stepped out, stopping on the sidewalk a few feet away from where I stood. We hadn't seen each other since Skyler's party, and when our eyes met, I felt the air around me grow still and warm. I felt totally transparent, sure he could tell how much I'd been thinking about him lately.

He opened his mouth like he was about to say something to me, and then an older boy who I didn't know bounced out of the door behind him and yanked on Nate's backpack, jerking him backward.

Nate's attention slid away from me to his friend, and the two of them turned and walked in the direction of the bus.

My heart pounded in my chest.

As I walked to the spot where Mom would be picking me up, I wondered when and how I would ever get to be alone with Nate again.

chapter

thirty-six

Mom came in to my room on Saturday and sat on the edge of my bed.

"Hey, baby," she said. "It's eleven. Time to get up."

Mom smelled clean, like she'd already showered. She was wearing a yellow T-shirt and khaki shorts.

"I'm still tired," I grumbled.

Mom leaned in toward me and started untangling a knot of hair next to my ear. "Lima, do you ever brush your hair?"

I liked when Mom got super-close to me and I could see the freckles on her skin and smell the good Mom smell underneath the smell of her shower products.

"Sometimes," I said. "When I feel like it."

"You know it's Daddy's birthday tomorrow," Mom said, gently unwinding the strands of hair.

"I know. I didn't forget," I said. "What are we gonna do?"

We always spent Dad's birthday with Nana, and I had been getting more and more worried about it as the day approached, knowing that we couldn't do that this year.

"He said he just wants to go to Gladstones for dinner. Just the three of us," she said.

Mom and I hated Gladstones, with its soggy, fried food and tacky Malibu tourist paraphernalia, but that was a secret we kept from Dad. It would literally break his heart if he knew.

"Sounds good," I said.

Whatever sadness Mom and Dad had about Nana was tucked neatly away, out of sight.

Meredith called me while Mom and I were doing the breakfast dishes. Meredith never texted.

"Hi, beauty," she said when I answered. "What are you up to?"

"Nothing," I said. I hadn't seen Meredith since before the holidays, and it felt good to hear her voice.

"There's a really amazing silent movie playing at the New Beverly this afternoon," she said. "Want to come? We can eat at the old farmers' market afterward."

I glanced outside at the perfect sky and ocean, and I thought about all the clatter in my head and decided a silent movie was probably exactly what I needed.

I got ready quickly, and silently stared out the window while Mom drove me to meet Meredith.

The theater was in a busy part of the city, trafficky and bright and polluted. Meredith was waiting out front, wearing aviator sunglasses, a long floral dress, and a suede jacket.

"Meredith looks so grown-up," Mom said as she pulled up to the curb.

"Yeah," I agreed. "She has really cool style."

"Hmm," Mom said, her mouth forming a straight line.

Meredith came over to the car, and I got out. She wrapped her arms around me and held me protectively under her arm while she talked to Mom.

"This movie is going to be so special—thank you for bringing Lima all the way out here," Meredith said to Mom. Sometimes she really did seem like a grown-up.

Mom smiled and nodded and told us to have fun. As we walked inside, I thought how weird it was that no matter how polite Meredith was, Mom always seemed suspicious of her.

The movie theater had red velvet chairs, and the screen was smaller than regular movie theater screens. It even had a heavy curtain that parted when the movie started.

Everything felt like an antique, touched with the magic of all the people who had been here over the years. Maybe it's because LA is kind of a new city, but there aren't that many places that I've been that are really old.

In the cool, dark theater and the wordless universe of the movie, I actually felt a good wave of calmness. Maybe the world was bigger than I thought. Not just all about Hailey and Nate. I almost, for a fleeting second, glimpsed a life that might exist after high school. I tried to catch it, but the feeling vanished as quickly as it had emerged.

When we got out of the theater, it was night.

"There's this incredible taco stand at the farmer's market," Meredith said. "I'm starving."

The old farmer's market in West Hollywood wasn't a real farmers' market like the ones Mom and I went to for fresh produce. It was a bustling, rowdy outdoor food court that resembled a county fair more than anything. Tourists and locals swarmed through the labyrinth of exotic food stands and wine bars. I followed close behind Meredith, trying not to lose sight of her in the crowd. Meredith ordered us six tacos, and we ate them standing up at a yellow plastic counter. We must have gone through a hundred napkins, wiping salsa and sour cream and that red oil from the carne asada off our mouths.

"I love Louise Brooks," Meredith said, talking about the movie we had just seen. "She says so much without saying anything. It is so sexy."

Nobody at school talked like Meredith. Nobody said stuff like "sexy."

"You have that quality, too," Meredith continued. "You say so much with your face. I can just watch you."

I blushed. "I think you're like that!"

Meredith smiled. "No, I just try to be like that."

"You do?" I said. "Like, how?"

Meredith shrugged, pushing the remainder of the taco into her mouth. She blocked her mouth with her delicate hand.

"Did you go out last night?" I asked.

It's weird how Meredith almost never talked about anything personal. Even asking what she'd done the night before felt like prying.

Meredith frowned, staring off into space. "My memory is terrible. Last night? Oh, yeah, Walker and I didn't do anything. We listened to music. We video chatted with our father in Marrakech for a while. I wish I was there. I can't wait for next year."

"What's next year?" I asked.

"Walker and I are going travel," she said, straightening up. "We're starting by visiting our mom in Paris and then from Paris we're going to Istanbul and then we don't know. I want to ride the trans-Siberian railroad. And Walker is obsessed with Japan. We are keeping our plans open."

"Wow," I said. "That's amazing. And that's okay with your parents? Like not going to college?"

"We might go eventually," she replied vaguely.

"Are you deferring for a year?" I asked.

"We didn't apply. We went on a college tour last summer and it all just seemed so wrong. We couldn't picture it. Being in some dorm. The whole thing," she said, frowning a little. But then she brightened. "But who knows. Maybe I'll want to go to college after seeing the world."

I wondered if Mom and Dad would let me travel for a year before going to college. Everything always sounded so sensible the way Meredith said it, but I could already imagine the millions of questions my parents would ask if I tried to suggest something like that.

"I want to travel, too," I said. "That's why I like that Joni Mitchell song 'California.' It makes me glad to be right here."

"I know, it's a perfect song for being glad to be in LA," she said. And then she took her cell phone out of her pocket, glanced at the screen, and sighed. "There's a party in Hollywood later. Walker wants to go, but I don't feel like it. I'd rather just go back to your house and sit on the beach."

I was surprised. Meredith had never slept over. "Really?"

"Walker wanted to see some girl. I think he'll probably bring her home with him," she frowned.

"Oh," I said. "Walker has a girlfriend?"

"No," she chuckled. "It's not like that."

"Definitely come over," I said.

We left the farmer's market and Meredith drove us back to Malibu.

"What does Walker do when you take the car?" I asked.

She dragged on her cigarette before she answered. "We have another car," she said. "My dad's Mercedes."

"That's nice," I said.

And then she laughed. "It's so funny that Walker has to drive that thing."

I liked when Meredith laughed, but I also felt excluded. She had so many private jokes with herself. She laughed hard for about another minute, and then she took a long, steady breath and turned on the stereo. The singer was a man. His voice was soft and broken and coaxing.

As we drove west toward Malibu, the city changed. It went from urban to suburban and finally to the wide, dark expanse of the beach.

"Who are we listening to?" I asked as we turned onto the PCH. The gravel of his voice matched the grinding, unsmooth gears of Meredith's old car.

"Leonard Cohen," she said. "Isn't it beautiful?"

I nodded, and then laughed. "Like your cat!"

"Like my cat," Meredith agreed, and then cut off the ste-reo. "I'll teach you to sing it. It's one of those really easy ones to sing."

"Okay," I said. "I'd like that."

I felt so lucky to get to hang around Meredith. Her friend-ship felt like a prize, or a secret, or a key.

chapter

thirty-seven

Yuri was assigned as my partner for the spectra lab. It was an outside-of-class lab, and the only time we could find to meet up was Tuesday after school.

The room monitor that day was a young-looking assistant from the dean's office. She sat quietly behind Patty's desk reading a magazine.

"Let's do hydrogen first," Yuri said, nodding toward a glass tube that radiated a bright blue light, like a neon glow stick.

I positioned the spectroscope in front of it. "You go first."

Yuri bent down and looked in. "I think it's continuous, not linear. You check."

He stood up and lightly touched my arm, gesturing for it to be my turn. Yuri was one of those people who had to wear his regular glasses inside of his lab goggles, which made him look really silly. Even so, there was something handsome about him with his dark wavy hair and dimples. He'd had the same girlfriend all year, a senior named Ziyue, who walked him to chem every day.

I bent down and peered through the eyehole. I had been sort of excited that this lab had to do with light, but the spectroscope converted the glowing blue of the hydrogen into something dry and boring. Just a numeric equation.

By the time Yuri and I had finished, the February sun had already gone down and it was dark out. I had never been in the science classroom at this hour, and the night sky turned the big glass windows into mirrors.

I texted Mom to come get me, then I grabbed a granola bar from my locker and walked over to the patio behind the administration building. I thought hopefully that maybe Nate had a meeting with the dean today and would still be there, but the patio was empty. Disappointed, I wandered back to the main campus through the student parking lot. I wove in and around the remaining cars, to see if I recognized anyone's. Meredith and Walker's spot was empty. Skyler's spot was empty, too.

When I realized I didn't know who the few cars belonged to, a dense loneliness settled on my chest like a weight.

I walked to the computer lab, resigned to getting a head start on my homework while I waited for my mom. As soon as I stepped in, my heart literally leaped. Nate was there. Alone. Sitting at a computer, his face illuminated by a glowing screen. I had hoped for a situation like this so many times over the last few weeks that I almost felt like I had willed it into being.

When he saw me, he gave me a small acknowledging nod and I returned it.

I sat down at a computer a few stations over. I was careful not to sit too close to him. I could feel his eyes on me, though, watching my motions, doing that uninhibited staring thing that he had done in the past. I resisted looking in his direction. All I had wanted lately was the chance to be alone with him, and now that I had it, I was too shy to even speak.

"Long time no see," he said finally.

I allowed myself to turn and meet his eyes. I nodded in agreement.

He cocked his head and looked at me curiously, like he was putting something together.

"Want to take a break?" he asked. "We can go up to the roof."

I left my backpack in the computer lab and followed Nate up a set of stairs at the back of the building. People always talked about sneaking up on the roof to smoke or make out or skip class, but I'd never been. At the top, Nate pushed open a door and held it for me as I walked outside.

The roof was weird. Big bulbous vents were clustered like bushes. The ground was covered with a strange, soft gravel.

There were no lamps so it was darker than the rest of the school. LA spread out all around us. The lights of cars, office buildings, streetlamps, and storefronts lit up the city like a giant, flat Christmas tree.

I turned to Nate. He picked up a pebble from the ground, tossed it up, and attempted to kick it midair. He missed. He did it again. This time, the pebble grazed his shoe. He sighed, and squinted out at the city. I felt like I could watch him do anything and never get bored.

An ambulance drove by, and its siren blared like an opera over the low groan of traffic.

"What are you doing here so late?" he asked when it had passed.

My vision had adjusted to the dark, and I could see that his blue eyes were swimming.

"I had a chem lab," I said. "What about you? Did you have a meeting with the dean?"

"Nope, other stuff," he said. And then he cracked a smile. "But good memory. About the dean."

His smile melted something inside of me.

"Hey," he said, his tone changing. "How is your grand-mother?"

"She died," I responded quickly. The words hit the air like stones hitting a wall. It was weird, for the first time since Nana had died it actually seemed real. I felt the unyielding, irreversible truth of it. I would never see her again. Hot tears stung my eyes. I couldn't repress them, so I pressed my forearm hard across my eyes, blocking the tears from spilling down my face with the sleeve of my sweatshirt.

After a minute, I dropped my arm. "I'm sorry."

"Don't be," he said softly. He stepped toward me and put his hand on my shoulder, like he was going to pull me in for a hug. But instead he just let it rest there for a moment before dropping it back to his side.

His hand left a burning imprint on my shoulder, as if the place where he had touched me was on fire. We looked at each other for a moment. The city swirled around us, cars and electronic billboards and helicopters, and we were separate. In our own, secret pocket of dark.

Just then, my phone vibrated. A text from Mom saying she was here. A bubble of disappointment swelled inside me. I really didn't want to leave.

Nate walked me downstairs. We didn't talk, but our silence felt rich and active, like even without speaking we were saying things. In chemistry, Patty was always reminding us that air isn't negative space. It's full of molecules in motion, and when I was around Nate, I really understood what Patty meant.

Back in the computer lab, I picked up my backpack and swung it over my shoulder.

Nate watched.

"Okay," I said, trying to hold his gaze, feeling gripped with a sudden shyness. Was I supposed to give him a good-bye hug? I just stood there, frozen.

He stuck the palm of his hand out to me, as if he wanted me to give him a high five.

I slapped his hand and he caught it, his fingers wrapping around and through my own. My awkwardness vanished. Nate was so comfortable, so confident, it made me feel safe. And the sensation of our bodies touching, even just our hands, was so overwhelming my mind kind of went blank.

After a minute he said, "You should go meet your mom."

I nodded. I dropped my hand and drifted outside.

On our drive back to Malibu, the city looked clearer, more vivid than it had in forever. I noticed the rich green of the street signs, and the array of colors of the cars on the freeway. When we turned onto the Pacific Coast Highway, the ocean greeted us, moonlight sparkling on its surface like a zillion flickering stars.

chapter

thirty-eight

"We're going to let you in on a huge secret," Meredith said.

"Take it with you to the grave, Court and Spark," Walker joked, using his nickname for me.

We were sitting in their living room after a long and chaotic dinner that Friday night. Meredith had asked me to help her make ravioli from scratch, but she got so drunk on red wine during the process and took so many cigarette breaks, that we ended up making a box of mac and cheese instead. The kitchen was trashed, with discarded bowls of flour and eggs and butter sitting on the counter. Now, Walker was tuning his guitar and Henry and Lily were stretched out on the floor with their legs intertwined.

"We are obsessed with Justin Bieber," Meredith declared, looking me right in the eye.

I laughed. "You are not."

"We are," Walker said, and started strumming his guitar softly while Meredith sang the words to one of his songs.

I clasped my hands over my mouth. "That actually sounds pretty when you sing it."

"I know," Meredith said. "He has an amazing songwriting team."

Someone knocked on the front door and Walker answered it. I craned my neck, peering around Walker to see who was there and was surprised to see Ryan standing on the doorstep. And then my heart somersaulted when I noticed that lingering just a few feet behind him was Nate.

They came inside and said hi to the twins and then Nate walked over to me, his hands stuffed into the pockets of his jeans. I tried to smile calmly, but my nerves were jangling like crazy. Nate's appearance had split the normal path of the evening into a million exciting possibilities.

"Funny seeing you here," Nate said. "I didn't know you hung out with these kids."

"I do," I explained. "I'm friends with Meredith. Have you ever been here?"

"No. Ryan comes here sometimes now 'cause his dad lives nearby. But his house is nothing like this." Nate scanned the room. "This house is insane."

"I know, it's amazing," I said.

Nate looked out the glass doors to the balcony. "Can we go out there?"

Nate and I cut through the living room and out the sliding doors to the back deck. He gestured to a stone staircase that led to a lower, private deck. "Let's go there."

"I don't know if we're allowed. I think that's their dad's area."

"Is he home?"

"No, he's, like, always away," I said. "I've never seen him."

"I'm sure they won't care," he said, and started down the stairs. I followed.

"So you and Meredith are pretty tight?" he asked.

"Yeah," I said. "She's really cool."

"Really." Nate didn't say it like it was a question.

"Don't you think so?" I asked.

"I don't know," he said. "This scene doesn't seem real."

"What do you mean?"

"You know," he said. "Not to talk shit. But they just try so hard to be cool."

I thought about this for a moment, wondering if it could be true. Meredith had only ever seemed authentic to me.

"But I really don't know them, so, you know, whatever," Nate added when we got to the bottom of the stairs.

Unlike the upstairs deck, which was flooded with light from the house, the downstairs deck was completely dark.

I couldn't hear the sounds of the others at all now, only the buzz of cars below us on Mulholland Drive.

Nate looked out at the view and ran his fingers along the worn wooden banister.

"Isn't it so pretty out here? Before I was friends with Meredith, I never got to come to this part of LA," I said, rambling nervously. "But I love the views. You can see the Hollywood sign, like, perfectly clearly from Walker's balcony. Have you ever been there? Walker said you can hike to it."

Nate stopped fidgeting and turned to look at me.

"I never see you," he said.

"I saw you this week at school," I said.

"That's not what I mean," he said.

And something about the way he said it made me grow suddenly still.

"I've tried not to bother you. You're always hanging around with Hailey and I got the sense that maybe because of her or because of something else, you didn't want to—" he hesitated, searching for the words. "Talk to me."

I had a choice. He had given me the perfect opportunity to say what I was supposed to say: You should go for Hailey.

Instead, I said, "I do want to talk to you."

He nodded, taking in my words, his eyes fixed steadily on mine for a moment. And then, he stepped toward me, took my head in his hands, and kissed me.

It happened so quickly that my stomach dropped, giving me that half-seasick, half-amazing feeling you get from going down a roller coaster too fast. I closed my eyes and let myself kiss him back. His mouth was salty and soft and sweet all at once. Heat blossomed inside me.

After a moment, Nate stopped, took a small step back. His eyes were still burning into me.

"I've been wanting to do that for so long," he said.

I stared back at Nate, unable to speak. I felt as if I'd been turned inside out. The air was velvet against my skin.

Nate's phone beeped in his pocket. He pulled it out and read the screen. When he looked back at me, he frowned.

"Ryan's looking for me," he said. "He wants to go."

"Okay," I said, and my voice was a raspy whisper.

"So, what are you going to do with the rest of your night?" he asked. He reached out and tucked a strand of hair behind my ear.

"Oh, you know. Waste it," I said. My heart still pounded in my chest.

Nate laughed. "You're so funny, Lima. I never know what's going to come out of your mouth."

"I am?" I asked shyly. I didn't even think I had a sense of humor. Hailey had always been the funny one. I looked at the ground, unsure what to say next. So many things were happening so fast, I felt like I was dreaming.

"Hey," Nate said, and he gently kicked my shin with one of his sneakers.

When I looked up at him, he wasn't smiling anymore.

"Hey," I replied.

"So, can I get your number?" Nate asked when we got to the front porch. I watched as he punched the numbers into his phone and slipped it back into his pocket.

He looked like he was about to say something else when Ryan stepped out through the front door.

"Dude, where'd you go?" Ryan asked. I looked at the ground, suddenly shy to be caught alone with Nate. I wondered if Ryan could sense everything that had just happened. I felt so changed by Nate's kiss, it was impossible to imagine he couldn't see that.

"Lima showed me around," Nate said protectively. "Did you get your game?"

"Yeah. Not the one I wanted, but another one that's supposed to be really cool," Ryan said, not acting weird. Maybe he didn't notice anything different about me after all.

"Walker has video games?" I asked.

Ryan laughed a genuine, satisfying laugh that made me giggle, too.

"Good question. You know, I think they're his dad's. He has all the newest games, and Walker lets me borrow them 'cause he's never around. Anyway, let's go. This place makes me paranoid."

Nate ignored Ryan and turned to me.

"We're going," he said softly.

"Okay," I said.

"See you around?" he asked. An amused, warm light flickered in his eyes.

I giggled, bit my lip, blushed, suddenly unable to find my voice, so I just nodded.

I watched the two of them walk down the driveway, Ryan talking the whole way. As they got farther away they began to disappear into patches of dark. After a minute or two, I saw one last streetlight catch on Nate's shoulder and then they faded completely out of view.

My hand moved instinctively to my mouth. Nate's lips had felt softer than air. As much as the kiss had begun to ease all the tightly wound tension that had built up between us, it wasn't nearly enough. Now that we had started, all I wanted was more.

I wanted to savor this feeling and think about Nate, but I couldn't push away the thought of Hailey. This thing between me and Nate was official now. Not a fantasy. Not a suspicion. There was no going back.

• • •

Everyone had moved upstairs to Meredith's room while I'd been gone. They were all squeezed onto the bed watching TV, Meredith in the middle with Henry and Walker on one side and Lily on the other.

"Yay. Lima," Meredith said droopily when she saw me. "Come here."

I climbed onto the bed, next to Lily and tried to get comfortable.

"Lily, make room," Meredith commanded.

"I'm trying," Lily replied.

Leonard Cohen sprung up onto the bed and coiled himself into a shape like an *O* on Meredith's stomach. Meredith stroked him, running her black painted nails through his fur and went back to watching TV. They were watching a rerun of *Law & Order* and I wondered why, with all the millions of channels they had, they would watch this. But all of the twins' tastes seemed significant and carefully chosen, so I didn't ask.

Besides, I didn't care what we watched. My head was still spinning from the kiss. It had been perfect, seamless, almost unreal. And the feeling was lingering, like the first blissful hour after waking up from a good dream.

"Lily, can you stop chewing so loudly for like two seconds?" Meredith snapped out of the blue.

Lily was systematically working her way through a bag of

Twizzlers. She froze, stopped chewing for a second, and then swallowed uncomfortably.

"I'm just chewing. What am I supposed to do?" she asked. An embarrassing pink blush bloomed up at the base of her neck.

"Just, I don't know," Meredith said. "Haven't you had enough? You ate like that whole bag."

Lily's face was bright red now, but she acted cool. She scooted down to the edge of the bed and stood up. "I'm going to get some water. Anyone want anything?"

Walker and Henry shook their heads.

"I'd love a ginger ale. They're in the second fridge in the hallway behind the kitchen. You know the one?" Meredith asked. She didn't even lift her eyes off the screen to address Lily.

After Lily had gone, Henry propped himself up on his elbows and leaned across Walker to ruffle Meredith's hair.

"You're so bad," he whispered. Meredith didn't look at him, just swatted his hand away, but there was a wicked smile painted on her lips.

Without Lily, I rolled closer to Meredith and let my head rest on her shoulder. I tried to watch the show but it was halfway over and I had no idea what was happening. It really didn't matter though. In my mind, I was still standing on Meredith's balcony, Nate's fingers brushing against my cheek.

chapter

thirty-nine

The first thing I thought about when I woke up the next morning was the kiss. I spent the whole day Saturday reliving it, playing it over and over in my mind like pushing repeat on my favorite song. It took double the usual amount of time to finish my homework, and that night I couldn't even stay focused long enough to sit through a half hour TV show with Mom and Dad. The kiss was a magnet, sucking me back in time.

Mom and Dad were having a dinner party on Sunday night, and I offered to make a flourless chocolate cake. I hoped the challenge would be engaging enough to distract me from thoughts of Nate. The recipe was tough. I had to figure out how to sweeten the chocolate, how to use a double boiler, how to balance the chemistry just right.

I was standing over the stove, stirring together the butter and unsweetened chocolate mixture, when the doorbell rang.

Hailey was standing on the stoop in an oversized sweatshirt and baggy jeans, like the old Hailey.

I froze.

She heard about me and Nate, I thought. She's here because she knows.

"Did we have plans?" I asked, knowing that we didn't.

"No we didn't have plans," Hailey said. "I just really needed to see you, and I was worried that if I called, you'd say you were busy."

Panic spiked inside of me. I felt as if I was about to lose my balance.

"Where are your parents?" she asked.

"My mom is at the market getting bread for tonight, and my dad is on the beach. They're having a dinner party tonight."

"Oh, that sounds so nice." Hailey sighed, her eyes glossing over with genuine sadness. "I miss them."

I smiled a little, slowly letting my guard down. Hailey did love my parents. Maybe I wasn't in trouble after all.

"Can we go upstairs?" she asked.

I tried to remember the last time Hailey had been over. It must have been around Thanksgiving. Now it was almost March. I wondered if my room had changed. She looked uncomfortable in it.

"There are so many things I need to say to you," Hailey said. "I'm so sorry about everything."

I sat cross-legged on my floor, and Hailey sat with her back against my bed, her legs straight out in front of her.

"I've been a fucking horrible, terrible friend to you," she said. "I can't believe I didn't come to Nana's funeral. I can hardly think about it, it makes me feel so awful. Do you think your parents will ever forgive me? Will you ever forgive me?"

I looked at the floor. I couldn't manage to look at her.

"This is really out of the blue," I said. "That was, like, months ago."

"I know," Hailey said. "You might not get this, because you've never fucked up, but sometimes when you do something really bad, it's really hard to apologize. It's, like, acknowledging it makes it so much worse."

My eyes snapped up and met Hailey's. That I understood completely.

"I know it's stupid," she said. "But I've just been having such a manic year. I'm, like, I mean, you must know. You've seen me. I just don't know who I am anymore."

I nodded a little. I understood that part, too.

"And you," she continued, "you know me so much better than anybody else. Sometimes it's hard to be around you because I just feel like you see through everything I do."

Hailey dropped her head and covered her eyes with the heels of her hands. Bright red polish was chipping off her nails, and they made little misshapen blobs.

"My dad and Rachel are getting married."

"Oh, wow," I said softly. "When? When did he tell you?"

Hailey's hands collapsed in her lap. When she looked up at me, her eyes were wet. She pursed her lips, probably trying to stop herself from crying.

"He told me on Christmas," she said.

"Christmas?" I repeated. "That was so long ago."

Hailey ignored me and continued. "Rachel is pregnant."

"Oh, wow," I said again. And then I added, "Wow."

Hailey's dad left her mom for Rachel, his secretary, when we were nine. I had never met Rachel, only seen her once when they were dropping Hailey off. She was sitting in the passenger seat and I couldn't make her out behind all the reflected light on the windshield.

Hailey blinked, and wiped more tears away with the tips of her fingers. "I'm such a crier. I cry about everything."

I know Hailey was trying to be light, but I could tell she was faking.

"I don't know why I care," she went on. "It's not like I see them ever anyway. It's just that I'm gonna be, like, the weird old half sister who doesn't really exist in anyone's mind. It's like me and my mom won't even exist now that he has a new family."

I uncrossed my legs and reached forward to give Hailey a hug. She let me hug her, but then she kind of gently pulled away.

"I didn't come over here to make you feel bad for me, Li," Hailey said. "I was a bitch to you on New Year's and horrible about Nana, too. I just, I'm really sorry. I don't ever want to lose you. I don't want to push you away like that."

"I know," I said. A wave of guilt so gigantic and dizzying was swelling inside me. I felt like I might throw up. "I don't want to lose you either."

"Nobody knows about Rachel," she said. "I haven't told Skyler anything. I think it's gross. I'm so embarrassed. So can you, like, not tell your parents?"

"Why? It's not embarrassing," I said. "Lots of people's parents get divorced and remarried. Don't people say that half of all marriages end?"

"Just don't tell them, okay?" Hailey pleaded. "You don't understand because your life is perfect."

I felt suddenly defensive. What did Hailey know about what it was really like to be me?

"Fine, I don't understand," I said. It came out sounding hard, so I added, in a softer tone, "But you're gonna be fine."

Hailey wiped away a couple more tears. "I'm sorry. For

everything shitty I've done. For the shitty things I said on New Year's Eve. You are the most important person in my life."

I inhaled and exhaled slowly. "Do you want to stay for dinner?"

Hailey rested her head on my shoulder, and I could smell her unclean hair.

"You're so generous," she said. "I'd love to stay. I love you."

"I love you, too," I said. I knew what I had to do. I had to tell her about Nate. "And I have something I need to tell you, too."

Hailey looked perplexed. "Okay. What?"

Where do I start? I wondered. I couldn't start by telling her about the kiss. The kiss was only a part of a longer story. I'd have to start with all the conversations we'd had after school and at Clean the Bay, or the time he had touched my shoulder on the roof, or even the way we had studied Spanish together at the beginning of the year.

"Lima, what is it? You look insane," she scoffed.

"Nothing," I said quickly. If I tried to explain to her what was happening with Nate, she would shred it. She would minimize it and distort it, tear it up, and scatter all the pieces in the air like confetti. And what did I owe her, anyway? She couldn't just march in here and decide we were best friends again. I felt trapped.

"I know what it is." Hailey smirked. "I know your secret. You like Walker Hayes."

I let out a surprised gasp and then I laughed.

"No!" I squealed. "I don't."

"It's okay, Li," Hailey teased. "You're allowed to like whoever you want. No matter how dirty they are."

After our talk, we went downstairs, and I told Hailey what she could do to help me with my cake. I watched her back while she made the whipped cream. Everything was so twisted between us now. My feelings formed an intricate map of anger and guilt and sympathy. There were scars where she had treaded so carelessly across our friendship. Even with a big Hailey-style, bottom-of-the-heart apology, I wasn't sure if the damage would heal.

chapter

forty

∞

That Wednesday on the bus to Clean the Bay, I sat down in the front seat across from Leo. If Hailey wanted to sit in the back and hunt for Nate, she could do it alone. I was done helping her get his attention.

But when Hailey got on the bus a few minutes later, she sat down right next to me.

"So," she said, "your birthday is less than two weeks away. What are you gonna do? Sixteen is a big one."

"I don't know," I said. "I was thinking I'd do something at Meredith's house. Nothing major. Just watch a movie."

"Well, you know I'm not going to Meredith's house. I don't want anyone casting any Wiccan spells on me while I'm sleeping," Hailey deadpanned. "But maybe we can go out to dinner with your parents or something the next day?"

Nate climbed onto the bus and I kept my eyes glued to Hailey's, using all of my willpower not to look at him. Ignoring him was torture. I hadn't seen him since Friday night, and all I wanted to do was smile at him or make eye contact or do something to acknowledge him.

"Yeah, okay, something like that," I said, determined to keep the conversation going until Nate had passed.

At the beach, the sun was unusually hot and bright.

"I'm not wearing any sunscreen," I said. "So I'm gonna try and stay in the shade today. Like, under the pier."

"I'll come with you," Hailey said.

"Really?" I asked. Hailey was one of those people who was always trying to get a tan. It confused me that she would blow the opportunity to get some sun just to hang out with me, and her new clinginess was unnerving.

We wandered around for a few minutes under the pier without talking and then she said, "I've gotta pee. I'll be right back."

I watched Hailey trudge away toward the public bathroom in that awkward sand-walking way and then turned back to the ocean. Nate was walking near the water. He paused, bent down and picked something up from the sand, and then replaced it. He stood perfectly still for a long moment, squinting out into the horizon, the sun beating down on his profile. Warm light caught on his nose, his shoulders, his hands. Behind him, the surface of the ocean was a burnished sheet of metal. I thought about our kiss again, his fingers in my hair, the serious, focused look in his eyes the second before it happened. I thought about the moment we shared on the roof of the science building the week before and the way his palm had felt when he pressed it against mine.

"Lima?"

Hailey was back already.

"What are you looking at?" she asked. She turned her head, following the line of my vision until she saw Nate, and then her eyes moved slowly back to mine. The expression on her face was like she was solving a math problem.

"Nothing," I said. "I was just zoning out."

"Oh, okay," she said, sounding skeptical.

And then feeling a little weak, or worried or something, I took a step toward her and wrapped my arms tight around her neck.

"I'm just so glad we're friends again," I said. "I missed you."

That night, I left my cell phone on my desk. I hadn't been more than an arm's length away from it since I gave my number to Nate on Friday. Would he ever call? All I wanted was to see the screen light up with his number.

The waning evening sun washed into my room, streams of mild light stretching across my desk. Next week, we'd move the clocks forward and the days would get longer. Daylight Savings was always easy for me to remember because it usually fell within a day or two of my birthday. I always looked forward to it, too, maybe even more than my birthday itself. Turning the clocks ahead an hour was like switching the season from winter back to summer again.

Time was such a weird, subjective thing. The five days I'd spent wondering if Nate would call had felt like an eternity, and meanwhile the whole school year was slipping by like a ghost, too fast and elusive for me to catch.

chapter

forty-one

ast year, when I turned fifteen, my birthday had fallen on a Friday, and I spent that whole weekend at Hailey's. Double sleepovers had always been our specialty. All day Saturday we stayed in our pajamas, eating snacks and watching TV. Because it was my birthday weekend, Hailey had let me watch all the episodes of *Top Chef* that I'd missed, even though she hated that show. My TV at home was bigger and fancier than Hailey's, but I always preferred watching TV at her apartment. Her TV room was small, carpeted, and windowless. There was an inside-ness to it that I could never find in my own house.

We didn't even leave Hailey's apartment until Sunday morning when we walked to the Baskin-Robbins on Venice Boulevard and had ice cream for breakfast. Ice cream for breakfast for our birthdays had been our tradition since fourth grade.

It had been my idea to go to this Baskin-Robbins, but once we got there, my excitement deflated. The strip mall was dingy in the broad daylight. A group of men were smoking cigarettes outside of a liquor store, shouting to each other in a language I didn't recognize.

"We should go home," I said to Hailey. "This is depressing."

"Are you kidding?" Hailey responded. "You have to have ice cream for breakfast on your birthday weekend. It's good luck."

All the details from that weekend were seared into my memory, and now, on the eve of my sixteenth birthday, one moment in particular kept coming back to me. After our *Top Chef* marathon and an impromptu dance party, and after trolling around online looking at boys from other schools, we climbed into bed and whispered about turning fifteen. We talked about whether we would ever have boyfriends, and wondered what it would be like to have sex. It didn't seem possible that those things might be in our futures.

I lay awake after Hailey had turned off the lights, not tired. As my vision adjusted to the dark, I scanned her room and my eyes landed on the drawings we had done on the back of her door. I glanced at Hailey. Her back was to me, but I could tell from the slight puff of her exhale that she was already sleeping. I remember looking at the back of her head, the straight line of her back and rib cage, her legs under the sheet, and thinking, or actually kind of knowing, that she would get a boyfriend and have sex before me. It's like I just always believed she was going to leave me behind.

chapter

forty-two

The night before my birthday it rained. I went straight from school to the twins' house. Walker drove and Meredith sat shotgun, and I sat in the backseat, watching the rain splash hard against the windows of their car.

Back at their house, Meredith lit candles and the three of us listened to music and ate leftover Indian food.

"This is so good, where is it from?" I asked Meredith.

"It's from this amazing vegetarian place on Sunset near Franklin. It's the best," she said. "We went there last night."

"Just you two?" I asked.

"Yeah," Meredith said, like it was obvious.

I had never really asked myself what Meredith and Walker usually did for dinner, and now it occurred to me that they probably went out every single night. I could picture it easily, the two of them, sitting across from each other in restaurants around LA night after night, ordering glasses of water or soda and then waiting for checks, looking for parking spots, climbing in and out of the car. Their life, which always seemed so glamorous and wild, struck me suddenly small and lonely.

"You're not coming to the movie?" I asked Walker, when he didn't put on his shoes after dinner. He was lying on his back on the couch, his phone resting on his stomach like a pet.

"Nope," he said. "Do you know how many times she's made me watch *Darling*? And once was enough."

"Why are you being an asshole, Walker?" Meredith asked calmly. "You've seen it once and we didn't even finish it. Don't lie."

He mumbled something inaudible, not looking at either of us as we left.

The city was slippery and dark in the rain. We ran from the parking lot to the theater without umbrellas and were soaked by the time we got inside.

I was waiting on line to use the bathroom before the movie started when my phone beeped.

What r u doing this weekend?

And then a second later:

This is nate

My pulse quickened. I stepped out of the line to let an

older woman go ahead of me. I wanted more time to craft my response.

> At a movie now. Tmrw is my birthday so
> spending time with fam.

I replied, deliberately not mentioning Hailey.

> !!! happppyy birthday

I wrote back, thanks.

By the time I got to my seat, I was giddy.

I put my phone into the silent position and looked up at Meredith.

"I'm so glad you're excited about this movie," she whispered, misreading my enthusiasm. "It's going to break your heart, I promise."

chapter

forty-three

The next day, the sky was a post-rain, shiny blue. Perfect beach weather.

"You guys all know each other, right?" I said awkwardly as Hailey climbed into the backseat of the twins' car. We had made a plan to pick Hailey up on the morning of my birthday and all go to the beach together.

Meredith and Walker smiled and nodded, and Hailey tried to smile, too.

"Happy birthday, Li! How does it feel to be sixteen?" She asked, handing me an enormous bag of candy. I recognized the stamp on the clear plastic bag, and I felt a stab of guilt as I realized she must have gone all the way to Santa Monica just to go to the best place. The bag was full of all my favorite candy: cotton-candy jelly beans, sour belts, and chocolate-covered gummy bears. "Since we couldn't do ice cream for breakfast, I thought candy for breakfast would be the next best thing."

"Yay, thank you!" I ripped open the seal on the bag, and held it out to her. She popped a jelly bean in her mouth. I offered the bag to Meredith and Walker, but they turned it down.

"Thanks for picking me up," Hailey said nervously to the twins. She tucked her hands under her thighs so that they smashed into the car seat. "What did you guys do last night?"

That was such a typical question for Hailey, and something Meredith and Walker would never answer. It was weird watching Hailey try to relate to Meredith. It reminded me of trying to get the positive ends of two batteries to touch.

"We went to a movie," I said. "What about you?"

"I went to this party that Skyler told me about. It was so dumb. I was sure Nate was gonna be there because it was totally his scene. But he didn't come," she sighed. "Ryan said he's been being really antisocial lately."

"That's weird," I said too quickly.

I looked out the window, but not before I caught Meredith's eye in the rearview mirror. There was a little more focus in her eyes than I was used to seeing. She must have seen I was uncomfortable and I wondered how much she knew. Had she known that Nate and I had slipped off together that night when he'd come to their house? Did she even know who Nate was? I had never talked to her about him, but for some reason, I felt certain that she had deduced some version of the truth in that one instant.

And then Meredith's eyes flicked back to the road, and we sped along the PCH, the wind and salty air washing away all the remnants of the conversation.

Finally, we got out and climbed over a rocky wall to sneak down to a special beach that the twins had named "The Black."

Hailey seemed surprised at my adventurousness.

"Why do you call this beach The Black?" Hailey asked as we padded through the sand. "There's nothing black here."

Meredith and Walker exchanged a look. "It's a long story," Meredith said.

I was used to those kinds of answers from Meredith, but Hailey rolled her eyes.

On the beach, Meredith popped open a bottle of champagne and gave me a wooden beaded bracelet. It felt so magical and perfect that I even let myself have a few sips of champagne from the bottle. The alcohol went straight to my head, and I lay on the sand.

Meredith and Walker splashed in the water up to their knees, while Hailey and I watched. The space between us felt big and strange. I don't know if she noticed it, too; she seemed pretty content. But I couldn't stop thinking about Nate. My secret was so big and so real that it formed a huge barrier between us. It was weird how something you didn't say could be such a presence.

Suddenly, Hailey broke the silence.

"I have to tell you something," she said. "I'm kind of embarrassed, but I just hate having a secret from you."

Hailey covered her eyes with her hands. "I can't look at you while I say this. But I hooked up with Max last weekend. And then we kind of had sex at that party last night."

"Oh my God!" I was really surprised. I remembered Hailey mentioning she thought he was okay, but having sex with him was a whole other thing. How had she jumped from liking him a little to going all the way? And on top of that, Max was kind of unbearable. He was always flaunting his fancy car, designer jeans, and expensive haircuts.

She squeezed her eyes tight. "I know. It's horrifying. But it was just for a second. Basically it was just a lot of sloppy making out. I'm so grossed out thinking about it."

"So why did you hook up again yesterday if you're grossed out by it?" I asked.

She sighed, "I don't know. I mean, last night was a little better. And making out can be fun. Like, if I close my eyes and imagine it's Nate, I can kind of get into it."

I went livid. I was so sick of hearing Hailey talk about Nate like she really knew him. I felt suddenly protective of him. Her crush felt like a violation.

"I know what you're thinking," she said a little defensively.

I shook my head. "No, you don't."

"You're thinking I'm a stupid, dirty slut, right?" she asked. My anger turned into pity.

"No, not at all," I said gently. I tried to think of something generic to say so we could stop talking about boys. "I think you're probably normal."

She heaved a sigh of relief, and her body seemed to go a little limp.

"I love you, Lima," she said. "You're the only really good person I know."

Hailey stayed over that night and I waited until she was fully asleep to crawl out of bed. I'd kept my phone off all day because I didn't want Nate to text or call when Hailey was around, and now I was itching to see if he had. I grabbed my phone off my desk and tiptoed downstairs to check.

All the lights in the house were off, so the ocean and the sky outside look bright. I could hear the muffled sounds of the waves crashing outside the glass doors. I put some left-over cake on a paper towel, curled up on the living room couch, and turned on my phone. I watched the screen power up and after a minute, a text from Nate appeared on the screen. It was from nine thirty.

Happy bday ;)

It was after midnight now. All I wanted to do was text him back but I worried it was too late. I felt suddenly exhausted. I didn't know how much longer I could keep this thing with Nate a secret. I had to tell Hailey about us soon or I might ruin everything.

Back in my room, Hailey was sleeping on her stomach, her face smeared across my pillow. I turned off the lamp and climbed into bed beside her. She curled up behind me, her body folding neatly next to me like a shell.

It's crazy, I thought, how some things never change while other things change so drastically. From the outside, things looked exactly the same as last year: me and Hailey sleeping together in a bed like sardines. But inside, under the surface, everything was different. Patty had gone on a tangent recently about how the magnets at the North and South Pole are constantly shifting. They move too slowly for people to notice, but then, once every several hundreds of thousands of years, they just switch and everything starts moving in the opposite direction. I didn't totally understand the science, but it felt true. Lying there with Hailey's arm around my stomach, and this huge secret eating away at my heart, I wondered if that was what had happened to my life.

chapter

forty-four

"Hey," Mom said. She was standing in my doorway, her wet hair wrapped in a cocoon of towel on top of her head. "Don't forget, we're going to Santa Barbara this weekend to see Caroline."

"Okay," I said, looking down at my hands as I zipped up my cutoff shorts.

Hot, dry winds had started up just a day or two before. Santa Ana winds are violent, desert winds that ransack the city and give the days a strange, surreal quality. The waves on the ocean get loud and erratic, and everything, even your own thoughts, feels out of balance.

"What's wrong?" Mom asked.

It was amazing how Mom could sense the tiniest shifts in my mood. "Is it gonna be weird without Nana there? I'm kind of afraid to go back."

Mom frowned. "It might be a little sad, but I think it's

going to be okay. It will be nice for Caroline to have us there. Do you want to bring a friend? Hailey?"

I know Mom added "Hailey" because she was afraid I was going to invite Meredith. But there was no way I could spend a whole weekend with Hailey without telling her about Nate. It was out of the question.

"I'll think about it," I said.

Later that day, I saw Emily sitting in the library, typing furiously on her laptop.

"Can I sit here?" I asked.

"Of course," she said, "especially if you're going to talk to me and distract me from the most boring art history paper of all time."

Emily's skin look burnished. It was clear she spent every second that she wasn't in school on the beach. That was probably why she was always trying to get her homework done during lunch.

"Hey, do you want to come with me to my aunt's house in Santa Barbara this weekend?" I asked.

"Wow," Emily said, surprised. I was pretty surprised that I'd asked her, too, and maybe it was a bad idea, but the words had escaped my mouth and now I couldn't take them back.

"I know it's random," I said, embarrassed. "But there's a

pool, and it's close to the beach and stuff. You can probably even surf if you want."

"Surfing in Santa Barbara is awesome," she said. "I wouldn't go alone. But yeah, totally, I'd love to come." And then she paused and added, "Really? You're sure?"

"Yeah," I said. "It's not that exciting. You might want to bring your computer and do homework. I usually get a lot of homework done when I go there."

Emily smiled. She was one of those people who smiled with her whole face, not just her mouth. "This is gonna be awesome. I'm so there."

chapter

forty-five

Loading up the car before we left Malibu felt like standing under the nozzle of a hair dryer. A blast of wind came at me as I dumped Mom's suitcase into the trunk, and it whipped my hair across my face so that a few strands stuck to the ChapStick on my lips.

What if bringing Emily to Santa Barbara was a mistake? I thought as I climbed into the backseat. What if we had nothing to say to each other? I really didn't know her very well.

But as soon as we got to Emily's house and I saw her standing out front wearing baggy jean shorts and a big T-shirt with a Quicksilver logo printed on it, I felt better. She was not intimidating at all.

"I can't believe this heat," Dad said as we drove up the PCH with the air-conditioning on high. "I guess summer is here early."

"I know, it's crazy," Emily agreed. "It's not even April yet."

"It'll cool down again," Mom said. "Santa Ana's come and go."

Emily turned to me.

"Can you believe tenth grade is like three-quarters over? We have eleven weeks left not including spring break. I counted."

"That's weird," I agreed. "That means high school is eleven weeks away from being half over."

"Unbelievable!" she said, her eyes popping out of her head.

We talked for a little while longer, and Emily was super-nice to Mom and Dad, clearly answering their questions about what her parents did and how long she'd been surfing. But then she looked out the window and zoned out, a vague, contented smile painted across her face.

Caroline greeted us at the front door. She had cut her hair super-short, and it made her look like a dandelion.

"Ah, the new Hailey!" Caroline teased, when I introduced her to Emily.

I gave Emily a tour of the house, and she dumped her backpack in the guest room where she would be sleeping.

"This place is really nice," she said politely.

"I know," I said. "I love it."

Emily glanced out the window at the hard, cobalt blue sky.

"Want to go swimming?" she asked brightly.

Emily stripped off her clothes by the side of the pool. She wore a black racer-back swimsuit, like athletes wear.

"Can you dive?" she asked, climbing the ladder up to the diving board.

"I mean, I kind of dive," I said. "Like, it's not technical or anything."

"I'm really into diving," she said. "My brother and I always rate each other on a scale of one to ten. Will you rate me?"

I was sitting on the edge of the shallow end, my feet dangling in the velvety pool water. "Sure," I said.

Emily had a stocky build. Her legs were solid and tough-looking. She wore her fat like a seal or a whale, thick and smooth. She bent down and touched her toes and then arched her back, her arms slicing through the blue sky behind her. Her dive was breathtaking. She seemed to move slowly, hovering in the air for a second before making her vertical descent into the water. The pool's surface barely seemed to break as she entered. It was the most graceful, elegant thing I'd ever seen.

When she came up for air, her face glistening with water, her hair smoothed back against her head, she was transformed.

I clapped my hands enthusiastically. "Ten! That was a perfect ten!"

"Really? No way!" Emily said, laughing. She seemed surprised, too.

I think if some people did a perfect dive like that, it could seem like showing off. But with Emily, it didn't.

I dropped into the water and floated around. I alternated from my stomach to my back, feeling the warm sun on my body and listening to the quiet, uncity sounds of Santa Barbara as the afternoon wore on.

Later, Emily stayed by the pool while I helped Mom and Caroline make dinner. Dad sat on a bar stool at the kitchen counter, drinking a beer. I chopped garlic for a salad dressing. I liked trying to get the pieces so tiny that they were like pulp.

"My little brother, Jim, is used to being surrounded by women," Caroline said, putting a bowl of tortilla chips and salsa in front of Dad.

"I'm a lucky guy," Dad said. "I can't complain."

It was so weird to think of Dad as a little brother. Caroline was a few years older, but I wasn't sure how many. I thought about Nate and his sister, Liz, and tried to picture Dad and Caroline young and close like that. It was impossible to picture them in high school.

"Li, someone's calling you," Mom said, gesturing toward my cell phone, which was vibrating on the counter. "I'd get it, but my hands are covered in dough."

I put down my knife and walked to the phone. I looked at the screen. It was Nate. I didn't want to answer it right here in front of my parents so I let it go to voice mail.

"Who's calling?" Caroline asked, a slight teasing in her voice.

I must have been blushing, because Caroline was looking at me as if she was seeing right through me.

"Nobody," I said. I could feel my face turning red.

Mom and Dad both looked at me then, and I could tell they knew there was something going on. I just absolutely wanted to disappear.

"Does someone have a boyfriend?" Caroline was full-on smiling now.

"No," I said. "It's nobody, or I don't know who it is—it's a number I don't know. I don't have a boyfriend."

Caroline must have been able to tell I didn't want to talk about it. She looked at Dad inquiringly, and Dad just shrugged.

I went back to chopping garlic. I was dying to listen to the voice mail, but I didn't want to show all the grown-ups that I cared, so I put it out of my mind.

One of the things I liked about being at Caroline's house, away from the city, is that when it gets dark, you just kind of make your way to bed. Just as we were finishing dessert, Caroline opened another bottle of wine, which I knew meant that the grown-ups were going to stay up late talking and drinking.

After Emily and I had watched an hour of TV, we went up to our rooms. Finally alone, I listened to Nate's voice mail.

"Hi, Lima. Calling to say hey, seeing what you're up to tonight. Yeah, okay, call me back."

My heart skipped at the sound of his voice. I put down my phone and stared out the window into the dark, quiet night. I wanted to call him back, but I was afraid of seeming too eager. I didn't want to be pushy with him like Hailey had been.

I changed into my nightgown and looked at myself in the room's full-length mirror. The lamp cast everything in a warm yellow light. I had gotten some sun in the pool. I pressed my thumb hard into my shoulder and watched it go white and then flush with color again. That was how Hailey had taught me to check for a tan. I felt gripped by a sudden pleasure at my reflection. In spite of being dirty and sunburned, I looked vivid and alive. Like a person Nate could want. I wished he could see me just like this.

I grabbed my cell phone and pressed talk. I held my breath while I waited for Nate to answer.

"Hello?" Nate said, panting.

"Hi, Nate," I said. My voice sounded tiny. A moment

ago I had felt kind of grown-up. Now I felt like a kid. "It's Lima."

"I know," Nate said. "Hang on."

There was fumbling on the other end of the line, and then he came back. "Hey, Lima. Yeah, I called you earlier."

"I know," I stammered. "I'm calling you back."

"I'm glad," he said. "What's up? Where are you?"

I unclenched my eyes and took a breath, starting to relax a little.

"I'm in Santa Barbara, at my aunt's house," I said. "It's really nice here."

"Oh, that's cool," he said. "Yeah, there was some party tonight, and I was gonna see if you were going, but I guess not."

"No, not tonight," I said. "Are you going?"

"No," he said. "I didn't feel like it. I've just been riding my bike around."

There was a moment of quiet, and then I asked, "Is this a good time to talk?"

"Yeah," he said. "I just sat down on the sidewalk. I can talk."

Then there was another pause, but it felt warm and full. Almost the way it was when we were together.

"I don't really have anything interesting to say," I confessed.

"That's okay," he said. "Tell me about your aunt's house."

I stood up and walked out onto the balcony, then rested my elbows on the railing. "I know Santa Barbara isn't, like, technically rural or whatever, but it feels really remote out here."

And then we just started to talk. I told him about Caroline and Emily, and I told him about the amazing super-garlicky salad dressing I made for dinner. He told me about how he had video chatted with his sister earlier, and all the complaints she had about her school. I asked him if he wanted to go to an East Coast college like Liz, and then we talked about the future. College. Going versus not going. California versus New York. Traveling in Europe. Family vacations.

"My sister is probably the funniest person I know," he said. He told me about how they smoked pot together, and she made up songs about this hamster they had when they were in elementary school that Nate had accidentally killed. And he told me stories about the soccer team and riding his bike through his neighborhood at night, and I told him about how I was always afraid of the ocean. We talked about everything. Everything except Hailey.

"I've always wanted a dog," I said at one point. "But my mom's allergic. I'd want to name it Almond."

Nate laughed a little. "Almond. Good name. My stepdad named our dog Buster."

"That's a cute name," I said.

"It's the most popular dog name in the world," he said. "Liz said he named it that so he could just buy the collar and the bowl and everything with the name already on it. He's really cheap."

Our conversation unfurled in unexpected ways, like taking a hike on a new trail, and I felt alive and curious, just the way I would if I were actually exploring.

"Lima," he said finally. "I should go. I still have to bike home."

I liked how he said my name. "Okay."

"Thanks for calling me back," he said.

I bit my lip. I couldn't speak.

"Hello?" he asked.

"I'm here," I said softly.

I heard him take a sharp breath, and we fell into another silence. This one felt heavy.

"Okay, see you at school?" I said finally.

"Yeah," he said.

"Bye," I said.

"Bye."

"Bye."

"Bye."

chapter

forty-six

"What makes something wrong?" Hailey asked.

We were sitting in her mom's parked car in the big gated parking lot of their apartment complex the following weekend. Hailey and I always hid out in the car to talk in private when her mom was home.

"What do you mean?" I asked.

Hailey put her hands on the steering wheel and glided them around as if she was driving. "Like, why is it wrong for me to drive without a license? I know how to do it. I've already finished driver's ed. So is it wrong just because it's illegal?"

"I don't know," I said, nervous about where this was going.

"It doesn't hurt anyone," she said, "to break that kind of rule."

"I guess not," I said.

"But, cheating on your boyfriend or girlfriend," she continued, "is wrong because it can hurt people."

I couldn't look at her.

"Like, all the lying and stuff that must go into an affair," she said. "I've been thinking about that a lot lately. Like, it's not just the big lie of 'Oh, yeah, I'm, like, fucking my secretary,' but the millions of little lies. Like, when you ask someone about their day, and they just leave out this whole part of it because it involved the other person."

I knew she was thinking about her dad and Rachel, but it felt as if she was talking about me and Nate. And she was so right. That was how I felt all the time, buried in the small lies.

I turned and looked right at her, and I braced myself for her to tell me that she knew. Maybe Ryan had told Skyler that Nate and I had disappeared that night at the twins' house.

Hailey looked at my expression, and something twisted and inscrutable passed over her face. Suddenly, she grabbed the car keys, stuck them in the ignition, and turned the car on.

"Hailey, what are you doing?" I practically shrieked.

Hailey started laughing while the engine roared. After a few long seconds, she turned the car off again and dropped the keys in her lap.

"Sorry, I'm just messing with you. You looked so serious all of a sudden!"

I tried to smile, but my heart was racing. All of her actions seemed motivated by her knowing the truth.

"I'm sorry I scared you," she said. Her voice had turned suddenly soft. "I'm a mess right now. I'm so, like, ugh about my dad."

"I know," I squeaked.

"It's just confusing," she said. "I've been thinking so much about him and Rachel because of this whole wedding thing. You know how I've always hated him for being a cheater?"

I nodded.

"The thing is," Hailey said, "even though Rachel is a zero, she and my dad really love each other. I mean, they're getting married. They're, like, for real in love. I think they're, like, more meant-to-be than my mom and my dad."

Hailey was doing that opening up thing again that made me feel all stiff. Like anything I said would sound trite and awkward.

"So what was he supposed to do?" she went on. "Rachel is, like, the love of his life. I'm sure it sucked to meet her when he was already married, but, like, I believe in following your heart. What if he was actually just being true to himself? What if he did the right thing?"

I looked at Hailey. Was she really asking me, or was this a rhetorical question? I felt certain she knew about me and Nate now. This was all code. My face was burning. My palms were sweating. I knew I was supposed to say something, but I was buried so deep in my own pit of guilt that I felt a million miles away.

Finally, I managed to speak.

"What your dad did was not the right thing, Hailey," I said. "He could have done it differently."

"How?" Hailey asked. And then, suddenly, tears spilled out of her eyes.

To my surprise, I felt hot tears in my eyes, too. "Because of you. Because he made you feel like he was choosing Rachel over you, too."

Hailey's sob caught in her chest. She kind of choked a little and squeezed her eyes shut.

"I'm so mad," she said. "I just get sick when I think about their baby. It makes me sick."

I was crying now, too. It was a million things. It was the queasy feeling I got thinking about Rachel and Hailey's dad, and it was how much I loved Hailey, and how immeasurable that kind of love was. It couldn't be weighed against Nate or anything else in the world. I knew right then, no matter how shitty of a friend Hailey had been, that she never for one second did anything to deserve the pain that she was going to feel when she found out about me and Nate.

chapter

forty-seven

It rained on and off the whole week before spring break. I'd been studying for the big chemistry test every night, but my mind was like a sieve. I felt as if all I thought about anymore was Nate and Hailey.

I was running flashcards during lunch the day before the test when Lily appeared in front of me. She had on an orange-and-white-checked vintage dress, like something a waitress at a retro diner might wear.

"Hi," I said. I almost never saw Lily at school, and we had never spoken in public. We seemed to have an understanding that our friendship was bonded to the twins' house.

"Have you talked to Meredith lately?" she asked.

"Not since the weekend," I said. "Why?"

Lily pursed her fire engine red lips, thinking.

"She hasn't been at school in a few days," Lily said, dropping her voice. "And she hasn't been returning my calls. Can you try and call her?"

I pulled out my phone and dialed Meredith. She answered after a few rings.

"Hey, Lima," she said. "Whatcha doin'?"

"I'm at school. You know, high school? Like, where we're all supposed to be right now?"

Meredith sighed. "Oh right. School. School is so bourgeois."

"She's fine," I told Lily after I hung up.

Instead of seeming relieved, Lily just frowned.

"What's wrong?" I asked.

"Nothing, that's all. Thanks," she said, straightening up. She pivoted and left the library, her Mary Jane heels rapping softly on the carpet.

Rain sloshed against the window of the library and I tried to refocus on my chemistry cards. Tomorrow's test was the most important one of the year. Due to the fact that there were so many seniors in Honors Chem, the class was going to wind down in intensity after spring break. This was basically our final exam.

For us non-seniors, it was crucial to do well because it would determine who could take AP Biology next year. I didn't care about taking AP classes just for the sake of it, but I was dying to take AP Bio because of the trip. Every year, the twelve students in the class went to Costa Rica to watch the sea turtles hatch. People who went said it was the most amazing week of their lives.

My phone beeped.

Staying after school for meeting with dean.
Can you stay late?

Nate. I hadn't been alone with him since the night we kissed. I bit my lip.

Say no. I looked down at my chemistry cards, but now they looked scrambled, underwater, remote. My thoughts were way too tangled up in images of Nate to focus on anything else.

chapter

forty-eight

ate said he'd meet me in the computer lab at three forty-five, but it came and went. I tried to study while I waited, but my concentration was terrible. I stopped every two minutes to look at the clock, and kept losing my place in my work.

When I saw it was already four thirty, I began to worry. I hadn't memorized a single chemical formula in a whole hour. And on top of that, I'd begged mom to pick me up at five, even though I knew it would to screw up her whole day. And for what? To sit in the cold, damp computer lab, hungry and distracted?

"Sorry I'm late."

I jumped. Nate was standing in the doorway.

"It's okay," I said. His hair was damp.

He dropped his backpack and shrugged off his jacket. Then he grabbed a wheely chair, swiveled it around, and sat down in front of me. He grabbed the arms of the chair I was in and pulled it closer to him, so close that his knees touched mine.

"What are you working on?" he asked softly.

"Science. Chemistry. We have a test tomorrow," I replied, biting a nail.

"Are you nervous about it?" Nate asked.

"Super-nervous," I replied quickly.

I let my hand fall to my lap and sighed. And then Nate reached out and picked up my hand. He held it between his own two hands and inspected it carefully, as if it was a seashell he'd found on the beach. I stayed perfectly still on the outside, barely even breathing, but on the inside, my heart was pounding.

"It's not raining anymore," he said after a minute. "Do you want to go up on the roof?"

I nodded.

Outside, the rain had stopped. Swatches of bright blue sky broke through the cloud layer like fault lines in the earth. New, perfect clouds, white and bright as porcelain, hung low across the sky.

"I love it after it rains," I said, my teeth chattering in the chilly post-rain air. I shivered and folded my arms around my chest for warmth.

I turned to Nate. In this light, colors appeared extra

vivid. The blue of Nate's eyes, the lavender circles under-neath them, the red of his lips were even more saturated than usual.

"Sorry it took me so long to get to the computer lab. We had to go over all my progress reports," he said.

"How were they?" I asked, but I was detached from my words. All I could think about was that we were alone.

"They were fine," he said.

"That's good," I said.

He took a step toward me so we were less than a foot apart. My eyes rested on the collar of his shirt. I lifted my face up toward him, careful not to knock my nose against his chin, and he looked down at me. We still weren't touching, not even our sneakers, or our knees. The space between us felt pressurized and heavy. Being this close to Nate made my whole body hum. I felt like if I had to wait another second to kiss him, I was going to literally explode.

I reached for his hand at the exact same second that he pulled me toward him and then we were kissing. I wrapped my arms around his neck and then moved my hands down his back so that I could actually feel the back of his rib cage through his shirt with my fingertips. I stopped feeling cold as time melted away.

Suddenly, my phone vibrated in my pocket and I got slammed back to reality: We were on the roof, we were still at school, it wasn't even dark out yet. The sounds of the world returned. I had gone temporarily deaf while we'd been kissing. Now, I could hear people talking on the patio below. A door slammed. A car horn beeped.

The text was from Mom.

10 mins

When I looked up at Nate, my face must have been full of disappointment, because he looked like he understood. His hair was a mess from my hands being in it, and I imagined that mine was, too.

"It's my mom."

He nodded and shook his head like he was shaking something off, and then he ran his hands over the front of his shirt to smooth it.

"Do I look okay?" I asked. "I feel like she's gonna know."

"Know what?" he asked.

I was about to answer him but when I saw the amused flicker in his eyes, I laughed.

"That's not helpful," I said.

"Stay still," he said, suppressing a smile. He took a step toward me and combed my hair clumsily with his fingers.

"You're probably just making it worse." I giggled.

He laughed a little and backed away.

"So," I said. "Are you hanging out with Ryan this weekend? Like maybe going to Meredith's house one night?"

He blinked. "I'll probably see Ryan. I don't know what he's up to, but I usually see him."

"Okay," I said. "Well, I'm going over there on Friday."

Nate's eyes strayed from mine and he looked out into the space behind me, his face clouding over in thought. I wanted him to promise me that I would see him on Friday night. We hadn't talked on the phone since Santa Barbara, and I was tired of waiting, of just hoping we'd have a chance to be alone together.

"So?" I said again. "Friday?"

Nate snapped back to reality and looked at me. "Right, yeah. I'll ask Ryan."

chapter

forty-nine

There were twenty questions on the test. The first three were okay. Composition of the atom and chemical reactions were clear in my mind. I understood the principles so well I felt like I could roll them around like marbles and look at them from all sides.

But then, after that, it was like gibberish. The blank white of the paper vibrated and pulsed, taunting me. My empty test was like a mirror to own my empty mind. I couldn't access anything we had learned about stoichiometry last semester. I had never in my whole life failed a test. I wiped sweat from my forehead. I was sinking.

People started finishing, handing in their tests and leaving around noon. Emily left at twelve ten, flashing me a sympathetic smile as she headed for the door.

When everyone was gone, and it was just me and Patty, Patty spoke.

"Time's up," she said, from behind her desk. "It's over."

I dragged my test off my desk as if it weighed a thousand pounds, walked up to Patty, and dropped it front of her.

She took it and looked it over, noting how empty it was. We both knew I had failed.

"What happened?" she asked.

I opened my mouth to speak and hot tears stung my eyes. My mouth was full of sand.

"I love this class," I blurted. "And I want to take AP Bio so bad. I really think I could handle it."

Patty handed me a tissue.

"I don't know what happened today. I studied," I sniffled, looking at my shoes. "But I just have a lot going on."

How had I turned into one of those girls who claimed they had a lot going on just because they were hung up on some stupid boy? I had always hated girls like that. I was supposed to be better than that. Humiliation swelled inside of me.

Patty rearranged the pens on her desk, stalling.

"Listen," she finally said. When she looked up at me, disappointment was written all over her usually mild expression.

"AP Bio is a demanding class, and a popular class, so I can only enroll students who are really up for working that hard."

"I know," I said. "But I really think I can do it."

"Well, this is your opportunity to show me." Patty looked at me thoughtfully for a moment before she spoke. "You can retake the test. The first day back after break. And I'll average the two grades and that will be your grade."

"Really?" I asked, blotting tears away with the sleeve of my sweatshirt.

"Different questions. Same material," she said.

"Okay," I sniffled. "Thank you so much for giving me a second chance."

She nodded, but she didn't smile or say anything else to me as I packed up my things and left.

chapter

fifty

The next day, Friday, was the start of spring break. I had plans to go straight to the twins' house from school, and since Meredith was still absent, Walker gave me a ride. We had never really been alone together, and I felt self-conscious sitting in the passenger seat with him driving. He had a manliness that differentiated him from other boys at our school. I remembered how Hailey thought I had liked him, and the thought made me blush.

"I should eat," he announced, swerving off Sunset Boulevard into an In-N-Out drive-through. "It's good to eat something before you start drinking. You want something?"

"I'm not hungry," I said, wondering if Walker even knew that I didn't really drink. After months of hanging out, I'd never once gotten drunk, but I wasn't sure he'd noticed.

Walker ordered two cheeseburgers and a milk shake and ate while he drove.

"Is Meredith okay?" I asked. "She was absent all week."

"She's fine," he said. "She had a cold for a couple days and then she didn't feel like coming yesterday or today. The last day before a break is always pointless."

He crumpled up his first hamburger wrapper with one hand then reached into the bag for his second.

"So she just, like, stayed home? She's not worried about her grades?" I asked.

This was the longest conversation Walker and I had ever had. He reminded me so much of Meredith, the way that he was surprisingly natural. It occurred to me that when they weren't drunk or stoned, they were more normal than most people.

He thought a moment. "We don't care so much about grades. Did Meredith tell you we're not going to college?"

I nodded. "She said you might apply next year. After a year off."

"Maybe," he shrugged. "Personally, I don't see it happening. There are other things that matter more than college, even if that's not what people tell you."

I smiled. That was such a Meredith thing to say. They both had this amazing way of seeing things that made it seem like everything was always going to be okay.

Walker turned up the volume of the music in the car, and I checked my phone to see if Nate had called. He still hadn't told me if he was going to make it to Meredith's house tonight. *No new messages.* Each time that I checked my phone and saw that he hadn't texted, I felt another ounce of happiness drain out of my heart.

When we arrived, Henry was lying naked on a lounge chair by the pool. He didn't seem embarrassed to be seen by any of us, not even Walker. Lily and Meredith were wading in the pool.

"Hey, friends," he said lazily when he saw us.

I wasn't attracted to Henry or anything, but I felt a really strange desire to examine his body. I had never seen a naked guy before, and I was curious. I forced my eyes not to linger on the dark region of his groin.

Meredith hoisted herself out of the water and sat at the edge of the pool, dangling her legs in the water. The water had made her bra and underwear totally see-through.

"Mer, where's the cord that connects the outdoor speakers to the stereo?" Walker asked, unfazed by her nudity. I could see the rosy color of Meredith's nipples and the dark patch in between her legs, and I wondered why it wasn't weird for Walker to see her like that, too.

"I think it's in the top drawer to the right of the stereo," she said, seeming as relaxed as her brother, "where you keep the remote control."

I borrowed one of Meredith's bathing suits and swam

until my skin was rubbery and raisined. Around me the others drank and smoked pot, ate chips and store-bought chocolate chip cookies.

I tried to enjoy myself, but I kept thinking about Nate. It was almost seven. What was he doing tonight instead? Why was he so impossible to pin down? I knew checking my phone every five minutes to see if I had accidentally missed a text wasn't actually helping the situation, but I couldn't stop. I told myself to try and be present and enjoy the afternoon with my friends, but it was useless. I kept finding myself hoping that Nate would surprise me by coming over. It was a persistent, buzzing kind of hope, like a fly that hovers around your ear while you're trying to fall asleep. I just couldn't make it leave me alone.

Why was it that nothing felt fun or important anymore unless Nate was involved? Even the twins' house, with its magic views and pretty music, was dull. It was strange, the way one person could seem so much more vivid and exciting than a whole group of people. It reminded me of something Hailey had said to me once after she made out with the bartender at my parents' anniversary party last year. For the few days after it happened, she was high on the whole experience, but within a week, she had resumed talking about Nate.

"Why?" I asked. "How can you just hook up with people

and then keep liking Nate? Doesn't it make you like him less?"

"You don't get it," she had said. "A million people can't replace the one person you love."

I got out of the pool before everyone else and went inside, feeling itchy and antisocial. Upstairs, in Meredith's room, I browsed her bookshelf. She had an archive of vintage *Vogue* magazines and a large, shiny book of Nan Goldin photographs.

I took the photography book, lay flat across her bed, and started looking at the pictures. The people in the pictures were flawed, deformed, and completely naked. The pictures weren't flattering like the pictures in magazines. They were the opposite. They were harsh, even disturbing. It was bizarre, though, because even though their bodies were imperfect and their flaws were exposed, there was an intimacy in them that I had never experienced from a photograph before. I couldn't look away.

"Hey."

I slammed the book shut, embarrassed to be caught and twisted myself around to a sitting position.

Nate was standing in the doorway. My stomach leaped into my chest with joy at the sight of him.

"Hey," I said back, trying not to act too excited. The house sounded quiet. I had no idea how long I had been up here. "You came."

He crossed over to the bed and sat down next to me. He was wearing a baby blue T-shirt and beat-up jeans. He looked super-cute.

"We just got here a few minutes ago," he said, taking my hand in his, winding his fingers through mine so they were knotted together like rope.

"I'm glad you're here," I said, my heart fluttering in my chest.

"They're all passed out down there," Nate told me. "Did they take horse tranquilizers or something? They look wasted."

Nate and I went downstairs together.

Meredith was draped across the couch, still wearing nothing but underwear. Her feet were in Henry's lap, and Henry's head was drooping onto Lily's shoulder. They were breathing slow, synchronized breaths.

Ryan emerged from the bathroom.

"I'm ready to leave," he said to Nate. "So I'm just gonna go wait for you outside."

"I want to leave, too," Nate said. And then he turned to me as if it was the most natural question in the world and said, "Are you coming?"

It's funny. I always thought the most important decisions

I'd make in my life would be ones where I'd have lots of time to deliberate. To weigh the costs and benefits, and play out different possible outcomes, even to make a pro-con list. But I was learning that really significant changes can be created in an instant. I just hoped my instincts were good.

The walk down to Ryan's house was dark. There was a steady buzz in the air, a combination of electricity and insects and faraway cars. I wasn't sure what our plan was but when we reached Ryan's house, we stopped.

"I'm so beat, I'm gonna go pass out," Ryan said to Nate, not looking at me.

Nate's face remained completely calm. "Yeah, okay. Talk tomorrow?"

"Yeah, sure," Ryan said. And then he looked down at me and the faintest flicker of understanding passed behind his eyes. "See you, Lima."

I felt so close to Ryan at that moment, I wished I could throw my arms around his neck and squeeze him tight. He had helped me escape from the twins' house and let me and Nate go off together without making anything awkward or weird. I wanted to thank him but instead, all I said was, "Okay, see you."

I turned to Nate after Ryan had gone inside, unsure what to do.

"Wanna go back to my house?" Nate asked mildly.

A yellow light turned on in one of the upstairs rooms in Ryan's house.

"Okay," I said, biting my lip. "Sounds good."

We didn't talk on the way to Nate's. The radio was on low and scratchy. While he drove, Nate rested his right hand on the gearshift and his left hand on the wheel. He had such an amazing way of seeming relaxed and alert at the same time. I sank back into the seat and closed my eyes, letting myself feel the bumpy road beneath the car.

Growing up isn't a steady process, I thought. There are actually specific moments, nights, or long strange days when you can almost feel yourself change. This car ride to Nate's house felt like one of those times.

I opened my eyes and looked out the window so I could watch the city go by. It was late. The streets looked foreign, wider, more anonymous than ever.

I couldn't believe how easy it was to break the rules. I had always imagined it would take planning and lying and scheming to get around them. But in reality, it was the opposite. Here I was: I just walked right out of Meredith's house. My parents had no idea. I wasn't allowed to get into the car with a driver they didn't know. But what would they think if they knew what was going on at Meredith's? I had slipped into a life where every choice I made was simply the lesser of two evils. There seemed to be no option that they would approve of. I would never in a million years be allowed to go over to Nate's house this late on a Friday night. And still, it was all so easy.

My mind flashed on the first time I swam in the ocean. I had been afraid of it for so long that it started to seem impossible to actually do it. But really, the other side is right there. You can just take a deep breath and walk into it.

"Do you want anything?" Nate asked as we drove past a gas station. "A soda or anything?"

"I'm good," I said. "Thanks."

I glanced at the clock on the dashboard. It was 9:46 p.m. What was Hailey doing right now? Maybe she was out with Skyler, dressed in sky-high heels and surrounded by thumping music. Or maybe she was getting ready for bed in her dim apartment in Mar Vista. I pictured her in frumpy flannel pajamas, her favorite teddy bear waiting for her on her pillow. Maybe she was doing a face mask and looking at pictures of people on the computer.

And suddenly—almost violently—I saw our love triangle clearly for the first time. It was simple. I was going after the boy that my best friend was in love with. I was greedy and selfish. My insides must have been made of something black and ugly and mean. I felt a wave of nausea.

"Hey," Nate said, bringing me back to the present. We had come to a red light so he turned to face me. For a moment he was still, but then he smiled a little and shook his head, almost like he was in disbelief about something. When he spoke, his voice was so soft that it seemed as if he was talking to himself more than to me. "Lima."

"Yeah?" I whispered.

"Nothing," he said quietly. "Just this."

I chose this, I thought. *I chose Nate and secrets and lying to my parents. I chose Nate over Hailey. I chose Nate over my perfect, unblemished life. I chose Nate over everything everyone has ever wanted me to be.*

chapter

fifty-one

n ate lived on one of those hilly LA streets with no side-
walks, where you enter each house from the back.
Before we got out of the car, I turned to Nate.

"Wait," I said.

"What's up?" he asked.

"This is really random, but do you think Ryan is going to
tell anyone that I came over here tonight?" I asked.

"Ryan is a steel trap," Nate said. "He won't say anything."

"Okay," I said. "Because, I haven't told anyone anything
yet. And it might be weird if it gets around or whatever."

"I respect that," Nate said. "That's fine. I won't. And Ryan
never would."

For a moment, it hurt to think about Nate and Ryan, to
remember what it was like to have a real, true best friend. I
was wrecking my most important friendship to be here with

Nate right now and he wasn't risking anything. I was hit by a fresh wave of guilt.

"Is something bothering you?" he asked, as if he could read my mind. He reached across the center console and touched my hair. I stayed still as he gently took a piece between his thumb and forefinger and ran his fingers slowly down to the tip.

"No," I said, letting out a deep breath. "I'm good."

"My parents are in their room," Nate whispered when we had stepped into his front hallway.

Everything about Nate's house seemed amazingly regular. There were pictures of the family on the walls, dog toys scattered on the floor, lamps and ornaments and flowers on the tables.

"Should we watch a movie? Or just go to my room and talk?" he asked.

I dropped my gaze, feeling gripped with an unexpected, crippling awkwardness. "Maybe just talk?"

His room was simple. A narrow bed with gray sheets. Two posters on his wall. One of a Brazilian soccer player and one of a band I hadn't heard of. There were textbooks and pens scattered all over his desk.

He walked over to his bed and turned on his bedside lamp. It cast long yellow leaves of light around the room. He sat on the edge of the bed, and I sat beside him. I tucked my hands underneath my legs.

"You sure you're okay?" he asked.

I nodded, and then he leaned in and kissed me. It was a more innocent kiss than the ones that we had had before. Then he stopped, pulled off his shoes, and lay back on his bed silently, not touching me.

I watched all of his actions, unsure what to do next. In some ways, I just wanted to sit there and be invisible and watch Nate do everything he would do if he was alone. This was what I had been fantasizing about all year: to see the real Nate. To just know him.

"Lie down," he said.

I untied my shoes and lay down next to him. He rolled onto his side so we were face-to-face. I wondered how often he had been in this position with other girls. Was this a regular thing for him? For me it was all so new it practically hurt.

"Are you really okay?" he said. "You seem quiet."

My heart was pounding. Words got stuck in my throat.

"Can I ask you something?" I asked, my voice sounding tiny. I could barely stand to look at him.

He nodded.

"Have you," I started, "you know, have you, like, ever had sex?"

I couldn't believe I'd said it. I squeezed my eyes shut out

of shame. When I opened them, he was looking at me in this really inquisitive way.

"Yeah," he said. "I have."

My heart sank.

"But never, like, with someone like you," he said.

It's weird, but all of a sudden I felt like I was going to cry. I don't know why. It's like I was getting pummeled with a million emotions at once.

"What do you mean?" I asked. "Like me?"

"Like, with a friend," he said. "Someone I really like as a person."

"I'm, like, a friend?" I asked.

He laughed. "Not like that."

"I've never," I started, "I've never done it."

"I kind of figured."

"Why?" I asked, feeling self-conscious. "How can you tell?"

"You just seem like someone who doesn't do stuff just 'cause everyone else is doing it," he said. "You're different than that."

I didn't say anything, and then neither did he. We just looked at each other. Neither one of us squirmed or said something stupid or teasing or anything. We just really held each other's gazes for longer than I've ever stared at another person.

"I think about you a lot, Lima," he said. "A lot."

"Have you thought about doing, about having it with me?" I asked.

He rolled onto his back so he wasn't facing me and took a deep breath in and out.

"Yeah," he said.

He had thought about it. His imagination would be so much more vivid than mine, because he had actually done it before. The thought made me scared and excited at the same time.

"I think about you, too," I said.

He glanced down his nose at me.

"C'mere," he said softly.

I climbed up onto his body. I liked lying on top of Nate, feeling every shape of his chest and hips underneath me. We started kissing and our mouths and bodies just started moving together. I thought I wouldn't know what to do, but making out with Nate was easy. I didn't have to plan my moves. I just did what felt right.

Nate rolled toward me and kind of gently pushed me onto my back. He lay on top of me, letting his weight press into me. He moved his hand slowly over my chest, slowly over my stomach, slowly over the bony part of my hip and then to my leg.

"Can I take off my jeans?" he asked. "They're kind of bothering me."

I nodded.

Nate stood up and unbuttoned his jeans, and I watched as he pushed them to the ground. And then once he had stepped out of his jeans, he took off his shirt, too.

"Sit up," he said.

I sat up.

"Put your arms over your head," he said.

I stuck my arms straight up like a little kid, and he pulled my T-shirt up over my head so I was just wearing a white cotton bra that I'd gotten with Mom at the Gap last summer.

Nate's body wasn't surprising, and I was relieved about that. His chest and stomach were smooth and hairless. If anything, the most foreign thing about his body was his legs. They were just such boy legs. All that hair, and the way they stayed so straight and bony all the way to the top. They were practically skinnier at the spot where they disappeared into his boxers than right above his knee.

Nate sat down next to me, and we started kissing again. There was a new carefulness now that we were only partly clothed. The sensation of his hands on my skin took getting used to. It was like getting into a too cold pool: You know you'll adjust, but at first it just feels like tugging.

Nate's hands moved all over my body. He was slow and careful. When his hand slid under my bra, I felt him tense up, and he almost made a sound. But he didn't, and I was glad.

I was sort of scared of all that heavy breathing and groaning you hear in the movies.

I let my hand move down to his boxers. Hailey always said penises were really scary, really gross and rubbery and weird. Through the fabric of his shorts, I couldn't tell what I was touching. It was a mystery—parts were super soft and other parts were hard as bone.

He took my right hand in his left hand and brought it inside his shorts. When I felt the strange soft skin of his penis, I made a gasping sound. It did feel weird. Nate's hand stayed on the back of my hand and he guided me. I tried to relax and breathe and even enjoy it, but it just felt overwhelmingly foreign. Even scientific. I felt myself clamming up, as if I was disappearing inside of myself.

"Wait," he said. He took my hand and brought it out of his shorts. He squeezed my hand really tight, and then he put it on his chest.

I was too ashamed to look at him. The shame of knowing I had failed was coupled by the bigger, darker shame of our bodies all together.

"Hey," he said.

I let myself look at him, in his face, and I felt immediately better. He looked really content, really mild. His cheeks were glowing pink. A lock of his hair had fallen across his

forehead in this adorable way that made him look like a little
boy.

"I'm sorry," I said.

He smiled. "Are you kidding? That was so nice."

"No," I said, biting my lip and turning red.

"Lima," he said, "you are so hot. You drive me crazy. You
have no idea."

I let out a little sigh of relief and let my head collapse onto
his chest. He stroked my hair and ran his fingers along the
edge of my ear.

chapter

fifty – two

I woke up when the light started creeping into Nate's bedroom. Everything in his room looked slightly dingier in the daylight. The light revealed the few cracks in the paint and the sort of cheap plastic of his swivel chair.

I was suddenly uncomfortably aware of how dirty I was, having not brushed my teeth or washed my face, and struck by a fear that Nate's mom would wake up at any moment.

I peeled my cheek off Nate's chest and crawled over him, reaching over the side of the bed to find my cell phone in the pocket of my jeans.

"What's up?" Nate grumbled softly.

"I should go before your parents get up. And I need to be back to the twins' house before my mom comes for me," I whispered. "I'm gonna call a taxi."

"No," he mumbled, wiping his eyes with the back of his hand. "I'll take you."

"Are you sure?" I asked. "You really don't have to."

He nodded groggily. "Yeah, yeah, no problem."

I pulled on my jeans and T-shirt and watched him as he did the same. I had the same feeling I'd had the night before: that I could just observe him doing regular things forever and not get bored.

He was barely looking at me. I got a wave of fear that I had screwed something up.

It's almost as if he read my mind, because he looked up at me before he tied his shoes. I was standing awkwardly, two feet away from the bed.

"What are you doing all the way over there?" he asked.

I sat at the edge of the bed next to him. He wrapped his arm tightly around my shoulders and pulled me toward him in a kind of headlock, and I knew everything was still okay.

It was really different to be alone in the car with Nate in broad daylight. It was the first time I felt like we were boyfriend-girlfriend.

"My mom hates McDonald's," I said as we drove past one. "She's all into, like, natural food and stuff."

"That rules," Nate said. "McDonald's is, like, the most fucked-up corporation in the world."

I wondered for a second if Mom and Nate would get along, and I felt a pang of longing to have everything be out in the open. She would like him if she met him. I just knew it.

Being around Nate, I felt that I was exactly where I needed to be. It didn't matter if we were talking or not talking, if I had or hadn't brushed my teeth. Right here, in this beat-up old Honda, at the corner of La Cienega and Wilshire, was the center of the universe because Nate was there.

The front door was unlocked and I let myself into the twins' house. I walked into the living room and froze in the entrance. Meredith and Henry were making out on the couch. They were clothed, but their bodies were intricately locked together, churning rhythmically like gears in a machine.

Meredith paused when she heard me come in, and she looked as surprised to see me as I was to see her. She pushed Henry off of her.

"Sorry, so sorry," I stammered, backing out of the room.

"Wait," Meredith said, stumbling off the couch.

I turned away.

"Lima," she said gently. "Hey, wait."

I stopped and faced her. "I didn't see anything."

She laughed. "That's not true. I know you saw us."

"Did Henry and Lily break up or something?" I asked.

"No," she said. And then she sighed exasperatedly. "It's complicated."

I didn't say anything.

Something hardened in her expression and she said, "Where are you coming from? What happened to you last night, anyway?"

"Oh," I said, "I just, like, went back to Nate's house 'cause you guys were all sleeping."

"Mmm," Meredith said, and I could see her piecing together my story. Whatever moral leverage I had a moment ago was gone now.

"I guess we all have our secrets," Meredith said, and this time, I genuinely couldn't read her tone.

"I'm really tired," I said. "I'm gonna go lie down."

Meredith didn't object, but I felt her eyes on my back as I walked away.

I curled up on a couch in her sunroom, hoping to sleep for a little before Mom came. I peeled off my sweatshirt and draped it over my eyes, creating a makeshift darkness. I was tired and wired at the same time. My mind was reeling, running through all the things that had happened during the last twelve hours. For the next two hours until Mom picked me up, I drifted in and out of brief, restless patches of sleep.

chapter

fifty-three

∞

I took the make-up chemistry test before school on the first Monday back after spring break. Patty worked quietly behind her computer while I sat at a desk and made my way through the exam. This time, I nailed it. When you knew what you were doing, getting the right answer was like digging for something you had buried in the ground. You might not be totally sure where it was at first, but if you were close enough, you found it eventually. I knew if I didn't get a perfect score on this test, I had no chance of getting into AP Bio next year, so I had studied like crazy every day over break.

Each day of spring break had been prettier than the last. The sky got bluer, the ocean got brighter, the jacaranda trees around LA bloomed. Nate was out of town the whole time visiting his sister, and Hailey was in San Diego visiting her dad, so I didn't have any distractions from studying besides hanging out with Mom. And balancing schoolwork with

Mom-time was easy for me because I had so much practice at it. Sometimes, when Mom and I were making dinner after a long day of studying, I felt like the old version of myself. The girl I'd been last summer. No secrets. No broken friendships. No knowledge of her own capacity for doing bad things.

I finished the chemistry test twenty minutes before first period. Unsure what to do, I decided to go walk across campus and get a cup of tea from the student center. Outside, sunlight broke through the morning marine layer and glistened in the puddles on the concrete, bouncing light back up toward the sky.

Nate and I had texted over break and talked on the phone one night for twenty minutes while his sister slept, and I was excited to see him. But my excitement was laced with fear. Even after the whole two weeks of vacation, the memory of touching his penis still made me feel squeamish, even queasy. It was weird how separate that experience had felt from my general attraction to him. When he looked at me a certain way, when we held hands, even when he walked into a room that I was in, something moved deep inside me. A warm pit seemed to grow in my stomach. But that feeling didn't have anything to do with the actuality of his body. After my quick brush with it the other night, I wondered if sex could ever feel like it synced up with all the other feelings I felt for Nate.

I cataloged all the people I knew who had had sex, trying to figure out who I could talk to. I guessed that Emily was a virgin. But Meredith had had sex. Walker, too. And Lily and Henry. And probably all the grown-ups I knew. Leo the Clean-the-Bay supervisor wore a wedding ring and definitely had it. Even though I wasn't sure if Patty was married, I was sure she'd had it, too. Weird that so many people I knew had done it, and there still was no one I could ask for guidance. The only person I really felt comfortable enough to talk about sex with was Hailey.

After I got my tea, I walked back across campus and watched people roll out of their cars with spring break tans and new sunglasses. Girls wore colorful dresses and sandals, and seniors wore sweatshirts baring the name of the college they would be attending.

From across the patio, I saw Nate. He wasn't facing my direction, but I recognized the particular blue of his backpack. A girl I didn't know walked by him and smiled. I wondered for a second what it would be like to have our relationship out in the open. Would we walk to class together? Would we meet in the same spot every morning like Hailey and I used to? There were a million questions floating around my mind, and I had the crazy, sinking feeling that there might not be one set of right answers.

chapter

fifty – four

At the beginning of lunch, I spotted Meredith crouching down to open a locker in Upper School East. I had called her a couple of times during the break, but her phone went right to voice mail and she never called me back. Was she embarrassed that I caught her and Henry? Angry with me for sneaking away to be with Nate? Each night when I checked my phone and saw she hadn't called me back, my fear that I had upset her grew. Now, I was eager to see her, to find out more about her and Henry and to apologize if I had made her mad.

"I didn't know you had a locker," I teased.

She closed the door and stood up.

"Hey, you," she said, giving me a quick kiss on the cheek.

Her hair was pulled back into tight ponytail, and she was wearing a white polo shirt, khaki shorts, and bright white

Keds. It was a total good-girl outfit, but everything looked a little bit bad on Meredith.

"Want to go out to lunch?" I asked. "It seems like the perfect day to go get a hot chocolate from the 21st Street Bakery and be late for fifth period."

She smiled a little. "It does seem like a good day to be late for class. I like how you're thinking, Lima. Let's get outta here."

"Okay, good," I said. "Because I feel like I haven't seen you in so long. It's like you disappeared during spring break."

Meredith laughed and wrinkled her nose, confused.

"I'm serious. We haven't talked since that night, or morning or whatever," I said, trying to casually ease into the discussion. "And I don't know. I just hope that nothing is weird with us."

"What night?" Meredith said, her black eyes widening like two seeds blossoming. "I don't know what you're talking about."

"Really?" I asked. "But, like, you were so hard to reach during the break."

"I was? You're crazy," she said, looking at me completely innocently. "I was just busy."

I scanned her face to see if I could detect a lie, but she seemed to really believe what she was saying.

• • •

In the car, Meredith played Fleetwood Mac while she smoked a cigarette. Wind burned through the car and set her hair wild in electrified lines. I watched her mouth on the cigarette, her hands on the steering wheel. I thought about her and Henry and what I had seen.

She glanced at me out of the corner of her eye. "What are you thinking about, Missy?"

"So, can I ask you about Henry?" I asked. "Is he going to break up with Lily to be with you?"

She dragged on her cigarette, and I wondered if I detected a little tremor in her hand at the mention of Henry.

"No, it's not like that," she said, and her voice was plain. "He's cheated on Lily before. Lily knows."

"About him and you? Or about the other girls?" I asked.

She sighed. "Both. She knows about me."

"Whoa," I said. "That's so weird. So she doesn't mind?"

"She minds. She just doesn't want to break up with him," Meredith said.

"Do you wish they'd break up so he could be your boyfriend?" I asked.

She blew a skinny stream of smoke out of her lips and then looked at me, pensively. "I don't want Henry to be my boyfriend. I don't want a boyfriend. I'm not in love with Henry or anything."

I tried to process that.

"And Henry doesn't love anyone besides himself," she added.

I was surprised to hear the word love used with so much certainty. Was I in love with Nate? Was Hailey?

"Perfect song, right?" Meredith said, turning up the volume on her car stereo.

Stevie Nicks's violin-like voice reverberated through the car.

Meredith laughed and threw her cigarette butt out the window. She smiled at me with her big, black mysterious eyes, and I realized, a little disappointed, that that was all I was going to get from her.

chapter

fifty - five

I decided that if I was really careful about it, I could ask Hailey about sex. I just had to pretend to be the old me. The pre-lying-and-sneaking-around-with-Nate version of me. I wondered if I even knew how to do that anymore.

Hailey and Skyler were sitting together at a picnic bench drinking Diet Cokes and eating Cheetos during lunch the next day.

"Wow," I said, dropping my backpack and sitting across from them. "I just overheard the most awkward conversation in the bathroom."

"About what?" Hailey asked.

"Some girl was talking about having sex with her boyfriend," I lied.

Skyler guffawed. "What did she say?"

"I don't know, it just sounded painful or something," I said vaguely. "Have you—like—are you a virgin?"

Skyler took a long sip of Diet Coke through a straw before she answered. "No. I lost it in ninth grade to my Spanish foreign-exchange student, Alberto. You didn't know that? I thought everyone had heard that."

I actually had heard it. "What was it like?"

"Whoa, Li!" Hailey said, laughing. "What's going on? Sex on the brain much?"

I tried to play dumb. "I don't know! Maybe! I mean, I am, you know, sixteen."

Hailey reached across the table and gave my hand a condescending squeeze. "You are so cute. I love you."

"Do you have someone in mind?" Skyler asked. And something about the way that her eyes fastened onto me made me scared that she knew about Nate. It wasn't impossible that something would have leaked out.

"No, of course not," I sighed. "Never mind. I was just, I don't know, wondering."

I knew right then that I was never going to think my way out of my questions about sex. The only way to get answers was to do it.

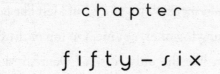

chapter

fifty — six

"Have you given any more thought to what you'll do this summer?" Mom asked. She was giving me a ride to the twins' house. Afternoon traffic on Sunset Boulevard was heavy and claustrophobic.

It was the beginning of May. The school year was doing that crazy speeding-up thing that it always did between spring break and the end of the year, as if time was getting sucked up by a vacuum cleaner. Summer was only six weeks away and I still had no idea what I was going to do. Patty had given us a list of science-related internships a few weeks ago, but I still hadn't gotten around to reading it carefully. I had been meaning to sit down and choose a few to apply to, but I kept forgetting to actually do it. I cringed, realizing I had probably already missed a few deadlines.

"Not really," I said distractedly. I stared at my cell phone, debating calling Nate. I wanted him to come to Meredith's house so we could sneak off together, but I felt like he should initiate our getting together, not me. On top of that, I didn't want it to seem like the only reason I went to Meredith's house was to try and see Nate. Everything used to feel so magical there, but after the last time, it just felt different. Was Nate the only reason I was going back?

"What's going on?" Mom asked.

"What do you mean?" I asked, snapping out of my daze.

"You've been clutching your cell phone this whole car ride," she said with a wry smile. "Is there someone you're hoping to hear from?"

"Oh," I felt embarrassed. I tossed my cell phone into my purse as if it was contaminated. "I don't know. No."

"You know," Mom said tentatively as we waited for the light to change on Laurel Canyon Boulevard, "you can tell me anything."

"I know," I said. But the truth was, I couldn't tell her everything. She would kill me if she knew I was involved with the same guy that Hailey had been in love with forever. She always took Hailey's side when the two of us fought.

"Like, if there's a boy . . ." she trailed off. "I don't want to be nosy. But I did have a boyfriend when I was your age. So I do know a thing or two."

I smiled a little. I was kind of curious about Mom's high school boyfriend, but I needed to steer her away from this topic. I wished there was some little part of the story I could share with her that wouldn't involve explaining the whole, messy thing.

"Mommy," I said, "if you're asking if I, like, have a boyfriend? I don't."

She let out a relieved puff of breath.

I'm not sure why I didn't just tell Mom everything. If there were no Hailey, would I tell her about Nate? Could I ask her advice? It felt like a stupid question. Everything that happened was so intertwined, I couldn't just like pull it apart and look at one thing on its own, in a vacuum. Everything depended on everything else.

"Cheers," Walker said, handing Meredith a whiskey. The ice made an elegant clanking sound against the glass.

I had only ever watched TV in Meredith's bedroom, but tonight we were going to watch the Bob Dylan documentary, *Don't Look Back*, in the screening room. It was amazing how even after all this time at Meredith's house that there were rooms I had never seen and rituals I was still being initiated into.

The opening credits were on when we heard the doorbell. Walker went to answer it, and when he returned a minute later, Ryan and Nate were with him. Nate lingered a little behind, wearing that nice shirt he wore for visits with the dean.

"Look who I found," Walker said, jumping over the back of the couch to reclaim his seat.

Meredith twisted her body around so she was facing Ryan. "Hey, neighbor. Did you come over to watch with us?"

"Yeah," Ryan said. "Is that cool?"

"Of course," she smiled.

Ryan looked at her a little strangely, and I knew he was seeing that unexpectedly sweet side to Meredith for the first time.

Nate and Ryan sat down on the adjacent couch, and I groped for the right way to behave. Should I give Nate a hug? A kiss on the cheek? Unsure, I ignored them. I turned to Meredith and pretended to be suddenly interested in her necklace.

When the movie had started over, I finally glanced at Nate, whose gaze was glued to the screen.

I couldn't focus on the movie at all. All I could think was that Nate was only a foot away and I was totally unable to interact with him. I was panicked that the whole night would slide by and we wouldn't get a chance to talk. I hated myself for being so awkward and reserved. Hailey always made people feel welcome.

After what felt like forever, Nate stood up.

"I'll be right back," he said.

"Pause it?" Walker asked.

"Nah," Nate said. He ran his hand along the back of the couch, and when he passed behind me, he grazed my shoulder with his fingers and quickly squeezed.

I made myself count to sixty before I followed him.

Nate was standing by the glass doors staring out at the city. All the indoor lights were off, so he was silhouetted by the sparkling lights of Hollywood and the valley behind it.

"Hey," I said.

Nate glanced at me and then turned back to the window. I felt, as always when I was around him, that I could see the energy coming off his body, like colorless light. I walked up to him and stood next to him, and then, without thinking about it, I let my head tip onto his shoulder. He wrapped his arm around me pulling me to his side with an ease that made me feel as if we had done this exact thing a million times before. We stood there like that for a long moment, watching the planes take off from Burbank Airport deep in the valley. Each plane was a tiny red blinking light, arcing up into the night sky like an electronic shooting star.

"That movie makes me think about my dad," Nate said, still staring outside. "He loved Bob Dylan."

"Really?" I asked. His arm was still draped around my

shoulder and I reached up and took his hand in both of mine, winding my fingers through his.

"Yeah," he continued. "He took me to a concert when I was like five or six. I remember it well. It was raining and it was an outdoor concert. It's one of my clearest memories of him. That whole day."

"I bet it was fun," I said. "I bet you were cute."

He made a little half-laughing noise. "I don't know about that."

"Was he sick for a long time?" I asked.

"It didn't seem that way to me," he said. "It felt like it happened overnight."

Nate bit his lower lip and looked at me.

"It's okay," he said. "You know, I'm not sad when I think about him exactly. It's just weird. It's been almost ten years. I just can't believe how much he's missed."

I didn't know what to say so I just squeezed his hand tighter. Nate pulled me into him, letting his face fall into my hair and I hugged him back. I could feel his heart beating, his breath going in and out. After a minute, Nate said, "Thanks."

"For what?" I asked.

"I don't know, just, whatever, listening," he said. Then he took a step toward the back door. "Let's go outside."

I followed Nate past the pool and down the stairs to the lower deck.

Big, dark trees surrounded us, concealing the city lights and the traffic below. I liked feeling separate from everything and everyone except Nate. It made me wish we could go away together, somewhere where we could take as much time as we wanted to get to know each other.

"So," Nate said. "Hailey called me tonight."

I dropped back away from the railing as if I'd been hit in the stomach. It was the last thing I'd expected him to say.

"Whoa," Nate said. "Are you okay?"

I nodded.

"She asked me if I was going to some party she was going to. It's weird that she doesn't know about us."

I felt dizzy. "I just don't know what to tell her yet."

"Just tell her what's up," he said. "She's your friend, right?"

"She's my best friend," I said defensively.

"What's wrong?" he asked.

"Nothing," I said, shrinking farther away. "It's just complicated."

"It's not such a big deal, Lima."

"If it's not such a big deal, why do you care so much?"

Nate was quiet for a moment before answering. "I think because it just doesn't seem like you. You don't seem like you're afraid of what anyone thinks."

I knew he was trying to give me a compliment, but I bristled.

"You don't get it," I said. "Hailey isn't just anyone. She's my oldest, best friend and she is gonna be really mad at me."

"All I'm saying," he said, "is the Lima I know, the one I like, is an honest person."

"Oh my God," I said. "I can't believe this."

Nate might have been right, but it didn't matter. I was risking my entire friendship with Hailey just to be with him, and now he was going to stand there and tell me how I should behave? Angry tears stung my eyes.

"How can you lecture me about being a good person? You're the one who started this whole thing," I said. "You kissed Hailey and then just ignored her. You're the one who is coming between me and my best friend. Why don't you just leave me alone? That would fix everything."

Nate's mouth hung open for a moment in surprise, and then he just looked hurt. He stumbled backward.

"Wait, Nate, I'm sorry," I whispered. "I didn't mean that."

"No, it's okay. You're right," he said, and retreated back up the stairs.

chapter
fifty-seven

With Nate gone, the night air clamped down on me and I suddenly couldn't breathe. My head was spinning. I stepped toward the house, then grasped at a door handle and practically fell into Meredith's dad's bedroom. I moved through the dark and collapsed on his bed. I lay there in the silent room, and the bad kind of quiet enveloped me. This was the opposite of how tonight was supposed to go.

I hated myself for getting upset at the mention of Hailey. The night up until then had been going so well. I could feel how much Nate trusted me. He was opening up to me more than ever. But instead of letting him in, I had lashed out and ruined everything.

I heard a rustle and opened my eyes. Nate was standing in the doorway.

"Can we talk?" he asked.

I nodded and dragged myself into a sitting position, and he came over and sat down next to me on the bed.

"What you said out there—" he began.

"I take it back," I interrupted. "Please believe me."

"Let me say this," he said. "You're not wrong. That stuff you said, it's kinda true. I've fucked up a lot of shit in the past. Like, with girls. Not just Hailey. But her, too. I don't trust myself. And I don't want to do that to you. Not ever."

Why would you? I thought. A dark well was widening beneath my feet, threatening to suck me in.

"But with you, it's different," he said. "I've never liked someone so much or for so long."

"Really?" I asked.

A smile spread across his lips. He reached into my lap and picked up one of my hands. "Yeah."

We stared at each other in the dim room. Even in the dark, I could see his blue eyes were blurry with feeling. There were so many things that had happened between us and suddenly there was this beating inside of me, like something in my heart that needed to come loose.

I reached up and touched the rough part of his cheek and he pulled me toward him. We started kissing and then we lay down onto the bed clumsily, our legs getting all tangled in the transition. The room got warm and then hot and I felt the edges of our bodies softening, as if we were actually blending together.

"Lima," he said, pushing a strand of hair off of my forehead, "you are so important to me."

"You're important to me, too." I whispered. We kissed again, and this time I could feel a blind, intense longing opening up inside of me. Nate kicked off his shoes, and I sat up to take mine off, too. Then I lay back down and we kept kissing. We rolled over and under each other, his knees pressed my knees apart, and then my hands ran down his body and inside his clothes. Everything seemed to be coming undone. Buttons. The snap on the back of my bra. The zipper of his jeans. This time, I didn't think about the strangeness of his body or wonder about how I looked as my shirt came off. Something between us was changing and I was certain that Nate felt it, too. Like we were slipping into a dream.

"Should we stop?" he asked. He was lying on top of me. When he spoke, he shifted his weight the tiniest bit and a new line of sensation lit up inside of me.

"Do you want to?" I asked.

He frowned a little in the dark. "I'm not sure. Sex changes things."

"I know," I said, running my finger along the edge of his collarbone.

"I really don't want you to do something that you might regret later," he said.

I looked up at him and his eyes were burning, drowning.

"I don't think I'll regret it," I said. "I don't think I'd regret anything with you."

I reached for one of Nate's hands where it was resting on the pillow beside my head and wound my fingers into his. His palm was sweaty and for a moment I thought maybe he was shaking.

"Are you nervous?" I asked.

"Yeah," he said plainly.

"Me too."

I watched the rise and fall of his chest as he breathed slowly in and out.

"I just," he said, and for the first time, I really saw him straining for the right words. I wasn't sure if I'd ever seen Nate not know what to say.

"I know," I whispered. "It's okay. Do you have something?"

"Yeah, I have a condom," he said, rolling off of me. He reached for his pants in the dark, and I could hear him shuffling through our clothes. When he found it, he lay on top of me again, this time supporting his upper body with his elbows so that he hovered a little bit away.

I reached up and touched a strand of his hair. We kissed again. I could feel the heat radiating off of him. He rolled onto his back, fumbled with the condom, and after a minute, came back to me.

And then it was happening. I could feel Nate breathing and I could practically feel the blood pumping in his veins, too. I ran my hands down his arms and over his back. My toes, my fingers, my lips, everything was buzzing with Nate. And all those parts of Nate that I'd always wanted to touch, like his elbows and his shoulders, even his knees, I felt as if I were touching them all at once.

"Was that okay?" Nate asked when it was over.

"Yes," I whispered.

We kissed and then he pulled me tighter to him and buried his face in my hair.

Now that we'd had sex, kissing Nate felt like the most natural thing in the world, like something I had been doing my whole life.

"Are you okay?" he asked.

"Beyond okay," I whispered.

We lay naked, our bodies mashed into a single puddle of heat and dampness. Slowly, our heartbeats began to steady. A night breeze blew in through the open doors and I looked outside. Funny, I thought, how the whole world outside of this room was totally unchanged. Exactly as it had been when we came in here. But everything in this room, and everything between the two of us, and even all those things inside of us that we couldn't see or name, was different.

chapter

fifty-eight

When Nate and I awkwardly re-entered the screening room, the movie was still going. I sat down on the couch and tried to act nonchalant. I had splashed my face with water and combed my hair with my fingers, but I felt disheveled and undone in a way that I couldn't conceal.

I could feel Meredith's eyes on me, so I turned and met her gaze. She didn't smile. Her eyes were dark. She looked at me for a long, slow minute then flicked her gaze back to the movie screen without saying anything.

Did she know what I had done? I could hardly believe it myself. I shifted uncomfortably on the couch, my insides still feeling warm and loose, like they might spill out of me if I wasn't careful. My whole body had been kneaded, softened by having sex with Nate.

• • •

After the movie I walked Nate and Ryan to the front door. Nate and I couldn't stop looking at each other and smiling and blushing. There was a renewed shyness about both of us now.

"That was a fantastic movie," Nate said to me over his shoulder as he and Ryan walked out onto the porch.

We both laughed.

"Such a good movie!" I added.

Ryan rolled his eyes. "You guys are idiots. You saw five minutes of it."

Ryan knew Nate and I had snuck off together, but I didn't care. And Nate didn't seem to care. The only thing that mattered to me right then was us. I watched Nate climb into the car, glimpsed his hands, his bony ankle peering out from beneath the hem of his jeans. The memory of sex was slippery, hard to hold on to. It was already impossible to imagine how close we had been to each other an hour before.

I showered before I got in bed with Meredith. I stripped down in her bathroom and looked at my reflection in the mirror. Having sex was a weird mix of familiar and unfamiliar sensations. My body was doing a foreign thing, but it was still just my body doing it. It felt different and uncomfortable, but not scary. Nate was still Nate. I was still me. It was disorienting to look at my body in this artificial light now and realize that it was capable of all that.

Meredith's shower was hard and hot, and I scrubbed my skin with her loofah. A sadness was starting to creep into the edges of my mind. Maybe it was just the inevitable comedown from an experience so intense. I wished Nate was still here. I wanted to climb into bed beside him. If I were with him right now, I wouldn't feel lonely.

I turned and faced the showerhead and let the water beat down on my face. If I had lost my virginity to anyone other than Nate, I would have called Hailey right then. Even though our friendship wasn't perfect anymore, she would still be amazing to talk to about this. She would have helped me sort through all the things I was feeling. I tried to remember what she had said when she told me about losing her virginity last summer. There was something obscure about her that day that I hadn't understood at the time, but now I felt like maybe I could. Suddenly, I genuinely missed her. I hadn't truly missed her like that in months, and the intensity shocked me. But the feeling was quickly followed by the suffocating fear that choked me every time I imagined telling her about Nate.

Emotions and vague disappointments spun around inside me, as elusive as fish in a pond. I wanted to catch them and understand them, but they kept squirming out of my grasp.

chapter

fifty-nine

On Saturday night, I watched TV on the bed with Mom and Dad. I wore a pair of flannel pajamas with puppies on them that Aunt Caroline had given me. I lay in between Mom and Dad, nestling my head on Mom's chest. Now that I wasn't a virgin, I wanted nothing more than to feel like a little kid again. I knew it was an itch I'd probably never be able to scratch. There was no going back.

The landline phone rang in the middle of a show. Mom answered.

"Hi, Hailey," Mom said. And then, "Me too, sweetie."

I could hear Hailey talking, but I couldn't make out her words.

"Of course we can," Mom said. "Okay, here's Lima."

Mom covered the receiver with her hand before she passed it to me.

"I told Hailey we'd take her with us to the farmers' market tomorrow," she whispered. "She knows we always go on Sundays."

"Hi," I said into the phone. "I'm in the middle of a show—can I call you back?"

Mom frowned at me.

"Yeah, yeah, of course," Hailey said. "I'm gonna see you tomorrow. Bye, Li. Love you."

"Love you, too," I said.

After I hung up, I could feel Mom's eyes boring into me for just an extra second longer than normal before they drifted back to the TV.

chapter

sixty

I usually loved the Palisades farmers' market on Sundays. Salty air from the beach blew into the street and made the smells of food extra potent. Local farmers always gave out samples of their freshest fruit and vegetables.

"Mmm," Mom said, closing her eyes with pleasure as she bit into a grape. "Try this."

She handed Hailey and me each a grape with a toothpick stuck in it.

I took a bite. It tasted perfect. I wished I could share it with Nate.

"That's good," Hailey said. "I'm gonna get another. You want, Li?"

I shook my head. Friday night felt like a lifetime ago. Gaps of time between seeing Nate were feeling longer and longer and more and more intolerable.

"Watch the cart," Mom said, and disappeared to go pick out vegetables.

"Are you wearing makeup or something? You look different." Hailey said, once we were alone.

I flushed.

"No," I said. "No makeup."

She rolled her eyes. "God, you're so annoying. Can you just stop being so pretty for, like, five minutes so I can think about something else?"

I tried to smile.

"So," Hailey said, "I have to tell you. I had a fight with Skyler on Friday."

Of course there was a reason why Hailey wanted to hang out with me.

"Hmm," I said absently, biting a nail.

"She thinks I should just get over Nate. She said she's sick of hearing about him and that basically it's just, like, never gonna happen."

I ripped off a shred of nail with my teeth and spit it out.

"Li, that's gross, don't do that," Hailey said. "But can you believe that Skyler said that?"

I sighed. "I don't know. I mean, why are you mad at her about it? It sounds like she's just trying to protect you."

Hailey scoffed. "Don't defend her. She just thinks I'm not hot enough to get him."

"Did she say that?" I asked.

"She didn't have to," Hailey said. "I know she thinks she's the hottest girl in school."

I didn't want to defend Skyler, but the truth was, she was in a million ways a better friend than I was.

"Do you think I'm hot enough to get Nate?" Hailey asked.

I hated this game. A bright, cold wind swept through the market, and I took a deep breath.

"Of course," I said.

"Thank you!" she said, sounding a little wronged. "I'm glad someone believes in me."

Mom came back and dropped a bag of spinach into the cart.

"What did you do this weekend?" Hailey asked me as we followed Mom.

For an instant, I tried to imagine telling the truth. I could just say, "I had sex with Nate Reed." Hailey wouldn't even believe me if I said it. The thought made me giggle.

"What?" Hailey asked, her eyes narrowing on me.

"Oh," I shrugged. "Not much. Went to the twins' house on Friday."

"Hayes-Schmayes," Hailey said. "I'm ready for that phase of your life to be over."

"Meredith is amazing. You just don't know her," I replied.

Hailey frowned. "You know what? Take me with you the next time you go there."

I froze. "What? Why?"

"I don't know," she said. "Maybe they're not so bad. And I'm sick of Skyler anyway."

"But I thought you hated the twins," I said, feeling trapped.

"Geez, Lima, hate is a strong word," Hailey teased. "They can't be so bad if you like them so much. Maybe I'll like them, too."

Hailey would screw up everything if she started coming with me to the twins' house.

"Actually, I don't know if you'll like them," I said, trying to sound light. "They might not be your kind of people."

Hailey stopped walking.

"Oh my God," she said.

I turned and looked at her. She stared at me. The morning sun caught the tiny flecks of brown in her hazel eyes.

"Do you not want me to come with you or something?" she asked, her voice tiny.

My stomach clenched. Guilt and anger wrestled inside me, twisting into a million microscopic knots.

"Don't be silly! Of course I want you to come," I lied.

"Okay, good," Hailey said triumphantly. "'Cause we haven't hung out enough lately and I miss you. I need a big dose of Lima."

chapter

sixty-one

"What if I'm not cool enough for them?" Hailey asked during the car ride over to the Hayeses' a week later.

"Don't be silly," I said. I had my window down, and a hot wind brushed against my face. I kicked my feet up onto Mom's dashboard.

"Take your shoes off the dashboard," Mom said. And then she did a double take. "Lima, those shoes are filthy. I'll take you shopping for new shoes this weekend."

I looked at my red Converses. I liked the way the world had faded the laces and eaten away the white rubber.

"Sorry," I said, placing my feet on the floor in front of me.

"That's about as much trouble as I've ever seen you get into." Hailey deadpanned from the backseat.

After Mom dropped us off, I showed Hailey around

the twins' house. Even though she didn't act impressed, I could tell she was nervous. She lit a cigarette the instant we stepped onto the back deck and as soon as it was done, she lit another. Meredith gave her a drink and she downed it quickly.

I thought I'd be annoyed with Hailey for trying to be cool around the twins, but instead I felt bad for her, which was way worse. Ever since the whole Nate thing had started, I couldn't feel love toward Hailey without it being accompanied by an awful, sickening sadness.

Lily and Henry showed up after the sun had already gone down. I hadn't seen the two of them together since I had learned about Henry and Meredith, and they looked different to me now. I had always seen them as carefree and glamorous. Now they seemed older, sadder, even less attractive.

Henry lit up a cigarette, and stood by the edge of the pool barefoot with his toes gripping the concrete lip like claws. Meredith walked up to him, took the cigarette out of his hand, took a drag on it, and handed it back.

I glanced over at Lily, checking to see if she had also observed this intimate gesture. Her face was expressionless. She turned and walked into the house.

A splash startled me. Walker had jumped in the pool.

"I'm going in," Hailey announced. "Everyone here is too drunk to care about my fat thighs."

Hailey cannonballed into the water. I wondered if I should go inside and talk to Lily. But what could I possibly say?

"Bring me that vodka, Lima," Walker called.

I picked up the bottle and leaned over the pool to hand it off.

Walker reached for it, but just as I was close enough to give it to him he ducked away.

"I can't reach it, Lima. Come closer," he teased.

I leaned farther, lost my balance, and crashed into the water, all my clothes on, vodka bottle in hand.

When I came up for air, everyone was laughing, the half-empty vodka bottle floating on the surface of the water a few feet away.

I dove under and swam to the bottom of the pool. Underwater, the silence throbbed. My clothes tugged at my skin, like heavy wings, as I moved.

Suddenly someone was grabbing me, gripping at my sides and my arms. I flailed and sprang up to the surface. Hailey had her wet arms tight around my neck.

"Holy shit, Lima," she whispered, water and spit spattering on my face. "Nate is here."

In the bathroom, Hailey rubbed lip gloss into her cheeks while I sat on the porcelain toilet bowl lid and shivered in my wet clothes.

"This'll probably make me break out," she explained as she mushed it into her skin, "but at least I'll look halfway decent for Nate."

"You look fine," I said. My clothes clung to me, sticky and cold. For a moment, I let myself imagine what would be happening right now if Hailey hadn't come with me tonight. If she hadn't, Nate and I would probably be slipping off into some dark room together. We'd be whispering things and doing things to each other. We had so few opportunities to be alone, and Hailey was ruining one of them.

"This is the best lip gloss color," Hailey told me, narrating her actions. "Skyler gave it to me. She said it looks good on everyone."

I snapped back to the present. Nate and Hailey here at the same time was the worst possible scenario. I started to panic. Did Nate even realize that I still hadn't told Hailey about us? Would he be mad at me for being such a coward? And how long could I hide our relationship from her? What if I accidentally touched him in a too-familiar way?

"This house is really fun," Hailey continued, oblivious to my anxious state of mind. "I see why you hang out here all the time. I mean, this is awesome."

I knew she was talking to me, but Hailey was staring at herself in the mirror, angling her head this way and that.

When we stepped out, Nate was leaning against the wall, sipping a beer.

"Could you hear us talking in there?" Hailey asked, touching his upper arm.

"Nope," he said.

"I'm really drunk, so I, like, don't know what I'm saying," Hailey said, her hand still resting on Nate's arm.

He frowned. He looked at Hailey and then at me.

"You went swimming in your clothes?" he asked.

"I fell in," I replied flatly.

"Can I have a sip of your beer, Nate?" Hailey asked.

Nate held the bottle up to the light. It was more than half full.

"You can have it," he said. "I don't want this anyway."

"Come on," Hailey continued. "Don't be a party pooper. You should get drunk, too. We're all wasted."

"Here," Nate said, handing the beer to Hailey. "Have it."

Meredith turned up the music and Hailey shrieked.

"Madonna!" Hailey screamed. "I love this song! I'm gonna dance!"

I felt hounded as I walked upstairs alone to change my clothes. I just felt like going into a dark, quiet closet and listening to silence. I was sick of everyone and everything. Sick of Hailey. Sick of the twins. Sick of lying about Nate.

But more than anything, I was sick of myself and the voice in my own stupid head.

The lights in Meredith's room were off, and I stumbled and tripped over something in the dark.

When I flicked the lights on, I realized the thing I had tripped over was Lily. She was lying on the floor, on her stomach. She hadn't even reacted to me practically falling on top of her. There was an empty bottle of vodka lying next to her right hand. I immediately dropped to my knees, forgetting about my wet clothes.

"Lily?"

She didn't answer. I put my hand on her back and she felt eerily cold. I was suddenly filled with fear, shrill and loud as an alarm.

"Are you okay?" I asked. I had never seen somebody pass out like that, just in the middle of the floor. What was I supposed to do? How was I supposed to know the difference between someone being really drunk and too drunk?

Back downstairs in the living room, Henry and Meredith were dancing close. Their bodies moved together sweetly, knocking into each other and then pulling apart again.

I tapped Meredith on the shoulder. "I think Lily drank too much. She's totally passed out."

Meredith's expression was simple. "I'm sure she passed out," she said. "That's fine."

"Yeah," Henry said, his drunken eyes refusing to focus on mine. "We were drinking before we got here. Like, all afternoon."

"You should really see her," I said. "She's, like, not waking up."

Meredith looked at Walker, and they exchanged a wordless twin conversation.

"Okay," Walker said, hoisting himself grudgingly off the couch, "I'll check it out."

Lily was exactly where I had left her. A crumpled pile of person.

"Hey, Lily," Walker said, jiggling her with his foot.

She didn't respond. I searched Walker's face, scanning it to see if he was worried. He was drunk, too, and I wondered if he was really a better judge of Lily's condition than I could be. I was getting this terrible unsafe feeling, like a nightmare where you find yourself in the backseat of a moving car that no one is driving.

"Lily, I know you're wasted," he said. "Just say something so we know you're okay."

She was silent.

"Help me sit her up," he told me.

It was weird to move Lily's body. It's like, with her exerting no force at all, she was ten times stiffer and heavier than I would have imagined. Dread thickened inside me.

"Lily—you okay?" Walker asked, trying to look into her eyes. By then Meredith had appeared in the doorway.

"She's okay, right?" Meredith asked, sounding impatient.

"She's fine," Walker said. "Let's just get her some water."

We all looked back at Lily. Underneath her foundation, there were dark circles under her eyes. "I think we should call nine-one-one."

"No." Meredith said, as if it was a silly thought. "That's going too far."

"But she's sick," I said. "She could die."

Meredith looked puzzled for a second, and then she started laughing. Laughing so hard she had to cover her mouth with her hand.

"What's going on?" Nate said. He and Ryan and Hailey had all gathered in the doorway.

"I think Lily is really sick and we should take her to the hospital," I announced.

Nate raised his eyebrows in surprise, and then pushed his way past Meredith and knelt down next to Lily. He touched her face with the back of his hand, like a parent checking for a fever.

"Hey, what's wrong?" he asked her. "Are you too drunk?"

She didn't respond.

Nate ran his hand over his face.

"She's pretty fucked up," he said. "Maybe we should call someone. Or take her to the ER."

"What the fuck," Walker said, like it wasn't a question. "Don't call anyone."

Nate turned slowly and looked at Walker, and I almost got the feeling that Nate was going to punch him.

"Everyone is being so dramatic," Meredith sighed, flopping her head forward into her hands. "She's. Just. Drunk."

For a moment no one said anything, and I felt my concern start turning to panic.

"We're driving her to the hospital," Nate finally said.

Meredith and I stood side by side on her porch while the others helped Lily into the car. My clothes were beginning to dry. They felt as rigid as papier-mâché against my skin, and I shivered.

"This is really bad," Meredith said quietly, not looking at me.

"She's going to be fine," I reassured her.

Meredith scoffed. "No, not that. I know Lily's going to be fine. Taking her to the hospital is what's bad. Getting everyone involved. That's bad."

I turned to Meredith. The bright light of the house behind made her profile a flat, black silhouette.

"Lima, seriously, listen to me," Meredith said. "Let's just take Lily inside, make her drink lots of Gatorade and feed her greasy food. She'll be fine, I promise."

I wanted to believe Meredith. It would be easier to stay here than go to the hospital. But then I thought about the damp, cool feel of Lily's skin under my fingers and frowned. Lily was too sick to eat. Something was happening to her body that I wasn't sure we could reverse with food and Gatorade.

"I don't think that's good enough," I replied.

"You don't know what you're doing," Meredith snapped. "You have no idea what Lily's mom is like. And my father—"

This didn't sound like Meredith. "Your dad must know you guys drink when he's away. You're here by yourselves all the time. He has to know."

"Yeah, but he trusts us. He trusts us enough to do whatever. To let us travel alone," she explained. "If he thinks we aren't responsible enough he might not let us go at all. I mean, he can't like, physically stop us, but he could make it really hard."

"That's what you're thinking about right now?" I asked. I was stunned.

Meredith's gaze hardened. "Lima, this trip is everything. It's what we've been waiting for our whole lives."

Nate was climbing into the car. It was time to go.

"I'm leaving," I said.

I tried to give Meredith a quick hug, but she was completely stiff, unresponsive. I backed way. When I looked at her, I saw that her eyes had turned to knives.

"This is such a joke," she spat.

"What is?" I asked.

"This whole thing. Don't hug me. You think I don't know you just come over here to see your boyfriend behind your friend's back?" she hissed, nodding in the direction of the car.

I froze.

"You're a user, Lima," Meredith continued, holding my gaze with an eerie, unflinching calmness. "Just like everybody else."

Her words slammed into my chest like a hammer.

chapter

sixty-two

The road down the mountain was bumpy. We had placed Lily in the backseat between me and Hailey and her body sagged like a bag of rocks. I leaned my face close enough to hers to be sure she was breathing.

"All right, guys, can't we just lighten up now?" Hailey said. "We're taking the sick girl to the hospital like good Girl Scouts and Boy Scouts. Lily is gonna be fine. You can stop being all sober and concerned now. It's over."

Nate craned his head around and looked at Hailey for a second, really kind of contemplating her, and then he made a scoffing noise and turned back to the road.

I used my sleeve to dab a little bit of drool off Lily's chin. When I finished, Hailey was staring at me.

"You're so sweet and good all the time, Lima," Hailey said. And something about the way she said the word *good* made my skin crawl. "Don't you ever just want to stop being so good?"

Hailey was too drunk to know what she was saying, but still, her words bothered me. I was so not sweet and good. I was the opposite. I was the worst person ever.

"I'm not really that good," I said.

I glanced at Nate to see if he was paying attention. He was staring straight ahead, pretending that he couldn't hear.

The light in the Emergency Room was bright and dark at the same time, like an artificial twilight.

"Our friend is in the car, and I think she has alcohol poisoning," I told the receptionist. Nate and I had gone in to get help while Hailey and Ryan waited with Lily.

The receptionist shifted papers around her desk, unhurriedly. Then she handed me a clipboard and said, "Fill this out."

Nate and I sat down in the cracked plastic chairs of the waiting room. There were stacks of outdated magazines on the coffee table and local news flickered across a wall mounted TV.

"I don't know any of this stuff," I said, glancing at the questionnaire on the clipboard.

Just then, the double doors that led to the emergency room swung open and three doctors ran out to the parking lot.

"They're probably going to get Lily," Nate said, thinking aloud. "That's good."

He slumped down low in his chair, looking exhausted and antsy at the same time. I thought about the first time he had sat across from me in the library and I tried to remember what that felt like. Before I knew him. Before we'd ever really talked. Before we'd kissed. Slept in a bed together. Had sex. I could almost feel the sensation of time passing, of people changing, like a river rushing under my feet.

After a while, a doctor came out to talk to us. I had no idea how long we had been sitting there. It could have been five minutes or an hour. Something about waiting rooms made time disappear. Minutes slipped away like sand through your fingers.

"Your friend is going to be fine," the doctor said after introducing herself as Dr. Goel. She looked too young to be a real doctor. She was my height, and the scrunchie in her ponytail was the same bright pink as her sneakers.

"Really?" I gasped. "Can we see her?"

"She's sleeping now," Dr. Goel said. "Her mother has been called and she's on her way. You did the right thing by bringing Lily in."

Nate let out a huge, ragged sigh like the air going out of a balloon. Relief washed over me. Lily was going to be fine.

• • •

Nate and Ryan dropped me and Hailey at her apartment after the hospital. Hailey passed out right away, but I couldn't sleep. I stood on her balcony and tried to clear my head. The air was foggy and thick, claustrophobic as my own thoughts. Even though I knew now that Lily would be okay, so many things weren't ever going to be okay. Meredith, for one thing, had been horrible. What she had said to me—that I was user—rang in my ears over and over.

And had Lily been trying to hurt herself? Was it because of Meredith and Henry that she had drunk too much, or was it an accident? There were so many things I didn't understand about their world, and I felt suddenly stupid for ever thinking any of them were my friends. I didn't know any of them at all.

chapter

sixty-three

"So explain to me how it is that I dropped you off at Meredith's last night and now I'm supposed to come pick you up at Hailey's?" Mom asked.

I was sitting on Hailey's bed the next morning. Yellow light flooded the room, but the air felt stale.

"It's a long story," I said. "This guy Ryan drove us."

"You know you're not allowed to get in the car with drivers I don't know," Mom said.

"I know," I said. "But we had to leave. It was really important."

"Why?" she pressed.

"Mommy," I groaned, "please come get me. I'll tell you everything. And then I promise you can ground me for life if you feel like it."

After I hung up, Hailey reached out and put a hand on my leg.

"You're not gonna be in trouble," Hailey said to me in a froggy, hungover voice. "You weren't even drinking."

"I know, but my mom is gonna freak out when she hears that everyone else was and that someone got alcohol poisoning."

Hailey rolled onto her back. There was an imprint of the pillow etched into one of her cheeks. Her mascara from the night before formed charcoal smudges around her eyes.

"I can't believe how bad things got last night," I said. "Lily could have died."

Hailey looked at me with a somber expression. She was kind of like Meredith in that, when they weren't doing something or being funny, their faces just looked empty and sad. I wondered if that's what I looked like, too.

"She's okay now," Hailey said. "Everything is fine."

I nodded.

"Last night was insane, though," she agreed. "I was so drunk. Did I make a fool of myself? Tell me honestly? Do you think Nate thinks I'm a total stupid drunk?"

"No," I said. "You were great."

"I was?" Hailey asked eagerly.

"Yeah," I lied. "I'm sure Nate was glad you were there."

Why couldn't I stop lying?

Hailey let out a sigh of relief. "Oh my God. I hope you're right. He was nicer to me than he has been in a long time."

Hailey threw on jeans and walked with me to wait for Mom on the concrete stoop outside her front gate. The sky that day was hazy and polluted, and the sun was a pulpy orange smear.

I stood up when I saw Mom's car approaching.

Hailey gave me a hug.

"Last night was really fun—minus the near-death experience," she said. "Let's hang out with Ryan and Nate again next weekend. I think we're a good mix."

Mom and I didn't talk on the drive. When I started to explain what had happened the night before, she just said, "Save it, Lima. Dad will want to hear this, too."

Back at home, I told them both the whole story. I told them about how I found Lily on the floor, and how Ryan drove us to the hospital and then to Hailey's. They listened quietly and when I was done, Dad said, "And where was Howie Hayes during all of this?"

"He wasn't there," I said.

"Where was he? It was the middle of the night," he said.

"I think he was out of town," I stammered.

"You think?" Mom repeated, raising her eyebrows.

"Do you see him a lot when you're over there?" Dad asked. "Does he know you're my daughter?"

"I don't know," I lied, dropping my gaze. I had totally forgotten that Mom and Dad didn't know I'd never actually laid eyes on the twins' dad.

Sensing my nervousness, Mom said, "What's wrong?"

Dad was ahead of her. "Is he or is he not out of town?"

"He is," I replied.

"So you're saying there were no adults there?" Mom said, disbelief painted on her face like a mask.

I nodded.

"Has that happened before?" she asked.

"I think so," I said. "I mean, I don't know. I don't know when he's there or not, we just, like, do our own thing, like, upstairs."

"You don't know if their dad is there?" Mom squinted. "When was the last time you saw him?"

"I don't know," I said. "I've never actually, like . . . seen him."

Mom's face fell. I could see her pulling away from me, disappearing deep into herself. "So you've been staying over at a house with no supervision all year? And lying about it?"

"I haven't been lying about it," I protested. "It just didn't come up."

She stood up and dropped her ceramic mug of coffee into the sink. Without looking at me, she said, "That's another lie and you know it."

And then she walked out of the kitchen.

"Don't move," Dad said to me, following Mom.

I could hear them fighting in their room while I waited for my punishment on the couch downstairs. Outside, the ocean was a gray slab of wet clay.

When they came downstairs, Dad sat across from me and Mom walked right past us. She stood perfectly still, staring straight out the window.

"You're scaring us, Lima," Dad said. "If you're lying about this, what else are you hiding?"

"What do you mean?" I asked. Did he know about Nate? If Meredith knew, did other people know too? Maybe I hadn't been as discreet as I thought.

"Drugs," he said flatly. "Are you doing drugs?"

I almost laughed. At least this wasn't something I had to lie about.

"No." I declared firmly.

Dad looked at Mom and shrugged. She still wouldn't look at me.

"I swear I don't do drugs. I don't drink; I seriously am the lamest person ever. You can drug test me, do whatever. I swear, they're just my friends. What happened last night was an accident."

"I don't know what to say, Lima." Dad said. "But you're out of your mind if you think you are ever going back to their house. Those kids are trouble. They're just screaming for attention. Am I right?"

Mom turned and looked at Dad. She nodded in agreement.

Dad then informed me that I was grounded, and the room grew strangely quiet. Mom asked Dad if he wanted her to make lunch, and he said he just felt like ordering pizza. Mom said good, she didn't really feel like cooking. Then she turned to me.

"Is pizza okay?" she asked.

It was the first time she had looked at me since I had confessed that I never met Meredith's dad. There was something so deeply distant and disappointed in her eyes it made me want to scream.

How long would I have to wait for Mom to get over the fact that I had lied to her? What if she never did? Was that how people grew apart from their parents? Little, stupid lies chinking away at their armor of closeness? And then someday you're just a couple of grown-ups, meeting for lunch and talking about traffic and the weather and real estate?

"Pizza sounds good," I said, in a voice so clamped it was practically a whisper.

chapter

sixty-four

om and I barely talked on Sunday and the silence in the car on the way to school on Monday felt like glass. If it broke, it might shatter everywhere and slice us both.

There was a part of me that wanted to tell her everything. I wanted to tell her that Meredith hadn't returned any of my calls since Friday night and that I was freaking out. I wanted to tell her that I felt like my friendship with Hailey had fallen apart and then been put back together all wrong. But if I told her about my problems with either Meredith or Hailey, I would have to tell her about Nate. And that would be bad. She was going to be so disappointed when she found out what I'd done.

At break, I went to see if the Hayeses' car was in the parking lot. I walked past a pack of seniors, and I could feel their eyes following me. I had the sensation that everyone at school knew what had happened.

The Hayes spot was empty. I took a deep breath and pivoted, turning back toward the center of campus.

"Oh my God, Lima," Hailey said, looping her arm through mine. "Everyone is talking about Friday."

I looked at Hailey. She was wearing her heart-shaped sunglasses, and her cheeks were flushed so red they almost looked bruised.

"I had a feeling," I said. "Everyone's been staring at me all day. How did it get around?"

"I don't know, but literally, I feel like a celebrity," she cooed.

"I really want to talk to Meredith," I blurted out.

"Why?" Hailey asked, making a face like she'd smelled something bad. "You do realize she is completely bitchy and weird, right? I mean, I was beyond drunk, but even I could tell she was being a bitch."

"She was drunk, too. Maybe she didn't know what she was doing. Maybe she feels bad now. You just never liked her."

Hailey shook her head. "That's not exactly true. I mean, kind of, but I get why you liked her. And now that I've hung out there, I get why you liked it. It's cool and glamorous and kind of, like, I don't know, different."

I nodded.

"But after Friday," she continued, "I'd think you wouldn't really want to be friends with them anymore. They were assholes to all of us. They acted like you were being uptight for trying to help Lily."

I knew Hailey was right, but I wanted to give Meredith a chance to explain.

"I just want to know what she has to say," I said.

I glanced over my shoulder at the empty parking space and felt a pang of longing for the Hayeses' big vintage car. I pictured Meredith driving, her hair going wild in all directions from the wind.

chapter

sixty – five

nother day passed without Meredith coming to school. Finally, that Wednesday, I saw her car pull into the senior lot as I was walking toward first period. I only had five minutes before class, but I had to catch her while I had the chance.

As soon as Walker was gone, I rushed over to Meredith's side.

She was bending down through the open car door, rearranging things in her purse when I approached.

"Hey," I said.

She straightened up and looked at me, and there was a long moment before she smiled. It was almost like she didn't recognize me.

"Hey," she said.

"Can we talk?"

Meredith pulled her bag onto her shoulder and slammed the car door.

"It's time for class," she said.

"I'm upset about the other night. With Lily," I blurted.

"Yeah, I know," she said. "That sucked."

"But Lily was okay, so everything is okay now, right?" I asked hopefully.

"Okay now?" she repeated, and then giggled a mean giggle. "Lima, Lily didn't have to go the hospital. You and your friends made such a big deal out of nothing."

"I don't think so," I said. "I really feel like it was the right thing to do."

A hardness passed behind Meredith's eyes. She took a deep breath, and I could see her struggling to regain her cool before she spoke again.

"If you want me to tell you that I think you were in the right, I never will," she said, her tone still mild but firm. "I just don't. I'm never going to comfort you about this."

Comfort me? That wasn't what I was looking for, was it? Confusion swarmed inside of me.

"So, are you, like, mad at me?" I asked.

"I'm not mad at you, Lima," she said exasperatedly. "It ended up being fine. Lily's mom didn't tell the school or my parents or whatever, so nothing happened. We're fine. Everything can go back to normal."

What was normal? I wanted to ask her, but I knew I only had a minute left to find out what I really wanted to know.

"But what about what you said? About feeling like I use your house or whatever, to see Nate?" I asked. I so rarely said his name out loud, and never to Meredith, and it felt strange coming out of my mouth. "Do you really think that?"

People were moving faster now, hurrying to get to class under the May morning sun, a bright clutter of hats and backpacks and sunglasses swirling around us.

"I shouldn't have said anything," she said impatiently. "I don't care about what you do with anyone. At our house or anywhere else."

"But—" I was sinking, struggling to figure out what I wanted to say.

Meredith sighed.

"Oh, Lima," she said condescendingly. "You're stressing too much. Everything is fine now. Don't worry about it."

It was weird. As much as I hated fighting with Hailey, at least we fought. At least she owned up to her own actions, apologized, got angry. This was worse.

"I have to get to French, but let's get together soon," she said vaguely as she backed away, heading toward class.

"Yeah, right," I said.

As I watched Meredith disappear down the hallway, I felt

more abandoned than ever. Even though she had suggested we hang out, it was obvious she didn't mean it.

Was this how it was going to be? Maybe this was just how Meredith did things. Maybe she picked up friends when she felt like it and then dropped them when she felt like it, too. Is that what she had done to Lily? And now, was she doing it me? She had adopted me at the beginning of the school year like a new toy, and now that I hadn't done exactly what she wanted, she was discarding me. Frustrated tears stung my eyes. I wiped them away, angrily, and headed to class.

chapter

sixty-six

Mom and Dad and I ate on the back porch that night. I sat where I always sit, with my back to the house, facing the ocean. The sunset was fluorescent and fake-looking.

Even though Mom made roast chicken, one of my favorite things in the world, I was too preoccupied to eat. My mind kept circling from Meredith, to Nate, to Hailey, and then back to Meredith again. Even though Meredith had let me off the hook today, I didn't actually feel better. Her words from Friday night kept coming back to me.

I wished I could say she was wrong about me being a user. But hadn't I been using her house to meet up with Nate? I mean, I'd had sex in her dad's bed. That thought, that one action, which had felt so natural at the time, suddenly seemed filthy and selfish and the kind of thing only really bad kids did. I had thought I would lose my virginity at college, or in my own room. Not in someone's parent's bed. It was just sleazy.

"Lima?" Mom said. "Earth to Lima!"

My eyes snapped from the gooey sunset to Mom's face.

"Daddy can clear the table," she said. "Stay here. I want to talk to you."

We sat there quietly while Dad took our plates away. I felt passive, pliable, patient. I was no longer afraid of getting in trouble. No lecture from her could be as painful as this self-loathing I was feeling.

"Where are you?" she asked. "What are you thinking about?"

"I saw Meredith at school today. I tried to talk to her about what happened, and she just, like, blew me off," I said. "She thinks we made a big deal out of nothing. I feel like, she's just, like, over me."

"You did the absolute, one hundred percent right thing," Mom said without hesitating.

"But what else is going on?" she asked.

I stiffened. "Nothing."

Mom closed her eyes for a second and pressed her forefinger and thumb into her forehead hard. I had only ever seen her do that when she was really mad about something.

"Mom? Are you okay?" I asked.

"It hurts me that you're being so secretive about this boy," she said.

My heart caved in.

"Mommy, what—what boy?" I asked.

"Give me a little credit, Lima. I can tell there's a guy."

I felt cagey. I was tempted just to start spewing lies, denying everything, but something about Mom's expression stopped me.

I didn't know where to start, so I just blurted out the only thing I could think of.

"His name is Nate," I said.

I started talking. I told Mom about how Nate and I started studying together in the fall, and how I never meant to go behind Hailey's back. I thought Nate and I were just friends, and by the time I realized it was more than that it felt too late to tell her. Once I started talking, I didn't want to stop. It felt so good to share that a small part of me I even wanted to tell her that we had sex. But I didn't. And not just because I didn't want her to judge me. I actually felt protective of Nate. I didn't want her to think he was bad.

Mom listened, nodding and frowning, her brow permanently furrowed.

Finally she said, "You know, it's okay that you and Hailey like the same boy. That happens all the time. My best friend in high school, Ashley Petersen, she and I both had crushes

first there was forever ∞ **325**

on Trey Krieger. And he ended up going out with Ashley. I was devastated."

Mom had a nostalgic gleam in her eye, and it actually made me kind of angry. Mom liked Trey and he ended up going out with Ashley? It didn't match the intensity of what had been going on between me and Nate. I felt myself clamming up again.

"You don't understand. It's not like that. Nate is . . . " I searched for the word. "Real."

"Listen, Lima," Mom said. Her tone had turned serious. "You should talk to Hailey."

"I know I should," I said. "But I'm scared."

"We're a lot alike, you and me," she said. "I also have a big capacity to hold things in."

"Do I hold things in?" I asked.

She smiled. "I think so."

"Hailey is going to kill me. You don't understand. She is obsessed with Nate. She talks about him constantly."

"What do you do when Hailey talks about him?" Mom asked, looking concerned.

"I don't say anything," I said. *I encourage her.* But I couldn't tell Mom that. It was too twisted and shameful.

"Tell her before she finds out," Mom said. "Look, you were so afraid to tell me about him, and it hasn't been that horrible, has it? I've done okay, right?"

I knew Mom was right that I had to tell Hailey before she found out. But telling Hailey was going to be so much more complicated than telling Mom. I was scared she would hate me and judge me. I was terrified Hailey was going to find a way to take everything good I had with Nate and smash it.

chapter
sixty-seven

om and I rolled down the windows on the way to school the following Thursday and let the hot air blow through the car. It was the last week of May, but it felt like summer. The mornings had grown warm enough to sit outside without a sweater; the city smelled like a mixture of cement and salt. The sky seemed to have been drained of its springtime moisture and turned back into a hard, cobalt blue ceiling.

I'd spent the two weeks after the Lily episode grounded. The most social thing I had done since that night was talk on the phone to Nate for an hour on Sunday. I had to call him from the landline downstairs while Mom and Dad were at a movie because they had confiscated my cell phone as part of my punishment.

Nate and I didn't talk about any real topics, like what had happened to Lily, or Meredith, or what we were going to do with our summers. Instead, we talked about random stuff. We discovered a shared preference for winter Olympics over summer Olympics, and then I tried to explain to him why *Top Chef* was better than the other reality TV on the air. We talked for so long that the phone got hot in my hand.

Talking to Nate was insanely fun even though what we talked about was mostly meaningless. Just picturing him at his house, holding his cell phone to his ear and thinking about me, made me feel close to him.

"So, Hailey called the house phone last night to talk to me," Mom said.

I had sunk so far down into thoughts of Nate, I had almost forgotten I was in the car with Mom.

"She did?" I asked. "That's so weird. Why?"

"It was sweet of her, actually," Mom said. "She told me about the Memorial Day party she's having this weekend."

"She told *you* about it?" I was shocked. Hailey had been obsessing about her party for over a week. I couldn't go because I was still grounded, so I hadn't been paying much attention when she brought it up. "Wow, she is literally telling everyone."

"She told me because she said she knew you were grounded and she really wants you to come," Mom continued. "She wanted to see if we'd let you."

"You're joking," I said flatly.

"So Daddy and I discussed it and we said yes. You can go," Mom said with a conspiratorial smile, as if this was supposed to be good news.

The truth was, I had been glad to miss it. Hailey's party was the last place in the world I wanted to be and now I had no excuse not to go.

"Great, Mommy, thank you," I said, trying to sound happy.

"Have you talked to her yet?" Mom asked. "About you know who?"

"I haven't had time," I said quickly. "But I'm going to, like, today."

chapter
sixty-eight

The day of Hailey's party, we rode the bus home from school, like the old days. We didn't talk very much but Hailey's excitement was electric. Even though she wasn't saying a lot, she was buzzing with energy.

When we got to her apartment, we set up right away. We strung white Christmas lights around the living room, fastening them to the wall with duct tape and thumbtacks. They were sloppy and sagging, threatening to crumple to the floor at any second.

"Atmosphere," Hailey explained.

When Hailey took a break, I followed her onto the balcony. Sounds of traffic and black dust from car exhausts blew up from Venice Boulevard and seemed to crawl all over my skin. I missed Meredith's house. The magical twilight of the Hollywood Hills.

"Are you okay?" Hailey asked.

I didn't answer because suddenly I couldn't speak. I felt as if I might cry.

"What's wrong?" she pressed.

Everything.

"Nothing," I lied.

"I'm not trying to be mean or pry or whatever," she continued in a gentle voice, "but you're acting really weird."

"It's a weird day," I finally said.

She shook her head. "It's not just tonight. It's been lately. For, like, weeks. Are you mad at me or something?"

I felt heat rising to my face. Guilt. Lies formed on my lips, but I couldn't speak. I opened my mouth.

"Hailey, I don't think you should go for Nate anymore," I blurted.

Hailey bristled. "What?"

"I just"—I was trying to ease into the confession—"don't think it's a good idea."

"Look, Lima," Hailey said defensively. "I get that you're sick of hearing about him. So is Skyler. So I should probably shut up about it. I'll just keep it to myself."

"It's not that. I just think it seems kind of frustrating for you. I think you would be happier if you didn't worry about him."

Hailey looked away from me and sighed. She faced out

toward the city, rested her elbows on the banister and leaned out and over the ledge, thinking.

"The thing is," she said softly after a minute, "I could stop talking about him with you if you want. And I could even stop strategizing how to get him or whatever. But I can't stop liking him. It's not like a button I can push and make the crush go away. Trust me. I've tried that many, many times."

I was being choked. She really liked him. She couldn't stop herself. And I knew how she felt, because it was how I felt, too. There was nothing I could say to make the truth hurt less.

"I'm gonna get dressed," Hailey said to me. "This conversation is bumming me out."

She walked back inside, abruptly, leaving me on her balcony. I waited outside for another minute, but I felt weird being alone. Her sudden absence had a presence, like a fossil, or a footprint in the sand.

chapter

sixty–nine

Tons of random people from school came to the party. Even Emily showed up with her older brother. The apartment was packed. The music was loud.

I didn't see Nate arrive, but he found me where I was talking to Emily and came over to say hi.

"How's it going?" he asked us, sipping a beer.

"It's okay," Emily said in her usual straightforward tone. "I'm really happy it's a three-day weekend."

I liked seeing Nate and Emily talk. There was something sweet about it. I looked up admiringly at Nate, and he looked back at me and I felt that invisible string tugging at my chest. My mind flashed on to us having sex. Is that what it's like when you've had sex with someone? Like you can never look at them again without getting flashes to this dark, shapeless moment you shared?

Emily turned to me and launched into a story about her cousins who were visiting from out of town. I don't think Nate could hear Emily over the noise in the room, and he eventually drifted away and dissolved into the crowd. I was sad to see him go, but sort of relieved, too. Talking to him in public scared me. I didn't trust myself not to reach out and kiss him.

The crowd thickened and thinned as groups came and left. Hailey opened the windows so everyone could smoke inside. The apartment thumped. People kept switching the music in the middle of songs, trying to find the one that would get the most people dancing at once.

After a while, I went into Hailey's room to get a sweatshirt and found Nate sitting on the edge of Hailey's bed alone, talking on his phone. When he saw me he gave me an acknowledging nod.

"I gotta go," he said into phone. "Me too."

"Who was that?" I asked.

Nate snapped his phone shut. "My sister. She just drunk dialed me from school to complain about her roommate. She's so crazy."

Without thinking about what I was doing, I sat down next to him and let my head fall onto his shoulder.

"You having fun?" he asked, placing his hand on my thigh.

I giggled and shrugged. "Eh."

Just then the door opened. I jerked upright, and pushed Nate's hand away as Hailey tumbled in. She froze when she saw us.

"What's going on?" she asked.

I looked at Hailey. The room was spinning.

"Just tell her," Nate said to me softly. "It's okay."

"I can't," I stammered.

Nate stood. He looked at me, his expression a mix of pity and disappointment. Then he crossed the room and left.

When he was gone, Hailey moved her eyes slowly to mine. "Tell me what?"

"Hailey," I began. "It's—there's, well—I, I mean—we . . ."

My voice trailed off. The stretch of room between us seemed to grow wide and dark as a ravine. As soon as I told her the truth, it would swallow me up entirely.

"I'm sorry, Hailey, I've wanted to tell you, I just—" I tried again and stopped. I had no idea what to say. I wished I had memorized a statement, something concise and simple. Instead, I was going to have to go into the whole long story. I took a deep breath and closed my eyes. I would never be able to un-tell her.

Hailey rolled her eyes and scoffed. "Don't be so dramatic. Just spit it out, Li."

"It's Nate. We, like, like each other."

"You like each other?" she repeated.

I nodded.

"That's ridiculous," she said, and she started laughing. "He doesn't like you. If it's anything, he probably just wants to fuck you."

I was stunned. I thought about Nate and about what had happened between us over the last year. I thought about the conversations and the silences and the super-gentle way he touched my hair. Hailey was wrong. Nate liked me for real.

"So that's it?" she egged me on, staring. "You like Nate. Big surprise. I could have told you that. Everyone likes Nate."

The volume of the music in the living room spiked, and people shrieked excitedly as a song I vaguely recognized came on. It was exactly the kind of thing Hailey would have wanted to dance to, but she didn't even seem to hear it.

"So how do you know that Nate like-likes you? Did he, like, try and make out with you when he was drunk at the Hayeses' or something?"

"It's not like that," I said.

"Have you kissed him?" she asked.

I nodded.

Hailey's face fell, all the color draining from it like air going out of a balloon. When she spoke, her voice was tiny. "When?"

"I don't know," I said. "I'm sorry."

"You don't know?" she asked, her bottom lip trembling. "Last weekend? Today? Just now?"

"Hailey, stop," I pleaded. I stepped toward her and gently touched her shoulder. She pulled away from my hand like it burned. Until that moment, I almost wasn't sure if she was mad or upset or what. But when I touched her, it was as if I literally felt her pain.

"Don't," she said.

"I'm sorry," I said, my heart pounding. "Hailey, I'm so sorry."

"For what?" she said, shaking. "You haven't even told me what happened yet."

"We're sort of together," I said. "We have been for a while."

Hailey dropped back, leaning into the edge of her desk for support like she was too weak to stand.

"I'm so sorry," I choked. Hot tears stung my eyes. "I love you so much."

"Since when?" she asked.

I was too dizzy with anxiety to focus on what had happened with Nate. "We kissed for the first time like maybe a week or two before my birthday."

"Your birthday? In March? That was so long ago," Hailey said. Her tears were streaming fast now, cutting dark tracks through her makeup. Hailey never let her makeup get messed up, and for some reason the fact that she all of a sudden didn't seem to care wrenched at my heart.

"I know," I whispered.

Something thudded in the other room. A lamp getting knocked over? A picture falling off the wall? Hailey ignored it. It didn't matter. Nothing mattered.

"Why have you been telling me to go for him?" she asked. "Are you evil? Seriously. Are you pure evil? Who are you?"

"I don't know," I said, uncertain. "I wanted to tell you about us but I was scared. I've hated having a secret from you, you have to believe me."

Hailey shook her head. "I don't have to believe you, Lima. I don't have to do anything for you ever again."

"I didn't mean it like that," I stammered. "I never wanted to hurt you. But it's so complicated. Nate's not your boyfriend."

"He's not my boyfriend, fine," she hissed, "but then why keep it a secret? Don't even pretend that you don't know how fucked up this is."

"I know," I said. "I'm a terrible person. But I'm telling you now so that we can start to make it better."

Hailey's face contorted with a fresh wave of pain. She reached for a tissue off of her desk, and blew her nose. For a moment, she stood there silently crying, her shoulders shaking.

"Hailey," I whispered. "I'm sorry."

"I can't even look at you," she said softly. "Just leave."

"Hailey, I want to talk about it; I want to make it better," I pleaded.

"Seriously, Lima. I don't want to talk to you," she said. "I don't want to be around you. Ever again."

"What can I say that will make it better?" I begged.

"Nothing. I have no idea who you are. I thought you were my best friend," she began, but her voice caught on the word *friend* and she let out a ragged sob. "And it turns out you're a total stranger."

"Hailey, I'm so sorry," I sobbed.

"I seriously can't look at you," she said again. "Just go."

I looked at Hailey's door and my gaze snagged on a squiggly-looking tree that I'd drawn on the back of the door in green marker. I wondered if I would ever see it again.

"Now." Hailey hissed. "Leave."

I wrenched open the door, stumbled through the party and then down the stairs of Hailey's apartment building, blinded by tears, my sobs echoing in the cold stairwell. When I finally got outside, I pulled out my cell phone to call a taxi, but my hands were shaking so badly the phone clattered to the sidewalk and bounced away from me.

I was crouched down, cursing and crying and crawling to find my phone in the dark, when I heard Nate's voice.

"Hey," he said.

I looked up at him for second and then back down at the dark pavement.

"I know what you're thinking," I said. "And I know I should have told her sooner. I've told her now. Please don't make me feel worse than I already do."

"That's not what I'm thinking," Nate said softly. Then he bent down and picked up my phone. "Is this what you're looking for?" he asked.

I nodded.

"Let me take you home," he said.

Nate and I didn't speak or listen to music in the car. I tucked my knees up to my chest and stared out the window. The only motions I made were to wipe tears off my face. I wasn't even sure if I was breathing.

The city was indifferent. Sepulveda Boulevard was abandoned this late at night. It was all brown and black and mustard yellow in the streetlamps. The only sound we could hear was the gentle, patient ticktock of Nate's turn signal while we waited at a light.

"Let's go get something to eat," Nate said. "I'm starving."

I wasn't even a little bit hungry, but I nodded anyway. I didn't have the energy to argue. Besides, where could I go? Upsetting thoughts would chase me down anywhere I went.

"I love this one," Nate said as we walked into a glowing twenty-four-hour Taco Bell on Venice Boulevard. Synthetic music sprang from the speakers. Fluorescent lights paneled the ceiling, making the whole room feel brighter than daylight.

"Want anything?" Nate asked.

I shook my head no and wordlessly took a seat.

The fight with Hailey had been replaying in my head this whole time. It was more real, more vivid, than reality. Her words were jumbled and I couldn't straighten them out, but they were all there, surfacing and resurfacing. *I thought you were my best friend and it turns out you're a total stranger.*

"Hey," Nate said, sitting across from me with a tray of food.

He pushed a blue slushie across the table toward me. It had a fat red straw sticking out of it.

"That's for you," he said. "I know you like blue slushies."

"You remember that?" I asked. It was the first time I'd spoken since we left Hailey's.

He nodded. And then he ate his burrito in silence. When he was done, he scrunched the paper into a waxy ball and threw it four feet into the trash can. Even though he was finished eating, he gave no sign that he was ready to leave.

I glanced outside. A cop car with its siren light on zipped past us.

"You okay?" Nate finally asked. "Want to talk about it?"

"She hates me," I said.

I took a sip of the blue slushie, and it was so sour I practically spit it out.

"That's disgusting," I said. "It's gone bad or something."

"Do you want something else instead?" he asked. "A Coke?"

"No. We should tell the people who work here that there's something wrong with the formula."

My mind flashed again on Hailey's distorted, crying face, and I felt nauseous. Her pain had been so white-hot, I could see it. She didn't just look upset or mad, like I expected. She looked injured.

"The formula?" Nate replied, cracking a smile. "This is straight from nature, Lima. This is a native blue fruit that grows on trees in Mexico."

Nate was trying so hard to make me feel better.

This observation grew in me, changed shape. It seemed profound. Even though nothing could make me feel better about Hailey, I wanted Nate to think I was feeling better. I wanted to make him happy by showing him that he was making me happy. I realized that our own separate happinesses had grown intertwined.

I took another sip of the blue slushie and said, with a fake newscaster's voice, "Yes. This is definitely the blue slushie plant of the coastal region of Mexico. It is commonly used for candy and soda, but it also has ancient medicinal purposes." It was a stupid joke, and I was terrible at doing voices, but I saw a smile flash somewhere behind Nate's eyes.

"Right. Some tribes have been known to smoke it for its hallucinogenic properties," he said. He spoke in the same fake official tone of voice I had used.

"Those people are generally never heard from again," I added, pretending to hold a microphone this time.

"Or actually, they just materialize at Walker and Meredith's house," Nate said, dropping the fake voice. "With a flask of whiskey and pack of French cigarettes."

It was a mean joke, and for a second I bristled. But then I started to laugh. And not a little bit, but a lot. It was the first time we had joked about Meredith and Walker and all the bad stuff that had gone on there. It was weird how something that had felt so heavy and filthy could be looked at from another angle and all of a sudden seem funny.

"You like that joke?" Nate said, smirking a little, watching me laugh.

I nodded, still laughing. "I don't know why that's so funny."

Nate wasn't laughing, but he looked really happy. He slumped back in his seat, finally relaxing a little.

When my laughter died down, I let out a sigh. The fit of laughing seemed to have relieved a little bit of my tension.

Nate nodded his head a tiny bit, thinking something I couldn't read.

I reached across the table and placed my hand on his hand.

"Nate," I said. My heart was pounding.

He looked at me, his head tilting to one side inquisitively. "Yeah?"

Suddenly, I wanted to tell him that I loved him. I could feel the words forming in my mouth like a bubble, but something stopped me.

"So many people are mad at me," I said instead. I could feel his hand pulsing beneath mine. I wrapped my fingers around his.

"I just never want to ruin this," I said. "I never want you to be mad at me."

He didn't say anything for a second. "I don't think you'll ruin this. I don't want to either."

I guess that's the truest thing you can give another person, the simple agreement that you will do your best to protect the fragile thing that you have.

"Thanks for hanging out with me. I don't want to be alone."

"Yeah," he said. "Of course."

Everything had moved so fast all year and I needed us to slow down. We had already done so much together, and I kind of wished we could rewind and do it again more slowly.

I could save telling him I loved him for another time. I didn't want all of our firsts to already be in the past.

Our eyes clicked into each other, doing a magnetic thing that made me feel as if we were the only people in the room. *And besides*, I thought. *He already knows how I feel.*

chapter

seventy

The next day I slept until three. When I woke up, my room was full of orange and red afternoon light. The house was quiet. I stood up and peeled the clothes from Hailey's party off my floor and tossed them into the hamper, and then I crawled back into bed.

A hole was widening in my chest, and everything bad that had happened all year was falling into it. My own actions looked so ugly and mean. I had betrayed Hailey. She was right. I was spoiled. I was sneaky. I was manipulative. How had I become this person? Everything I assumed about myself—that I was a good friend and good person—had turned out to be untrue.

I was crying again. I had cried so much in the last twenty-four hours my face felt chapped.

I thought there'd be some relief from having everything out in the open, but what I felt was the opposite of relief. All of my secrets looked dirtier in the daylight. Like how sometimes when you put on a sweater and it looks okay in your closet mirror, but then when you stand in the sun you realize it was stained all along.

I got up and walked over to the window. Mom and Dad were walking on the beach directly behind our house. I couldn't hear their voices, but I could see that they were talking. At one point Mom looked up at Dad and laughed, and then he pulled her into his side so his arm was around her shoulders. They walked like that for maybe three or four seconds before she slid out of his grip.

I wondered if I could ever be like that with a guy. So close and so comfortable. Mom and Dad had spent so much time together, dating, falling in love, being married. It was unimaginable. I had only hooked up with Nate a few times, and it was so intense and consuming. What would it be like to have an actual boyfriend? To be with someone for years? To sleep in the same bed together night after night?

I stood there in a daze, my forehead pressed to the cool glass, watching them as they headed back toward the house. On the porch, Mom scooped up a blanket that she'd left to dry in the sun.

chapter

seventy-one

School the next week was torture. Luckily, we had less than a month left.

I avoided the parking lots and the patios and the hallways. I only allowed myself to use the bathroom in the old gym because I knew I wouldn't run into Hailey there. At lunch, I buried myself in books in the library.

Emily sat down across from me on Wednesday.

"I'm so excited we both got into AP Bio," Emily said. Patty had posted the list earlier that day, but I was too pre-occupied to feel anything about the good news. Nothing seemed important to me except making up with Hailey. "I can't believe Maria didn't get in. She seemed so pissed."

"I didn't notice," I said, staring at my computer screen.

"Are you okay?" Emily asked after a minute.

"Not really," I said. "I'm having a bad week."

"Want to go get a snack or something?" she suggested. "I'll buy you a cookiewich. The swim team is having a bake sale. I just had one, but I could eat another. It might make you feel better."

"I can't go outside," I said.

"Why not?" she asked.

"I can't deal with seeing people. All this stuff with me and Hailey has gotten really bad," I said.

"What stuff?"

"You didn't hear about it?" I asked. "I thought everyone knew."

She shook her head no.

"All this bad drama happened at her party on Friday. And now we are fighting, I guess," I said.

"Why?" she asked.

"It's a really long story," I said. What would Emily think if she knew what I had done?

"Oh sorry," Emily replied, too quickly. "I don't know why I'm being so nosy."

"No, I'll tell you," I said. "But I'm too tired to get into it right now."

Emily nodded in agreement, but she was looking at me really intensely, like she was doing an equation.

"What?" I asked.

"It's just weird," she said thoughtfully. "I always thought

you, like, never had any problems. Like with social stuff or whatever."

"Me?" I was so surprised, I almost laughed.

"Yeah," she continued. "You hang out with Meredith Hayes, and Hailey, like, worships the ground you walk on. You're, like, the coolest girl in school."

I couldn't imagine anyone thinking that about me. I looked around the library. The tables were packed with people. Some of them I knew from class or elementary school or just from seeing them around, but they all looked anonymous.

"It's really funny to hear you say that, because I literally don't have any friends," I said. "Except you."

"I'm sure that's not true," Emily said, but I thought I saw her blush a little, anyway.

"Actually, a cookiewich sounds really good," I said, snapping my laptop closed. I hadn't eaten since breakfast and all of a sudden realized I was starving. "Want to come with me to get one?"

"Um, yeah!" Emily smiled. "I'm dying to get another one. I might be addicted to them."

Emily and I walked outside together and I felt a little safer being on the patio with her by my side. I just hoped I'd never have to tell her what happened with Hailey. I wasn't sure she'd still like me after she realized what a backstabber I was.

chapter

seventy-two

When I got home from school the next day, Hailey's mom's car was parked in front of my house. Hailey was sitting outside the front door wearing a big gray sweatshirt, her hair scooped up into a ponytail.

"Can we talk?" she asked when she saw me.

"Okay," I said. We walked through the house and out to the beach. When we got outside, Hailey looked at me and I saw that her eyes were swollen and red from crying.

"Hailey, I'm so sorry," I blurted. "You can't possibly know how terrible I feel. And how hard and horrible this week has been."

Hailey paused for a second, thinking. Then she looked right back at me.

"You want me to feel bad for you?" she hissed. "You are the worst person I have ever known."

I blinked, momentarily stunned.

"You have no idea, Lima!" she practically screamed. She was shaking and crying, angry tears spilling out of her eyes like faucets. "You betrayed me in the most insane way. You are the most horrible, self-involved, spoiled, twisted person in the world. You ruined my life."

No one had ever yelled me at like that, and I felt paralyzed with shock.

"I've been thinking about you and what you did nonstop since you told me," she said when she had regained control of her voice. "And it just gets worse and worse the more I think about it."

"I know," I whispered, my bottom lip beginning to tremble.

"You don't know," she fired back. "No one has been lying to you."

That was true.

"There are so many layers to what you did," she continued. "I don't even know where to start."

As I realized how far this conversation was from being over, I started to really cry. I was going to have to hear everything. Everything I'd been protecting myself against all year was finally coming true.

"First of all," she said, "I've been throwing myself at Nate all year and you never once stopped me. Do you know how psychopathic that is? It's not normal, Lima. Normal people don't keep secrets and lie to their friends and encourage them to go for people who they are secretly dating. It's seriously clinical, Lima. You should see a doctor."

"I tried to tell you," I said meekly.

"What does that even mean? You tried to tell me? Either you told me or you didn't," she yelled. "There's no in between."

"It's not like that," I said, feeling frustrated by the way Hailey had of always twisting the truth so my whole version seemed erased. "I just couldn't figure out how to tell you. It was like, every time I brought up Nate, the conversation always ended up being about you and him."

"Oh, so it's my fault?" she snapped, straightening up.

"I didn't say that," I protested.

"Whatever, Lima," she continued. "That's fine. You can tell yourself that this is partly my fault. But we both know that's bullshit. This is one hundred percent you."

"I'm not trying to blame you," I said exasperatedly. "I'm just saying. I felt like if I tried to tell you that Nate liked me, you wouldn't have believed me."

"What?!" She practically laughed, her jaw dropping. "Are you joking? Of course I would have believed you—look at you! You're beautiful. You're perfect."

How was Hailey so good at using compliments as weapons? I struggled for the right thing to say, to make her understand. Her words and feelings were so strong, I felt like they were strangling me.

"And that's a whole other layer," Hailey continued, but now her voice was subdued, sad. "It's just that you're you. He must fucking love you. And it kills me. I've loved Nate my whole life, Lima. You might think it doesn't count or whatever, because he didn't, like, love me back. But you're wrong. It still hurts so much."

"Hailey. I'm so sorry," I said gently. I had the impulse to hug her, to tell her that everything was going to be okay. But I fought the urge. All year, I'd tried to deny the truth in order to spare Hailey's feelings, but now the truth was winning.

Maybe it always does, in the end.

Hailey closed her eyes and tried to steady her breath. "Do you know how many times in my life I just wished I could be you? I used to wish for it on Christmas. I'd literally ask Santa if I could one day wake up and be Lima. Not Lima's best friend. Or Lima's sister. Or Lima for a day. But *be* you. Forever."

Hailey opened her eyes then and looked at me, shame and hurt swarmed in her expression. Her words sank into me, and I felt something inside me break under their weight. Even though we were face-to-face, I was sure that we would never see each other clearly again.

"Life is so unfair," Hailey whispered.

For the first time since we'd come outside, Hailey turned away from me. She looked out over the ocean, and a gust of wind whipped her ponytail across her face. She spit out a little bit of sand and turned back to me.

"You are so not who you think you are," she said quietly.

I shook my head, fought back more tears. I looked out at the ocean. White sun. Skinny streaks of clouds like loose threads. I turned and looked at my house, peaceful, quiet, calm. Even though it was only forty feet away, it looked like it was a million miles away, behind glass, inaccessible. I was trapped. This patch of sand Hailey and I were standing on had become a raft, or a lifeboat. If I ever wanted to get off of it, to go home, I was going to have to do better.

It occurred to me that Hailey wasn't right about everything, but at least she was being honest. She was telling me her version of the truth. And I realized I had to do the same. It was time to stop being afraid. Whether or not she ever understood what this year had been like for me, which she probably wouldn't, I had to try.

"Hailey," I said calmly. "I know you're mad. And I know you're jealous. Okay? I get it. I understand. I'd be jealous too if Nate liked someone else. I get jealous knowing that he kissed you."

Hailey's eyes snapped up toward mine. For the first time

since we came outside, she looked like she was actually listening.

"It's shitty," I continued. "That we liked the same person. It's the worst twist of fate that possibly could have happened."

Hailey didn't say anything.

"And I know it sounds like I'm trying to blame you for the fact that I kept it a secret," I said. "But I don't blame you. Not for a second."

"Okay," she said softly.

"I didn't want to like Nate. I tried not to," I said. "But once we started talking and being friends, it was really confusing. Because you know me, I've never liked anyone. I wasn't sure what was happening until it had gone on for so long that I just didn't know how to explain it."

She flicked away tears.

"I'm not saying it's okay that I kept it a secret," I said. "I know that was messed up. I was just so scared to tell you."

I took a deep breath. I knew I had to tell her the truth. It was the only way off this horrible lifeboat. I had to be brave.

"Hailey," I said, my voice breaking. "I know you don't want to hear this. But I think I'm in love with Nate."

Hailey closed her eyes and two enormous tears streamed down her face. I hadn't said those words out loud to anyone, and they felt so true and so important, I started to cry more now, too. Soon, we were both sobbing. Without thinking about it, I stepped toward her and hugged her and we stood there, hugging and crying for a minute. But then I felt her stiffen in my arms, backing lightly away.

"I can't be friends with you anymore," she said softly.

"Don't say that," I whimpered. "I'm so sorry. With every cell in my body, I am so sorry."

"I know you are," she said. "And I'm sorry, too. But I just can't."

She didn't look angry anymore. But there was something in her eyes that made me sick with sadness. A distance. A guardedness. It finally hit me that she would never trust me again. I had broken everything.

I stayed on the beach after Hailey left. I sat down in the sand and thought about the first time Hailey called her feelings for Nate love. It was fifth grade. We were on the playground after school one Friday. The sky was overcast and ominous. Hailey and I lazily swung on the tire swing, just letting it rock us back and forth slowly.

Things always felt magical after school. The way the playground emptied out and the classrooms were cleaned and locked. It felt mysterious and dangerous, as if anything was possible.

Across the concrete playground, we could see the soccer field where a group of boys were practicing. We were close enough to hear their screams, but not to make out the coach's orders. Even from across the yard, and without seeing his face, you could identify Nate. He wasn't the tallest or the fastest on the team, but he always had an intensity about him, an alertness. Even when he was standing on the edge of the field, watching the ball, he was so awake it almost seemed as if he was moving.

"Who do you think is the cutest boy in our grade?" Hailey asked, dragging her toes through the sandy pit beneath the swing.

I was embarrassed. I had never been good at talking about boys. "I don't know."

"You have to pick one," Hailey said authoritatively. "You have to rank number one and number two."

Everyone knew that Ryan was the cutest boy in school, so it would be the most obvious and therefore the least revealing answer.

"Ryan Masterson," I said.

"I knew you'd say that," Hailey said. "My number one is Nate Reed."

"Yeah, Nate is," I didn't know what to say about Nate. There was just something about him that made him stand out. "Nate is my number two."

Hailey halted her swinging. "No. He can't be you number two. He's my number one and my number two."

"Oh," I said. The rules of this game really seemed to bend themselves in Hailey's favor. "Why?"

"I am in love with Nate, Lima," Hailey said, looking me straight in the eye. "You should make Julian your number two. He's taller than Nate anyway."

And just like that, the rules were laid out. Nate belonged to Hailey. Forever.

Until now.

chapter

seventy-three

A week later, I was on my way to eat lunch in the library when I saw Hailey and Skyler, arms linked, backpacks on, going in before me. I froze. I had forgotten that the library always became the center of activity in the weeks before finals.

Suddenly, I felt overwhelmingly tired. I was hungry. I wanted to be by myself. I hated Hailey for being the victim. She had nothing to be ashamed of, she hadn't done anything wrong. She could walk around campus totally blameless. I, on the other hand, was a social pariah. I clenched my jaw tight, trying to fight tears. I really didn't want to cry at school. Girls who cried at school always seemed like they were trying to get attention and all I was trying to do was avoid it. But what was I supposed to do? Eat in a bathroom stall like girls do in bad movies about high school?

I turned away from the library, my lip trembling, and

walked quickly across campus to the patio behind the administration building. To my relief, it was empty. I sat at the dusty bench, wiped my eyes and pulled out my sandwich. While I ate, I willed myself to think only about how delicious it was. The perfect interaction of brie and bread filled me with pleasure. At least no one could take this away from me.

"Yo."

Nate's hands were on my shoulders. I jumped a little before I looked up at him. I tipped my head back so far it rested against his stomach.

Nate and I hadn't hung out at school together since the whole Hailey thing had exploded. Even though our relationship wasn't a secret anymore, I wasn't ready to be seen with him.

"What are you doing back here?" he asked. He climbed past me so he was sitting on the table with his feet on the bench.

"I'm just eating my sandwich," I said, not wanting to get into it.

"It looks like a good sandwich," Nate said, but I felt like he saw there was more going on with me.

"It is," I said. "Do you want the last bite?"

He shook his head. "You have it."

"It's probably almost time for class," I said when I finished. I stood up and prepared to leave, but Nate didn't move.

"What are you doing this weekend?" Nate asked.

"I'm going to Santa Barbara with my parents to help my aunt pack," I said.

Mom had told me the big news a few days before: Caroline was selling the house and moving to LA. I thought about the shadowy tiled hallways and the bright porches in Nana and Caroline's house. I was going to miss it.

"I'm sorry you never got to come see it," I said. "It's so beautiful."

"Sucks," he said.

"It's good for my aunt, though," I said. "My mom says it's weird for her to live there alone after living there with her mom and her kids for so long."

"That's cool."

"Yeah," I agreed, and I giggled a little and added in an imitating voice, "that's cool."

Nate lit up. "Was that supposed to be an imitation of me?"

I smiled. "Yeah, was it good?"

Nate laughed and flicked my arm. "No. It was terrible. That sounded nothing like me."

I laughed. "It totally sounded like you. Maybe you just don't know what you sound like!"

"Come here," Nate said, hopping off his seat on the picnic table and grabbing me as if he was going to wrestle me to the ground.

I squealed and tried to squirm away from his grip, but he wrapped his arms around me, pinning my arms to my sides and pulling me toward him. I tried to break free for a second, then gave in and let my body go slack, leaning all my weight against him.

Nate was smiling down at me and shaking his head in mock disapproval. It was amazing that he still had new ways of looking at me that made my insides melt.

chapter
seventy-four

om, Dad, and I spent the night in Santa Barbara, helping Caroline pack up the house. It was weird that the house was going to be sold and passed down to strangers.

On the car ride home, I stared out the window. The ocean was a deep turquoise laced with lavender foam.

"Dad," I said. "Remember that friend of yours who worked at the aquarium in San Diego? What was his name?"

"Of course," Dad said. "Mark Lanton."

"Do you think you could ask him if he has any internships for high school students this summer?" I asked. I had missed the deadline for the research internships Patty had mentioned, and until now, I hadn't known what I wanted to with my summer. "It might be too late, but I don't know, maybe there's something I could do there?"

Dad and Mom glanced at each other and didn't say anything.

"I've just been thinking it might be cool to, like, study the ocean," I continued. "Like marine biology or whatever."

"I'll call him first thing tomorrow," Dad said. "Good thinking."

Mom craned her neck around from the front seat and pushed her sunglasses off her face so they held her hair back like a headband. Her eyes scanned my face.

"What?" I said.

"Honey," she said seriously. "That's a brilliant idea."

I rolled my eyes at her and opened my window a crack. A loud rush of salty air sliced through the car.

"Anyone want to stop at Gladstones?" Dad asked as we got closer to Malibu, tossing a hopeful smile over his shoulder at me and Mom.

"Sounds great," Mom said, winking quickly at me.

We ate at Dad's favorite table in the corner of the restaurant. The thick glass window muted the sounds of the ocean outside. After we ate, we walked out the front doors through the patio to valet parking, feeling droopy from the greasy food.

"Look," Mom said. "Isn't that Meredith Hayes?"

I glanced in the direction Mom was facing and there she

was. Meredith, Walker, Henry, and Lily were seated around a big circular table. Lily? I couldn't believe it. I had just assumed her friendship with the twins had ended the same night that mine had. How could she stand to be around any of them after what had happened?

"Oh, wow," I stammered. This was all too much to process. It was disorienting enough to run into any of them here, even without the added shock of realizing that Lily was still hanging out with the twins. And I hadn't seen Meredith since the unsatisfying conversation we'd had in the parking lot weeks earlier. Seniors finished two weeks before the rest of the school, trickling out while everyone else stressed over finals and end-of-the-year deadlines.

"I think you should go say hi," Mom said, giving me a gentle push. "We'll meet you out front."

I walked tentatively up to their table.

"Lima! What a surprise." Meredith said. Her eyes were protected behind an enormous pair of vintage sunglasses.

"Hey, guys," I said awkwardly.

My eyes drifted around the table. Henry waved at me but didn't smile. Walker mumbled something and then reached for an oyster off of the bowl of ice in the center of the table. Lily didn't look at me. I hadn't seen her since that night, which felt like a lifetime ago. She looked different and I realized after a minute that it was because her bangs had grown out and she was wearing them swept over to the side, not coiled and sprayed. It made her look more conventionally pretty, even younger. I stared at her for a moment, willing her to acknowledge me, but she kept her eyes glued to her plate. And then, after a minute she turned away and reached for something in her purse.

"We've been up all night, so excuse us if we are weird," Meredith said. "We're just getting some brunch."

"Oh, cool," I said. It was so Meredith to call a meal at four o'clock brunch.

"Walker thinks raw oysters are the perfect hangover cure," Henry said.

"Does it work?" I asked, trying to match their casual tone.

"The verdict is still out," Walker said, finally looking up at me. There was a cautiousness in his expression that I hadn't ever seen before.

"I hope it works," I said quietly. "I should go, but I just wanted to say hi."

Meredith put her sunglasses on the table, pushed her chair back, and stood up, "I'll walk you out."

"Bye," I said to the table lamely, and was met with a few halfhearted byes.

"How have you been?" Meredith asked as we walked toward the valet.

"I've been not great," I said. "There's been a lot of hard stuff going on."

I looked at Meredith, and suddenly I realized this was my last chance to tell her what I thought. What did I have to lose anymore? I'd already lost everything.

"And I'm still upset about us. I'm mad and hurt and confused about the fact that we're just not friends anymore," I said simply, not dropping her gaze.

I expected Meredith to respond with one of her typical, elusive answers, but instead she sighed.

"I know," she said. "Me too."

Meredith's usually enchanting black eyes were marked with the opacity that people get from not sleeping. I'd seen it in my own eyes over the past few weeks.

"So, what happened? Why did you disappear on me?" I asked. "Was it because of Nate? Because I am so sorry about that. I never meant to use your house like that. I can tell you the whole story if you give me a chance."

Meredith shook her head. "We don't need to get into it. Besides, I don't really remember what happened. Everything has been crazy lately."

"We need to talk about it," I said. And then I added, "*I* need that."

Meredith paused. "I don't know. But I really do miss

you and I want to see you before I go," she said, forcing a smile. "Walker and I leave the second week of July. Things are gonna be kind of crazy until then, but maybe we can go swimming or something? You never taught me how to make peach crumble and you know that's all I want."

"You want to learn to make a crumble?" I repeated slowly.

"Yeah. Or like, I don't know, ravioli. Weren't you going to teach me to make ravioli?" she asked.

I bit my lip. The realization that Meredith was totally incapable of having a real conversation was making sadness blossom inside of me, spreading like dark ink. There were so many unsorted things about Meredith's life, things that she just refused to look at.

"Okay, sure," I said. "I'll come over."

We had reached the valet parking area now and I could see Mom and Dad double parked, waiting for me in the car.

Meredith gave me a hug.

"Bye, Lima," she said. A flicker of emotion passed behind her eyes, and I wondered if there was something she wanted to say but couldn't.

"Bye," I said.

I climbed into the backseat of the car and Meredith stood there, squinting and waving as we drove away. Wind and light ricocheted off the ocean and lit up strands of her hair like glitter. I knew after I left she'd go back to Walker and

Henry and Lily and their epic hangovers and their fabulous parties. And I knew I wouldn't go over to her house before she left to teach her how to make a crumble. I wondered if she knew it, too.

When I opened my computer that night, there was an e-mail from Lily with no subject. I hesitated and then opened it. All it said was "Thank you."

I closed my laptop, unnerved. It was weird that she had ignored me at lunch today only to thank me now. But the more I thought about it, the more it made sense. She must have been too embarrassed to say anything to me in front of the twins or Henry.

I opened my computer and wrote back. I typed, "Of course," and then clicked send. In the quiet moment that followed, it dawned on me that I didn't care anymore what Meredith and Walker thought about what I'd done at all. It didn't matter if they thought I was in the right or the wrong. I knew that I had helped Lily and Lily knew it, too. Maybe not every decision I'd made in the last few months had been terrible.

chapter

seventy-five

The morning of my first surfing lesson with Emily was bright and crisp. After talking about it over a couple of lunches, I had finally agreed to let her teach me. We swam out to a spot beyond the breaking waves and sat, straddling our surfboards and staring out at the horizon.

"This waiting is a lot of what surfing is," Emily explained. "Especially when you're a beginner."

The ocean gently rocked our boards up and down and side to side. A neat V of pelicans flew by, and we instinctively followed their path with our gazes.

"It's pretty mellow today," she said, turning around and squinting at me. A reddish morning sunlight lit up her body and caught swirls of metallic purple and green on the oily surface of the water.

The air was salty, rich, and vivid. The ocean water was briny and cold on my bare feet and in the places where it snuck underneath my wet suit. Getting into the wet suit had taken almost ten minutes, and I had face-planted in the sand twice, making Emily laugh so hard she said she was going to pee in her pants.

I fidgeted with the Velcro strap around my ankle, the one that secured me to my borrowed surfboard by a three-foot plastic cable. "Paddle!" Emily shouted suddenly, and she spun around onto her belly and started hurtling herself and her board in the direction of the shore to demonstrate what I was supposed to do.

I twisted around, trying to get onto my belly, but it was awkward and I could feel my limbs flailing. My leg got stuck in the cable and I lost time trying to untangle it, so by the time I was actually paddling, it was too late. I felt the wave billow up underneath me and then pass me by, leaving me bobbing on my board. I glanced over my shoulder and Emily was laughing hysterically, covering her mouth with two hands.

Seeing her laugh so hard made me start to laugh, too. I tried to splash her, but I had no momentum lying on my stomach, so I just kind of slapped the water. This made us both laugh harder.

"You'll get the hang of it," she said when she could speak again. She wiped away tears of laughter from her cheeks. Her wet hair was thick and it glistened in the sunlight.

The ocean was so full of secrets. Surfing showed me a whole other side to it that I could never have known just from looking at it from the beach. The ocean was strong and rhythmic and steady.

For a moment we were both still, and then we erupted again into a fit of giggles. I might be the world's worst surfer, but I loved it anyway.

chapter

seventy-six

fterward, Emily took me to the In-N-Out drive-through. It was only 10:00 a.m., but we both got burgers and milk shakes.

"Surfers are always the first people here," Emily explained. She spread her meal out across her lap and wedged her milk shake into one of the car's built-in cup holders.

I squeezed ketchup out of a slippery packet, trying to aim it at my burger.

"So what's the story with you and Hailey?" Emily asked, her mouth full of food. "I've heard some things at school, but I'm not sure what to believe."

I sighed. "You might hate me if I tell you the truth."

Emily rolled her eyes. "I doubt it. Honestly, I'm not exactly the biggest fan of Hailey and Skyler."

It was weird how Hailey and Skyler had become such a

pair. My whole life it was Hailey and Lima. Skyler had finally fully replaced me.

"Okay," I said. "But if you decide you think I'm a bad person and you don't want to hang out with me anymore, who's gonna teach me to surf?"

Emily laughed. "Shut up."

I told her about how Hailey had always been obsessed with Nate and how he and I had started to like each other and date in secret. I told her about how I lied to Hailey about it, and kept encouraging her to go for him until it all came out in the most horrible way imaginable.

"Whoa, that's intense," Emily said afterward. "It's so weird how you can like someone so much even when they are off-limits. Something like that happened to me once, too."

"Really?" I asked.

"Well, I mean, your situation sounds way, way worse," she retracted. "But, it was kind of similar. I had a crush on one of my brother's friends, and my brother was so pissed, he put an end to it."

"Why?" I asked.

Emily frowned. "He's just like that."

"Who was the guy?" I asked.

"My brother's friend, Tyler," she said. "We used to all go surfing together: him and me and my brother, and some other people, too. They were all my brother's friends, not my friends, but once I got good enough at surfing, I'd go out with them. And I'd always had a crush on Tyler, even since before we started surfing together."

"So what happened?" I asked.

"I'm not sure, but I think Tyler started to like me, too," she said. "He would text me and stuff. And he just gave me more attention than the other guys did. You know what I mean?"

"Yeah," I said. "It sounds like he liked you."

"Maybe. But I'll never know," she said.

"Why not?" I asked.

"My brother read one of Tyler's texts to me and flipped out," she said. "And the text didn't even say anything bad, it was just some inside joke we had. But my brother was pissed. He told both of us to stop talking and texting and everything. And I don't think my brother is friends with Tyler anymore, even though they still see each other on the beach all the time."

"That sucks for you, though," I said.

"Yeah," she agreed. "It does. I mean, I'm really picky. I've never really liked anyone else besides Tyler."

"And you never got to kiss him or anything?" I asked tentatively.

Emily shook her head. "Nope. But . . . well . . ."

Her voice trailed off.

"What?" I asked, curious. "Tell me."

"There was this one time when I felt like something almost happened," she said. "We were the last people out of the water. So we were, like, sort of alone. I mean, my brother and the others were, like, twenty feet away, but they weren't paying any attention to us."

"And?" I pressed.

"It's gonna sound really stupid if I say it out loud," she said, blushing.

"No it won't, just tell me," I said.

"Okay, well, he helped me undo my wet suit," she said, smiling a little. "He just unzipped the top part, like the part on my back that I can't reach. And he did it really super-slow. And then when I looked at him afterward, I felt like he was about to kiss me. Like if we'd been alone, he would have. Is that crazy?"

"No," I said. "I bet he would have."

Emily laughed. "Oh my God, I'm so embarrassed I told you that."

Emily's story reminded me of how things felt between me and Nate at the beginning of the year, before I knew for sure what was happening. Up until our first kiss, every single time we touched hands or bumped into each other, it was like my whole body got set on fire. Now that we had done everything, touching was different. It was a trade-off.

All that anticipation and suspense had been replaced with something else. Something less exciting, but more steady and meaningful and better.

"Anyway, my brother and I are really close, so it was horrible when he was mad at me. I'm so glad it's over," she said. And then she added, "Hailey might get over it, too."

"Maybe," I said.

Then I scooted my straw around the waxy bottom of my milk-shake cup and sucked up the last, sweet drops.

chapter

seventy-seven

Days came and went quickly during the last week of school, a blur of tests and papers and lame end-of-the-year pizza parties. After my last final, I ducked into the patio behind the administration building to dump my notebooks in the big trash bins. Later, Mom and I would shake my backpack out on the beach. All the dusty crumbs of graphite and ground-up paper that had worked their way into the seams would blow away. Then she'd toss it in the washing machine and lay it out flat on the back deck so the sun could dry it. That's how I'd know it was officially summer.

I was sorting out my recyclables from my trash when Hailey stepped out of the administration building.

We looked at each other and froze.

"Hi," I said.

"Hi," she said, her voice pinched.

I pursed my lips together, trying to smile, but it kind of felt more like a grimace. "What are you doing back here?"

"I had to get this thing signed," she said, waving a loose piece of paper she was holding in her right hand.

There was a pause.

"How were your finals?" I asked. We were like strangers. No, we were worse than strangers. It occurred to me that maybe the worst kinds of strangers are the people who used to be your friends.

"Fine," she said, and started to leave.

She walked right past me, looking straight ahead. I watched her back as she approached the small gate that lead to main campus. I noticed she was wearing this big yellow scrunchie in her hair that she had had since seventh grade. It was her good-luck scrunchie. She must have worn it for one of her finals. I felt a pang of love.

"Hey, Hailey!" I said suddenly.

She stopped and turned around to face me.

This time, I really smiled, and my voice didn't sound strained. "Have a good summer."

She seemed to relax a little bit. "Yeah, you too."

"And, you know," I said. "If you ever, like . . ."

"Yeah, I know," she said quickly.

I didn't know what else to say. I just stared at her.

"I gotta go, Li," she said.

It was startling to hear her call me that. For a second, it felt like nothing had changed. Like we were still just Lima-and-Hailey.

"Okay," I said. "Bye."

She turned again and disappeared back onto campus.

When she was gone, I let out a huge sigh. I hadn't realized it but I had been holding my breath that whole time.

I had been so focused on avoiding Hailey for the last couple of weeks that I hadn't really allowed myself to think about what was actually going on with her. Where was she headed today? Maybe she'd celebrate the first day of summer with Skyler. For the first time since our fight, I really tried to picture what her life would be like without me. And without Nate to chase after.

She would go to her dad's wedding. She would probably bring Skyler. She would cry about something that weekend, but being Hailey, she would bounce right back. She would find something to make fun of. There would be the sneaking of alcohol, the flirting with someone's cousin, the small, harmless chaos of an evening. And there would be inside jokes. New memories. New adventures that she would share with someone who wasn't me. The knowledge that I would ultimately be replaced was at once hurtful and comforting.

As jealous as it made me feel, the truth was that I didn't want Hailey to be unhappy.

My cell phone vibrated and I pulled it out of my jeans pocket. Mom had texted that she was waiting in the car-pool lane. I must have lost track of time. I tossed one last broken shard of pencil into the trash bin and headed out of school.

chapter

seventy-eight

When I got home, I collapsed on top of my bed. It was hard to believe tenth grade was over. High school was already halfway done. I rolled that fact around in my mind, trying to get a hold on it, but it kept slipping out of my grasp.

I stood up and opened the window. Air from the beach got sucked inside, as if my room itself was a giant lung, inhaling. It was already after four. Nate was coming over at six to have dinner with me and Mom and Dad. What was that going to be like? What would we talk about? I paced around my room nervously for a moment and then sat down awkwardly at my desk. After such a busy year, it was weird to have no homework and absolutely nothing I needed to do.

I turned on my iPod and flipped through my music, landing on a playlist that Meredith had made me called *Lima is the girl from Ipanema*. I pressed play and Leonard Cohen's ragged, deep voice ripped through the quiet in my room.

There are so many ways for people to disappoint you. Meredith had turned out to be such a disappointment. But I guess I had disappointed her, too, in the end. And she wasn't the only person I had disappointed. My parents. Hailey. Myself.

I crossed my room and sunk down onto the edge of my bed. Maybe I'm not better or worse than anyone, I thought. Hailey, Meredith, Walker, Lily, even Nate, we were all mixes of good and bad. We had all played our parts in the things that had happened over the course of the year. No one person was to blame. Maybe growing up was about being able to live with the fact that things weren't ever totally black and white.

Suddenly, I missed Hailey. She would have taken an empty afternoon like this one and filled it, turning it into something bright and meaningful. I pushed back against the feeling. She'd been a bad friend to me all year. I replayed the mean things she had said to me on New Year's Eve. But it was no use. I just missed her, I couldn't help it. I missed everything about her. Her spastic, self-deprecating humor and her way of being so disarmingly honest at the most unexpected times. And other, less describable things, too. I missed watching her zone out in front of the TV. I even missed how she'd sometimes try too hard to be cool in front of people who she wanted to impress. It was all a part of Hailey, and I missed all of it.

When Nana had died, the hospital gave Dad a cardboard box containing the clothes she had been wearing when she was admitted. A flowered dress and a pair of canary yellow sandals. There were imprints of Nana's feet on the insoles of her shoes and seeing that had made me sickeningly sad. Missing Hailey made me feel like I was those shoes. Permanently empty.

My phone beeped. It was a text from Nate.

What should I bring tonight?

It made me smile to think about him getting ready for dinner and maybe being a little nervous. He'd probably wear that cute button-down shirt that I loved. The thought made me blush. I texted him back.

Just you xx

I took a deep breath. The sharp feeling of missing Hailey had mellowed. It wasn't gone, but it had softened. It didn't press at my insides like a big boulder the way it had a moment before. I wouldn't miss her so much if I hadn't loved her as much as I did. And loving someone like that just had to be a good thing, even if we had to give each other up.

Outside my window, the glowing afternoon sun hung low. The sky was fading from blue to lavender and the ocean beneath it was a shimmering dark blue. Suddenly, all I wanted was to go swimming. Jumping into the bright, rough water would be like rinsing the remnants of the school year away.

Mom was reading on the back deck when I stepped outside in my bathing suit a few minutes later.

"I'm going in," I said, skipping past her to the sand.

"Be careful!" she called after me. "I'll be watching you from here."

Cold waves washed over my ankles, my calves, my thighs, sending chills up my spine like electric shocks as I ran into the water. When I was in too deep to stand, I dropped in and swam. Underwater, my hands grazed the sand on the ocean floor, and it was unimaginably soft, like velvet, or fur, or sifted flour. When I came up for air, I tasted salt, and felt the minerals all over my skin like crystals.

Off in the distance, the horizon line appeared to be swelling. A big wave was coming. I was too far in to go back. Dad had always told me it was better to dive a big wave than to try and run from it.

I took a deep breath and waited as the wave took shape, the edge sharpening against the sky like a mountain range rising out of the water. After a quiet moment, the wave began to crest. Precisely at first, a string of foam as delicate as pearls, and then faster, ripping across the horizon with a deafening noise.

When it was right in front of me, I dove. Underwater, my hands grasped at the sand. My eyes were sealed shut and darkness enveloped me. I stayed low while the wave passed over me. And then suddenly, everything was still. I paddled up to the surface, gasping for air. My head bobbed out of the water, and my eyes stung.

I couldn't see another wave coming, so I floated on my back and let the water rock me back and forth. I waved at Mom who was watching me from the deck, and she waved back. Behind her, our house looked strangely small. I looked up at my bedroom window. It was open, but I couldn't see in. For the first time in my life, it really hit me that I wasn't going to live there forever. In a few years, I'd go away to college and this house would just be a place that I would come and visit for weeks or months at a time. For some reason that realization seemed to make it shrink even more.

This year had turned out to be all about watching the things I always thought were permanent unravel before my eyes. I was starting to understand that absolutely everything and everyone, including myself, only existed in time. First, there was forever. Now, I realized, anything could change.

The current of the ocean twisted around my legs, as if it were alive. The hot sun mingled with the cold water. The ocean was another world. A parallel universe. It amazed me that it even touched our own. There I was, only feet away from my own bedroom and yet I was somewhere else entirely. I couldn't wait for my internship at the aquarium to start in a few weeks. Mark had told me over and over again during the interview that the work of an intern wasn't very exciting, but I didn't care.

I listened to the gentle sounds of water slapping water, and suddenly, an unexpected, vivid happiness bloomed inside of me. I wanted to shout at the top of my lungs. Tenth grade was over. The worst year of all time was officially done. And now there were so many things to look forward to: the internship, learning to surf with Emily, gardening all summer with Mom, and, of course, Nate. There was so much I wanted to share with him and so much about him that I still wanted to know. It felt like no amount of time that we could have together would be enough. The sky and the earth and the ocean stretched out in all directions around me. Colorful, incomprehensible ribbons of space and matter and time. I knew right then that everything was going to be okay. No, not just okay. Everything was going to be great.

acknowledgments

T his book would not exist without my agent, Logan
Garrison, and my editor, Stacey Friedberg. It's amazing to work with people who always see the ways in which a
story could get realer and more honest, and who love reading as much as you do. This book owes more to you two than
I can explain in this small space.

Logan, none of this would have happened without you.
Thank you for believing in this story from the very beginning
and for seeing the potential in it, even way back when. Your
notes challenged me to be a better writer than I thought I
could be, and you managed to support me through all of it
at the same time.

Stacey, you turned this manuscript into something beyond
what I imagined. Thank you for your high standards and for
your vision of what this book could be. I didn't know before
we started how many discoveries I would make during the

editorial process—thank you for showing me how much more the book could grow.

Thank you to everyone at the Gernert Company, Dial Books, and Penguin who have helped this book find its readers. Rosanne Lauer for the copyediting and Theresa Evangelista for the cover. And also, special thanks to Sarah Burnes and Lauri Hornik.

Thank you to my two very first readers, Lauren Strasnick and Michael Leviton. Your notes gave me the tools and the confidence to keep working. To my friend readers: Caitlin, Jordan, Lauren, Lily, and Sara. Also, Emily Parliman, Susan Chumsky, and SCBWI. And to Tula for teaching me to paint (and see).

I wouldn't have known how to do this without the conversation and company of the artists and writers who I am lucky to know both in LA and NY. Especially my boyfriend, Joel, your creativity and your belief in art is contagious. Thank you for being so okay with me always being glued to my *word processor*.

Finally, my family. This book is for you. My sister, Clarissa, thank you for inspiring me to write and for giving me the sentence that launched the whole thing. And thank you for always insisting *You play, too*. My parents, John and Nancy, a million *thank-yous* aren't enough—words cannot capture my gratitude.

Turn the page to preview
Juliana Romano's novel

SUMMER IN THE INVISIBLE CITY

Chapter 1

Memories are like plants: if you care for them, they grow. I've relived this one night so many times that what was once just a sapling has now become a tree, its roots twisting deep into the dirt.

I was standing on the roof at a New Year's Eve party during winter break of tenth grade. It was below freezing but we stayed outside anyway, because up there we could be reckless and loud. And sometimes the cold feels good, the way it holds your heart in its claws.

Below me, the city spread out in all directions. Sparkling lights lined up in the neat rows of Manhattan, and the bridges to Queens and Brooklyn draped like beaded necklaces across the glassy East River. Looking at New York from above at night is like looking at a galaxy full of stars.

"This is the best."

I turned and Noah Bearman was standing next to me. A lock of dark hair fell helplessly across his face, grazing the top of his sharp cheekbone and covering one of his dark eyes. He was wearing a sweatshirt that looked nowhere near warm enough. His hands were shoved into his pockets and his shoulders were hiked up to his ears, like maybe his muscles were cramping from the cold.

"What is?" I asked, trying to act like it was normal that he would be talking to me.

"This," he said, looking at the view. His breath froze when he spoke, making icy, geometric shapes in the night air.

I pulled a cigarette out of my pack and lit it. I hate smoking, but I thought it made me look cool. If Willa were there, she would have made me put it out. I sucked hard, hoping I looked experienced.

He watched as I took a drag and then asked, "Can I get one of those?"

"Sure," I said. I held the pack out to him. I was glad that I had painted my nails red.

He paused before taking a cigarette, and I willed myself not to stare at him. Still, I couldn't help notice the way the winter air had made his full lips even redder, and how it had turned his nose adorably pink.

"Which one do I want?" he murmured.

"What do you mean? They're all the same," I replied, confused.

He looked at me and his eyes twinkled. "Are they?"

Noah kept his eyes glued to mine as he reached into the pack and pulled out all the cigarettes. Then, he stuffed them all in his mouth so that they stuck out in every direction like crazy teeth. The whole time he kept looking at me.

I said, "Those are my cigarettes. They're expensive. Don't waste them."

Noah didn't answer me. He couldn't speak anyway, with his mouth full of cigarettes. He held out his hand for my lighter and I gave it to him. He flicked it on and wiped the flame across the tips of the cigarettes, torching them all. They lit up all at once.

I was aware that Noah was doing something so strange and twisted that it verged on being mean. But he was trying to tell me something. And anything Noah Bearman wanted to tell me, I wanted to know.

"What are you doing?" I asked, my voice tiny now.

He reached up and took the cigarettes out of his mouth, grabbing them with his full fist. Then he dropped them on the ground and stomped on them.

"I just did you a favor," he said. "Don't be mad."

"I am mad," I said, pouting. But I wasn't.

"I'm Noah," he said, as if I didn't know who he was.

"I'm Sadie," I told him.

"So the girl with the red jacket has a name."

Noah Bearman wondered about my name?

An icy wind howled, licking across the roof and whipping against us so hard that I had to turn my back on it and cower.

"You're shivering," he said, tapping my elbow with his own.

Even with the fabric of his sweatshirt and the thick wool of my coat between us, and even though it was just his elbow knocking against mine, Noah's touch made the cold night turn hot.

"Come on," he said. "Let's go inside."

So we did.

In some ways, it doesn't matter what happened next, or back at school, or in the year and a half since then. That night was perfect and I'll always have it. I'll hold on to the memory tight as I want, because it's mine.